ANOTHER PROVINCE
new Chinese writing from London

selected by Jung Chang, Lynn Pan and Henry Zhao

edited by Jessie Lim and Li Yan
assisted by Jenny Putin

Lambeth Chinese Community Association and *SIYU CHINESE TIMES*

Collection copyright ©Lambeth Chinese Community Association and
SiYu Chinese Times
Copyright in the individual pieces remains with the authors and
in the translations with the translators
On Another Province © David Yip
Foreword ©Jung Chang
Introduction © Henry Zhao

First published in 1994 by
Lambeth Chinese Community Association
69 Stockwell Road
London SW9 9PY
and SiYu Chinese Times
4th Floor, 16 Nicholas Street
Manchester M1 4EJ

Represented & distributed in the UK & Europe by:
Turnaround Distribution
27 Horsell Road
London N5 1XL

Lambeth Chinese Community Association ISBN 0 9522973 0 2
SiYu Chinese Times ISBN 0 9522974 0 X

ALL RIGHTS RESERVED: no part of this publication may be reproduced, stored in a retrieval system, or transmitted in any form or by any means, electronic, mechanical, photocopying or otherwise, without the prior written permission of the publisher.

BRITISH LIBRARY CATALOGUING-IN-PUBLICATION DATA
A catalogue record for this book is available from the British Library

Book cover artwork by Qu Leilei
Design by Samantha Ho
Typeset by Chinese Marketing & Communications
Printed and bound by BPC Wheatons Ltd

目 錄
CONTENTS

序 .... *i*
Preface

鳴謝 .... *iii*
Acknowledgements

On *Another Province*: David Yip .... *v*

前言：張戎（張樸譯）... *vi*
Foreword: Jung Chang

Introduction: Henry Y H Zhao .... *x*

Vivienne Huang: *Threshold* 1
黄慧文：門檻（趙毅衡譯）

Lab Ky Mo: *Dining Alone at Wong Kee Restaurant with Seven Men* 12
巫立基：在旺記餐館和七位先生獨自進餐（吳一明譯）

柳揚：江湖故事 29
Liu Yang: *Travellers' Tales* (translated by Peng Wenlan)

柳揚：流水帳 31
Liu Yang: *Daily Account* (translated by Peng Wenlan)

劉索拉：吃餃子歌 33
Liu Sola: *The Dumpling Song* (translated by Peng Wenlan)

劉索拉：人堆人（摘錄）..................................... 36
Liu Sola: From *The People Pile* (translated by Jenny Putin and Wu Daming)

虹影：鴿子廣場 48

虹影：最後的情節 56
Hong Ying: *The Last Episode* (translated by Jenny Putin)

虹影：情書 58
Hong Ying: *The Love Letter* (translated by Jenny Putin)

Maria Lin Wong: *Shadows* 60

浴缸：餓的故事 71
Bathtub: *The Hunger Story* (translated by Oliver Lim Bunnin)

浴缸：敦倫記（摘錄） 75
Bathtub: From *Notes From London* (translated by Ni Yi Bin)

劉洪彬：詞語 85
Liu Hongbin: *Words* (translated by Peter Porter)

劉洪彬：你是誰？ 87
Liu Hongbin: *Who Are You?* (translated by Peter Porter,
  Liu Hongbin and Jason Brooks)

喬林：蛻變 91
Chiao Ling: *The Metamorphosis* (translated by Chiao Ling)

Lili Man: *A Batty Metamorphosis* 93

喬林：心經 98
Chiao Ling: *Sutra of the Heart* (translated by Chiao Ling
  and Jenny Putin)

B. Y. H. Guild: *A Late Mixed Marriage* 100

Anna Chen: *The Next Wave Home* 106

顏展民：點點溫馨 119

Helen Soo: *Rosie* 121

曲磊磊：走進威虎山 131
Qu Leilei: *Walking to Tiger Mountain*
  (translated by Sally Church and Mau Sang Ng)

小芸：相親 142

Zibao: *A Transcription of Something I Heard* 146

乞靈：謝佩兒	153
乞靈：灣仔摘豆芽的老婦人	156
Tracy Cheung: *A Wayward Girl*	157
王家新：卡夫卡	161
Wang Jiaxin: *Kafka* (translated by John Cayley)	
王家新：日記	164
Wang Jiaxin: *The Diary Entry* (translated by John Cayley)	
Paul Wong: *Jerusalem*	166
Paul Wong: *Jugular*	167
Paul Wong: *Less Than Yellow*	168
吳洪強：沒有那樣黃（吳一明譯）	
Pui Fan Lee: From *Short, Fat, Ugly and Chinese*	179
胡冬：圖書館外的面具	193
Hu Dong: From *The Mask Outside the Library* (translated by Jenny Putin)	
胡冬：我想乘上一艘慢船到巴黎去	211
Hu Dong: From *I Want to Take a Slow Boat to Paris* (translated by Peng Wenlan)	
作者簡介	215
About the Authors	

序

《天外有天：倫敦華人新作》是一部華人雙語短篇小說及詩文選集。

近年來，英國有不少以中文或英文寫作的華人作家；然而，他們的文學創作環境仍欠理想。林拔芙華人協會為此發起這個出版計劃，希望可以突破英國華人文學的困境。這一項目得到倫敦藝術局的贊助，林拔芙華人協會聯合《絲語時報》，向倫敦區內華人徵求文學創作，並由作家張戎、潘翎、及文學評論家趙毅衡擔任評委。

本書總共收集了二十三位作者的作品。差不多所有用英文撰寫的投稿者都是有才華的青年新秀，在《天外有天》初試啼聲。以中文寫作之作者則來自中國大陸、香港、臺灣及馬來西亞等地；他們有些已是成名作家，通過這部選集，他們的作品得以獲得更廣泛的讀者。

從《天外有天》所登載的文選，可以看到在英國生活的華人作家不同的背景、風格、興趣、及觀點。我們希望這個先鋒計劃可以為華人作家提供更多的機會，協助他們的創作走上英國文壇。

PREFACE

Another Province: New Chinese writing from London is a dual-language collection of stories and poems by Chinese writers.

Its publication was initiated by the Lambeth Chinese Community Association to meet the needs of the emerging group of British Chinese writers, writing in both Chinese and English. Together with *SiYu Chinese Times* and with support from London Arts Board, the Association invited submissions of creative writing from Chinese people in London. The writers Jung Chang, Lynn Pan and critic Henry Zhao joined the editors to read and select from the short-listed entries.

The works of 23 authors are collected in this volume. Nearly all the authors writing in English are new, young talents, making their literary debut in *Another Province*. Those writing in Chinese have come from China, Hong Kong, Taiwan and Malaysia and many have had works published before, but will gain access through translations in this collection to a wider audience in Britain.

The writings in *Another Province* attest to the diverse backgrounds, styles, interests and perspectives of Chinese writers living in Britain. We hope that, in the wake of this pioneering volume, more opportunities for Chinese writing will follow to help establish Chinese creative writing as a vital and integral part of the British literary scene.

鳴 謝

本書編者對以下作出鳴謝：

評委張戎、潘翎、趙毅衡，感謝他們的支持和熱忱；

特別感謝 Margaret Busby 在編輯上的支持；

Mishti Chatterji、Yasmin Skelt 與 Jean Coppendale 吳秀桓、葉大衛、鄭偉壁、Steph Smith、Simon Jones、文坤李、蘇慧君、Matthew Crabbe、鄭亞英；對本書提供的意見；

本書封面繪圖由曲磊磊提供、
設計何超慧；
製作部梁秀晶、戴小萍；

倫敦博物館、Andy Topping；

林拔芙華人協會趙燕瓊、馮天嬌、溫萬儀、
杜銀新、連淑卿；

John Cayley 與 Peter Porter 允許本書重印他們的翻譯稿；

各位作家、翻譯員及熱心投稿人士；
並向這次未能登載的文稿的作者致以歉意。

本書出版者衷心感謝英中文化協會、倫敦藝術局、Paul Hamlyn 基金會在經費上給予的支持。

ACKNOWLEDGEMENTS

The editors wish to thank:

The selection panellists Jung Chang, Lynn Pan and Henry Zhao for their support and interest

With special mention to Margaret Busby for her editorial support

Mishti Chatterji, Yasmin Skelt and Jean Coppendale for offering advice

Siu Won Ng, David Yip, Zheng Weibi, Grace Lau, Steph Smith, Simon Jones, Lili Man, Helen Soo, Matthew Crabbe and Zheng Yaying for their encouragement and assistance

Qu Leilei for supplying artwork for the book cover
Samantha Ho for the design and typesetting
The production team Liang Xiujing and Dai Xiaoping

The Museum of London, Andy Topping

Yin King Chiu, Teng Kiu Fung, Manyee Wan, Georgina To and Elsa Lin of Lambeth Chinese Community Association for their invaluable help and patience

John Cayley and Peter Porter for permission to reprint their translations

The authors, translators and all the writers who sent in entries, with apologies to those whose excellent entries we had to leave out

The publishers gratefully acknowledge the financial assistance of the Great Britain-China Centre, London Arts Board and the Paul Hamlyn Foundation.

ON ANOTHER PROVINCE

David Yip

You can never say that you truly know an individual unless you have had some kind of dialogue with them. Seeing them is not enough; appearances can be deceiving. What you perceive can change radically once you have access to their thoughts and feelings. What is true for individuals is equally true for communities.

Based on the visits they make to Chinese restaurants, takeaways and other retail outlets, many people take for granted that they have some understanding of the Chinese community in this country. But their knowledge of the Chinese population is often distorted. The Chinese themselves have further obstructed communications by keeping outsiders at arm's length, not allowing them to see beyond the perfunctory smile and assumed deference. This approach has added to the ignorance and perpetuated assumptions and images which are often far from the truth. As a victim of these misconceptions, I have always wanted to try to make people realise that the Chinese community is made up of individuals. Certainly, we have a central core that holds us together, but there is a huge variety of elements which makes us stand apart.

Non-Chinese have written about us and typecast our image according to their own perceptions of what we should be. Their appreciation of Chinese culture is limited to what is presented during the Chinese festivals. Unfortunately, we have lacked a voice to express and show our diversity. However, there is an increasing groundswell of desire among the young Chinese generation to make their own representations: to explain what they want and how they want to be seen. And with the publication of this anthology, we are at last speaking in our own voices.

Another Province will give readers the pleasure and surprise of journeying into unexplored territory; perhaps, like missionaries, they will help spread the good news of what they find to the yet unconverted.

前　言

《鴻：三代中國女人的故事》作者張戎為《天外有天》寫這篇前言。張戎閱讀了這部精選集的每一篇作品，她也和其中的一些作者一樣，帶著對中國的回憶來到倫敦。在這篇前言裡，張戎告訴我們她是怎樣開始寫《鴻》。

張戎

當作家從來就是我的夢。十幾歲時，我在中國當農民，後來又做電工。當我在水田裡施肥，或者攀上電線杆檢查線路時，我總在腦海裡構思和推敲我的作品。但是出書，我想也沒想過，當時中國正陷入無休無止的政治迫害運動中，絕大部分作家受到批判，許多人被送進勞改農場，難以計數的書籍在1966年文革開始時被焚燒。即使寫給自己看也極端危險。1968年3月25日我16歲生日那一天，因為紅衛兵造反派突然來抄家，我不得不撕碎有生以來寫成的第一首詩，扔進廁所的馬桶。

1978年，我來到倫敦。在這個恍若另一個星球的世界裡，我開始有了要把在中國的生活寫出來的衝動。但下意識地，我不能進入記憶深處。在暴力橫行的文化大革命(1966-1976)中，我的家庭蒙受了巨大的苦難。我不想再重新體驗父親被關押、精神失常，母親跪玻璃渣和姥姥痛苦死亡的惡夢。

1988年，母親來到倫敦。這是她第一次離開中國。一天，她告訴我她最想做的事就是和我談談。

接下來的幾個月，母親幾乎每天都要談上一段往事。到她回國時，她留下了六十個小時的錄音帶，而我完全被她尋求理解的渴望所震動。遠離中國政治和社會的禁錮，她終於做到了從未做到的事情，自由地敞開思想和心靈。

我瞭解到母親許多九死一生的經歷，她的隔離審查，她的苦惱，以及她和把共產主義理想放在首位的父親之間的衝突。我還第一次聽說了姥姥雙腳被纏時令人髮指的細節：那時她才兩歲，為了符合當時女人的美的標準，姥姥的腳指被放在巨石下折斷，壓碎。可是，母親的故事並不淒慘、消沉，相反，它們自始至終充滿力量，使我振奮。

就好像這力量注入了我的心裡，我決定寫《鴻》：以20世紀動亂的中國為背景，寫出姥姥、母親和我三代女人的故事。兩年半的時間，我流過眼淚，也有過輾轉難眠的夜晚，但我沒有住筆的念頭。

出版的日期臨近了，就在我開始擔心這本書會有什麼樣的反應時，母親寫信來。她說，即使書出了沒人看，也不要失望。她能感到，通過寫《鴻》，我離她更近了。僅此一點，她就心滿意足，她就是一個幸福的人了。母親說得對：《鴻》使我對她更瞭解、更接近。不僅如此，《鴻》也是我對母親的愛和一生的一點小小的回報。

《鴻》結果是夢一般的成功。它帶給我和母親的還有作夢也想不到的快樂：母親以源源不斷的來信中讀到全世界千百萬讀者對她的理解。我呢，我成了作家。

張樸譯

原載：英國《獨立報》

FOREWORD

Jung Chang was on the selection panel for *Another Province*. Like some of the authors in this collection, she came to Britain with memories of China. *Wild Swans*, her moving depiction of the lives of three Chinese women - her grandmother, her mother and herself - against the background of modern China, was written in London and has been read by millions of readers. In this foreword, Jung Chang tells how she became a writer. We hope that her example will inspire readers, particularly Chinese women, who, like her, have dreamed of being a writer, to write stories of their own.

Jung Chang

I have always dreamed of being a writer. In my teens in China, I worked as a peasant and an electrician. While I was spreading manure in the paddy fields and checking power distribution at the top of electricity poles, I would polish long passages in my mind. But the idea of writing for publication seemed out of the question. China was consumed by endless political persecution in those days, and most writers were denounced; many were sent to prison camps. In 1966, when I was 14, the great majority of books were burnt across China. Even writing for oneself was extremely dangerous. I had to tear up the first poem I ever wrote, which was on my 16th birthday on 25 March 1968, and flush it down the toilet because Red Guards had come to raid our flat.

I came to Britain in 1978. In a world that felt like another planet, I began to develop an urge to write about my life in China. But subconsciously, I could not dig deep into my memory. In the violent Cultural Revolution between 1966 and 1976, my family suffered atrociously. I did not want to relive the nightmare of my father's imprisonment and insanity, my mother's kneeling on broken glass, or my grandmother's painful death.

In 1988, my mother came to London, her first trip out of China. One day, she suddenly told me what she wanted to do most was to talk to me.

She talked every day for months. By the time she left Britain, my mother had done 60 hours of tape recordings, and I had been overwhelmed by her longing to be understood by me. Here, outside the social and political confines of China, she was able to do something she had not been able to do all her life: open her mind and her heart.

I learnt about my mother's many close shaves with death, her spells in detention, her torments, and her emotional conflict with my father, whose first love was his ideal, communism. I also came to know the agonising details of my grandmother's footbinding: how her feet were broken and crushed under a big stone when she was two, to satisfy the standards of beauty of the day. And yet, my mother's stories were not unbearable or depressing. Underlining them was a strength that was all the time uplifting.

As if some of the strength were now injected in me, I made up my mind to write *Wild Swans*, the story of my grandmother, my mother and myself through the turbulence of 20th-century China. For two and a half years, I shed my fair share of tears, and tossed and turned through quite a few sleepless nights. But I persevered.

Then, near the date of publication, just as I was beginning to worry about how the book would be received, my mother wrote and told me not to be disheartened if people paid no attention to it. I had made her a happy woman because writing the book had brought us closer. This alone, she said, was enough for her. My mother was right: I had come to a new degree of closeness to her. What was more, I was happy I was now able, through the book, to pay her a small tribute.

Wild Swans turned out to be a success. It has brought my mother and me surprising joys beyond our dreams. My mother has found understanding from millions of readers all over the world in numerous moving letters. And I, at last, have become a writer.

(This article first appeared in *The Independent*.)

INTRODUCTION

Henry Y. H. Zhao

This is the first major selection of Chinese writing in Great Britain, and perhaps the first anthology, I believe, to gather between its covers works by Chinese writers both in their native and adopted tongues.

At the mention of the Chinese, most Westerners will almost inevitably evoke in their minds the image of a practical, hard-working people, the most well-behaved minority. Of course, this is a stereotype, but it is not totally groundless. The Chinese living abroad are nearly always regarded as the model minority because they are perceived to be culturally unchallenging, harmless or even invisible, except in the culinary field. The younger generation Chinese are more often than not model pupils. Chinese communities everywhere have perhaps the highest proportion of computer programmers or civil engineers among the young, but the proportion of students in the humanities going on to become artists and writers is small.

When one thinks of the glorious, long history of Chinese art and literature, and of London as one of the greatest cultural capitals in the world, one cannot help but feel sad about this. But the situation cannot remain unchanged. It is hard to imagine that an ethnic group, ambitious and capable of accomplishment in many fields, would let its culture remain neglected for long. Changes are bound to come sooner or later.

And changes have already come. In recent years a considerable number of Chinese in Great Britain have distinguished themselves in art and literature. Their examples have encouraged the younger Chinese generation to explore the pleasure and challenge of becoming artists.

These changes have been accelerated by another factor - the recent arrival in Great Britain of a large number of well-educated Chinese from Taiwan, Hong Kong and China either to seek higher education or to settle down. Many of these newcomers had already embarked on an artistic career before coming over and have continued to dedicate themselves to art in spite of financial and other pressures. London can proudly say that it has become one of the largest centres of gifted Chinese writers, alongside New York, San Francisco, Los Angeles and Paris. It is, I am sure, no exaggeration to say that we are on the eve of a British-Chinese cultural flowering. *Another Province* is testimony to this exciting prospect.

This is a dual-language book, symptomatic of a perplexing aspect of Chinese writing in another culture. The authors are split into two groups - some writing in Chinese and some in English. The choice of language was imposed upon them in their formative years. And with a few exceptions, the choice of languages marks a division more cultural than linguistic.

In most countries, these two sections of people rarely mingle. It seems that they do not have much to tell or ask each other. In fact they have great difficulty in communicating with each other. Language is not the decisive factor of the segregation; what divides the two is their cultural upbringing. It is, however, these very cultural issues that are the common ground between the two groups. In a sense, those who write in Chinese but live abroad are outcast· elements of Chinese literature, whereas the writing in English should be considered part of British literature. In these groups, one might say, Chinese literature and British literature overlap - the part of Chinese literature in exile in Britain and the part of British literature written by authors of Chinese origin. These overlapping parts might be marginal to their own mainstream literatures but history of literary influence has proved that it is exactly this overlapping part that serves as a bridge.

Whilst this overlapping does not translate by itself into the merging of two great literary traditions, even though the two groups of British Chinese literature are printed between two covers, we hope, nonetheless, in our effort to bring out the anthology, to give encouragement to this merger, or rather, to make more people aware of the possibility. The people who can benefit most from this prospect are the authors. Both groups can surely learn a great deal from each other.

As I mentioned earlier, many of the authors writing in Chinese began their writing career back in their homeland, some with national reputations. Let me start with fiction writers. Liu Sola was one of the pioneers of the Chinese New Wave fiction that started in the mid-1980s. Her short novel *You Have No Choice* became a *cause celebre* in Chinese literary circles when it was published in 1985 and was acclaimed as the first example of Chinese "beatnik" fiction. Back in China, Hu Dong belonged to the *Manghan* (boorish) poets which challenged the vestiges of elegance and grace in Chinese poetry in the early 1980s by using rude language and uncouth expressions in protest at the social and artistic status quo. And from the same province as Hu Dong - Sichuan, well-known for producing poets since the seventh century - is Hong Ying, who started her poetic career in the early 1980s and since coming to Britain has won a number of prizes. Her fiction has won acclaim as well.

For poets, we have Wang Jiaxin, who was active in the poetry revival in China in the 1980s. Then there is Liu Hongbin from Shandong Province. His poetry cries out with the pain of human suffering, born of rejection and alienation. Liu Yang spent his childhood in the Yangzi Delta, the cradle for modern ideas in China; his poetic writing inclines towards a new classicism with images reminiscent of the charm of ancient Chinese poetry.

But Mainland China does not have the monopoly on good poets, as the contributions from Chiao Ling, a woman poet from Taiwan, and Stephen Ng from Hong Kong demonstrate. Chiao Ling's poetry explores the complexities of human sentiment, whilst Stephen Ng's work is imbued with a concern for righting social injustice.

Chinese authors try their hands at different literary genres. Apart from poets, we have some excellent prose writers. Yen Chanmin from Hong Kong has a beautifully restrained undertone to his essays. In her story, Xiao Yun questions the traditional role of Chinese women in today's society. Qu Leilei's essay gives a nostalgic recollection of time spent in the countryside during the painful period of the Cultural Revolution. And Bathtub's wry observations of London life make amusing reading.

When we reach the works by the authors writing in English, we are presented with a very different picture. The language reads differently for sure, but so too is the approach. Whereas almost all the contributions in Chinese are by published writers, the majority of contributions in English are from new authors. Many of them are trying their hand at writing imaginative literature for the first time, with impressive results. What unites many of these writers is a concern with identity and their sense of displacement. It is understandable, given that many grew up acutely aware of being different from the majority of their peers. The publication of these experiences will surely lead to a better understanding of the Chinese community in this country.

Whilst these stories share a common theme - a preoccupation with their Chinese identity - their approaches and moods could not be more varied. Paul Wong has his tongue planted firmly in his cheek as he describes a torrid night-club encounter between a wealthy young Chinese student and a blond woman. Pui Fan Lee's one-person play narrating the experiences of a Chinese girl growing up in the UK is a masterpiece of tragi-comedy. No wonder the piece won the Race in the Media award from the Commission for Racial Equality. Lili Man's *A Batty Metamorphosis* tackles the identity dilemma head on with considerable humour. A Chinese woman wakes one morning to find herself with golden hair and blue eyes, a transformation that should have solved all her racial identity problems. Instead, it only compounds her confusion. Then there is Lab Ky Mo's cameo of life at London Chinatown's fabled Wong Kee Restaurant. The extremely entertaining descriptions of various people do not spare the Chinese waiters by paying cheap sympathy for their hardship. Such a sense of humour is rare in writing dealing with the issue of racial identity.

Not all of the stories where identity is a prominent concern are humorous. Beverly Guild's piece is a restrained, delicate exploration of the dynamics of a mixed-race relationship. Vivienne Huang's piece deals with a similar theme and is a fine example of stream of consciousness writing. It is marvellous to see a first trial of imaginative writing so mature in technique. Tracy Cheung examines the issue from the viewpoint of a completely anglicised girl who finds herself in confrontation with her mother's values. The protagonist does not seem to know whether what she is rebelling against is a western prejudice against Chinese or a Chinese prejudice against Westerners.

Not all the contributions in English, however, have Chineseness and identity as their main theme. Helen Soo's *Rosie* is a poignant tale about a teenage prostitute working in Los Angeles. Anna Chen's essay is a moving description of a mother's imaginary relationship with a daughter she never had. The language is simple but full of dramatic tautness. Maria Lin Wong's *Shadows*, on the other hand, is a sinister tale about the horrors of child abuse, seen from the perspective of a five year old girl. Zibao's piece is the most experimental in this anthology. The story is written in the form of a radio play. The author possesses a fine sense of the dramatic.

For all the stylistic and thematic variations, there is no difference in artistic value between the two groups of authors in this anthology. The spectrum our authors have exhibited in this anthology is a broad one. The authors here, taken as a whole, look well set to compete with writers of whatever groups. Their writings will certainly enrich the understanding of our life, our sufferings and happiness, and much beyond.

Vivienne Huang

Threshold

Rebecca leant her head against the smeared coach window. It was too hard to concentrate on the passing of now, the passing of time. Outside, hurtling faster than a romance, was the Sinai, drier than a relationship past its sell-by date.

She leant her head against the window, shaking in tune to the bumps on the single-lane road and fell gently into the sly embrace of half-sleep.

James, don't you remember? Ah, Tai Gong was always like that, like the photograph on the wall above the altar. Stern, with huge bags under his eyes. Burn the incense first, kneel, bow three times with all the dignity you can muster. Don't forget to bow at the same time as M & D, or else you'll feel the back of someone's hand on your neck, pushing.

Can we go into the garden? It does not seem possible, here in London, to have so much green. Emily, Natasha, you darling, Alex and I run to the bottom of the garden, to the rose bowers laden heavily with the summer pinks and red, warm from the afternoon sun, petals thick upon the green grass. There's the dense hedge, with the ragged hole. Typically, they're hesitating. Their nice dresses, their worries about our parents, their fear. We'll leave them behind.

James, you go first and I'll follow you wherever you go. You bend down swiftly, through the hedge, I close behind you. And out into the cornfield, the big blue sky, the heat of open ground. It's just you and me now, my Eurasian cousin, in the English countryside.

England. My first language is not English, that's my language of habit. In the beginning, it was our surrogate Grandma and her cronies cackling in Cantonese above the noise of the mah-jong tiles. But how can you make sense of a language with no sense of time? Life becomes too slippery.

I must be awake now, if I can think so rationally. Logic dies with sleep. Yes, I am awake. I can see him now, the man I think I'm going to marry, by my side as he has been for the last three years. Isn't he handsome? Look at his eyes, dark eyelashes, longer than is right. What is he like? Mostly brown, mostly macho. Broad shoulders, see, that little bit there where I rest my head? Large hands, twice the size of mine, his fingers long and broad, beautiful, strong, male hands.

He says he likes my small, neat hands, my small feet that can kick so hard. You think you can dominate me? I let you believe you can, I smile serenely, Buddha-like, and count to twenty because I know you need to feel like a man - sometimes.

An Englishman who has lived abroad for so long that he is both French and English. Neither French nor English. Somewhere in between, stuck in the Channel, shuffling backwards and forwards like a P & O ferry.

Where are we now? Ah, travelling through the Sinai on our ten-day escape from the City. It's good to be away from work.

What's this? The sapphire from my engagement ring is falling out - like a scream, it's running away from me. A sparkle, a flicker and it's gone. Grandma, don't say that it's bad luck, please. Help me find it.

Grandma is tucking her mobile phone into her apron now. She's just finished calling the police to help me find the stone. Auntie Chin gave her the mobile phone, to save her having to run at its call.

Grandma has a good life in that old people's home in San Francisco. Might even be the possibility of romance now, who knows? Auntie Chin saw two elderly black people flirting in the lift. He asked her for a date in the canteen and she had laughed a big laugh. Did they get married and share their grandchildren like short stories?

Love hardly begins with humour - no, more likely it begins with the silent stare of misunderstanding. He danced with me. We did not speak the same language but moved together as if through water, limbs so sweetly tuned as we danced the waltz. Footsteps stuttering in reply, drawing closer, closer, further. Negotiating a path of compromises across the floor and across time.

It would have been impossible. Be pragmatic, girl, after all, you're used to the good life. Hot showers, air conditioning, fast cars, cashpoint machines - and he could not offer any of those. He got so embarrassed about it, used to inflict these objects like a whip upon his back and swore that Chinese men were naturally the weaker. Did he want me to be responsible for his decisions? I gave up.

Like a fish in the sea, cool waters that flow so gently here, below the surface. No harsh sounds to penetrate my calm inner world. It's so good to be free, moving in a void, comforting blackness. Ah, sleep, embrace me.

Rebecca leant her head against the window. Her head drooped and her mouth slowly opened to form the beginning of a sentence.

John leant forward to look at her, the woman he planned to marry. He liked to see her asleep, so vulnerable. Preferred her that way - she was too strong sometimes, too demanding. Better asleep, infinitely childlike. He could protect her now.

Even now at 26, no trace of time had marked her face. So serene, so docile, like a mask covering the cracks of over-civilisation.

Outside, the desert lay broader than sleep, dust upon rock, shrub upon dust. Over the coach's loudspeaker came the wailing of a mullah, man to G-d or man to man? And what about woman?

He had met her at work. Eight till eight every day, in the City, five days a week, forty-eight weeks of the year. The same bloody tube, the same bloody journey. Unless surprised by the lethal incompetences of London Underground and the IRA, that journey was depressingly familiar, even down to the same people. Rebecca had not understood, she never got out of the house at the same time every day. She deliberately changed trains and was always late to work. "Life would be so dull otherwise!" she would say.

On the train, always with his *Independent*, smearing the contents in his brain, in his eyes; on his fingers, ink engrained into his suit. He would sometimes catch sight of himself, the reflection mocking his vanity. Look at those dark eyebrows, the dark eyes, the pristine pinstripe suit, the freshly shaven jawline, feeling that slow morning pulse beating gently against his blue shirt collar.

Rebecca would tease him if she caught him looking in the mirror for too long. "It's simple, you don't have to look - you're mostly brown, mostly macho!" If she was not too busy, she'd look at his reflection in that way, with those half-closed dark eyes, and they would make love violently in front of the mirror.

Three years. They had met at work. He had just finished a difficult client meeting. Clients wanted to iron out the bumps, they said, clear up any misunderstanding. So, he had given a fine performance of a youngblood and the clients had left assured their interests were being represented by such a good bloke.

His boss had turned to him to say, "John, fancy a celebratory drink at Dell'Ugo's? We nearly lost that bloody account. Thank God we don't have to go explaining to Steve about how we'll have to chase up something equally dodgy." And Rebecca walked past. All legs and black hair. Serene, smiling. *So, she's the new girl* - and she had turned and given them the open smile of a stranger.

The prowling had lasted for two weeks, circling like a hungry wolf, leaving trails of dinner and drinks invitations, marking out the boundaries with flirtatious phone calls. He had not wanted to introduce her to his parents too fast, but had instantly shown her to his friends.

John shifted. Right leg over left, now change with the hush of cotton against cotton. These seats were too small for his long legs, knees virtually jammed up against the back of the seat in front, and the air conditioning was stronger and colder than the wind of an English seaside summer.

What was I thinking of? My best man, Neil - the man with whom I have shared countless drinking sessions, relationship split-ups and pick-ups, car crashes even - had liked her as soon as he heard her speak. "Where did she learn how to speak such good English? Comes from Hong Kong or Singapore? Well assimilated, " he had drawled, always laconic.

I never thought of it that way. After all, it began as lust, curiosity, biological demands - who knows? Not a question of racial politics.

She keeps on teasing me for being so English, to wilfully distance me from her. But she's not the only one who wants it to happen. William, my genetic partner, that smoothie, always sweet-talking my parents, does not want our status to be confused. Like everything in his life, it's got to be planned and perfect, even though we're culturally half French. "Marrying a Chinese girl - well, what will our family friends think?" He's pathetic.

How I wish I could sleep as easily as she can. Look at her curled up in her seat like a cat, like a child. What will marriage be like? Endless dinner parties and soon the screeching of our own mixed-up children? Will she still be the woman I love now?

Rebecca's small naked foot lay close to his like an interjection.

Outside, beyond the window, the clouds gathered swiftly like partners to a dance. Darker and bigger they grew over the desert, until the growl of thunder and the first flash of lightning, purer than the rain that fell, came. Surely this was the kind of lightning that blinded Paul on the road to Damascus?

Rebecca stirred and the next moment was awake. "How long have I been asleep for?"

The rain fell heavily on to the heat-parched earth.

"Oh, hours," he said.

黃慧文

門檻

莉蓓卡頭抵著旅遊車蒙上灰的玻璃窗。要想集中注意力觀察此刻的消逝，觀察時間的消逝，太難了。車窗外，比浪漫史飛散得更快的是西奈沙漠，比過了出售時間期限的愛情更加乾燥。

她把頭靠在窗上，身體隨著狹窄公路的坑窪震動，漸漸地滑入半睡半醒的擁抱之中....

詹姆士，你不記得了嗎？啊，太公老是這樣子，像靈位上牆上的照片，神色嚴峻，眼睛下有二個好大的皮囊。先點香，跪下，三叩首，尊敬如儀，叩頭與父母同時，不然，會有個手按你的脖子。

我們能到花園中去嗎？在倫敦不太可能有大片草地。愛米麗，娜塔莎，你，我親愛的，阿歷克斯，還有我，直奔到花園頂頭，奔到玫瑰涼亭，夏季的妊紫艷紅，垂垂累累，日當正午，滿地落紅。後面是緊密的樹籬，有洞也是樹枝牽拉。自然，他們都不敢鑽。他們都穿著好衣服，怕挨父母罵。不管他們了。

詹姆士，你先走到哪裡我都跟著你。你迅速彎下腰穿過樹籬，我緊跟在後。然後我們就進入了一大片玉米田，無邊的藍天，原野的燠熱。現在就我們倆，我的歐亞混血表哥，在英格蘭的鄉野裡。

英格蘭，我的母語不是英語，英語是我習慣說的語言。起先，只聽得我們監護人外婆和她的密友們嘮嘮叨叨說廣東話，在一片麻雀喧聲之上。但不理解時間又如何理解語言？生活會變得太滑溜。

既然我能如此理性地思考，我現在想必已醒來。一睡著邏輯就消失。當然，我是醒著。我現在能看見他，我將嫁的男人，過去三年他一直在我身邊。難道他不英俊？瞧他的眼睛，黑睫毛長長的，也太長了一點。他長得怎樣？皮膚黝黑，很有男子漢氣慨，肩膀寬寬的，瞧，足可讓我把頭擱在上面休息。手好大，比我的手大一倍，手指又長又寬，漂亮，強壯，男人的手。

他說他喜歡我的手，小巧，潔淨，也喜歡我的腳，小但踢人挺狠。你認為你可以控制我？我讓你相信你能，我笑得明朗，像菩薩，數到二十，我知道你需要覺得自己像男子漢，某些時候。

一個英國人，但在外國住得太久，變成半法半英，非法非英，二不象，長在海峽裡，來回移動像輪渡。

此刻我們在哪裡？啊，在我們的十日之遊中，穿過西奈，不必上班真是愜意。

這是什麼？訂婚戒上的藍寶石掉下了，像一聲尖叫，從我身上溜走。一閃，一星兒光，就不見了，掉下地板。外婆，別說什麼了，霉運之兆，幫我找找。外婆正把她的無線電話裝進圍裙。她剛打電話叫警察來幫著找。金阿姨給了她這電話，免了她奔跑去按電話。

外婆現在在舊金山養老院過著好日子，可能還會談戀愛，誰知道？金阿姨看見二個老黑人在電梯裡調情，男的約女的在飯廳見，女的大笑。他們會結婚嗎？會像小說中那樣共享孫兒孫女嗎？

愛情不可能以玩笑開場，不，很可能以誤解的瞪視開場。他跟我跳舞，我們說的不是一種話，但像在水中一樣湊在一起。像華爾茲舞我們四肢合拍，腳步一前一後應答，接近，接近，又離開，談判出一條妥協之路，穿過舞池，穿過時間。

此事原應說是不可能。至少，得做一個講究實際的少女，你已經習慣了富裕的生活。熱水淋浴，空調，快車，自動取款，而他什麼也提供不了。對此他很窘，他承受這種事，像承受打到背上的鞭子,賭咒說中國男人一向性格軟弱。難道他要我對他的決定承擔責任?我不幹。

像海中一條魚,清涼的水柔和地流過,在水面之下。沒有刺耳的聲音,透過我寧靜的內心世界。多好,在虛空中,在使人安寧的黑色中運動。啊,睡眠,擁抱我吧。

莉蓓卡頭靠著窗。她頭垂下了,嘴慢慢張開,形成一句話的開端。

約翰傾身向前,看她,他準備娶的女人。他喜歡看她睡著,毫無防禦。他情願她這個樣——她有時太要強了,太作主了。還是睡著了好,無休無止地睡下去,像個孩子。他可以保護她。

她二十六歲了,但臉上毫無歲月的痕跡。如此明朗,如此柔順,像蓋在過度文明的裂縫上的一個面具。

車窗外,沙漠延展,比睡眠更廣闊,沙蓋著岩石,灌木壓著沙。旅遊車的揚聲器中傳來毛拉的哀訴,是人對上帝訴說,還是人對人訴說?那麼女人何在呢?

他是在辦公的地方見到她的,從八點到八點,在金融區,一週五天,一年四十八週。老是那倒霉的地鐵,同樣膩煩的旅程。除非倫敦地鐵和愛爾蘭共和軍的無能造成意外,每天來回熟悉得叫人喪氣,甚至同車的總是那伙人。莉蓓卡不懂這個,她從來沒有在同一時刻出門。她有意多換車,總是遲到。「不然生活不就太乏味了!」她老說。

在車裡他總是讀「獨立報」,內容亂塗在頭腦中,眼睛裡,手指上,油墨甚至弄髒了他的西服。他有時看得見自己,那形象是對自己的虛榮的一種嘲諷。瞧那黑睫毛,黑眼珠,古板的隱格西裝,刮得乾乾淨淨的下巴,他感到緩慢的清晨脈搏輕輕地拍打著藍襯衫的領子。

只要他朝鏡子裡端詳自己時間稍長,莉蓓卡就會嘲笑他。「一清二楚,你不用看――你皮膚黝黑,男子漢氣十足!」如果她不太忙,她也會來看鏡子中的他,看他的黑眼珠,然後他們就會在鏡子前瘋狂地做愛。

三年了。他們在工作地方見的面。他剛跟一個別扭的顧客談完。顧客總希望熨平所有的不快,消除一切誤解。因此他作了一個年少氣盛的出色表演,顧客走時心裡挺滿意,覺得自己的利益由好人在保護。

他的老板朝他說:「約翰,想到德魯果酒吧喝一杯慶功酒嗎?我們差點少了一個顧客,感謝上帝我們不必去跟斯蒂夫解釋,今後還得對付同樣難弄的事。」莉蓓卡這時正好走過,長腿,黑髮,爽快,微笑。這麼說她就是新來的小姐―她轉過身,給了他們一個陌生者的開朗笑容。

徘徊了二星期,像餓狼一般打圈,留下一路請吃請喝的蹤跡,邊界標記則是調情式的電話。他沒想把她帶給父母親看,還早。但他一開始就帶去見朋友。

約翰把重心從右腳移到左腳,一聲不響,像棉花碰到棉花。座位太小,他的腿沒處放,膝蓋頂著前面的椅背,空調器的風比英國夏日海濱的風還要強,還要冷。莉蓓卡小巧裸露的腳擱在他的腳邊,好像一個感嘆號。

我在想什麼?我的儐相尼爾,我和他分享了無數次飲酒,吵架,又和好,甚至分享過汽車失事,只聽她說了一句話,他馬上就喜歡上她。「她從哪兒學來這麼漂亮的英語?來自香港還是新加坡?非常西化嘛!」他拖長聲音說話,一向要言不煩。

我可從來沒這麼想過。起頭的原因可以是慾望,好奇,生物性要求――誰知道?但決不是種族政治。

她老是嘲弄我一副英國派頭,有意與我保持距離。但她不是唯一想把我推開的人。威廉,我的遺傳伙伴,八面玲瓏的傢伙,老是花言巧語跟我父母說話,他可不想讓全家前後為難。他生活中的每一步都得計劃週到，前後圓滿，哪怕我們只是半個法國人。要一個中國姑娘－－鄰居們會怎麼說？真是個可憐蟲。

我多希望能像她那麼容易入睡，瞧她蜷縮在座位中，像只貓，像個孩童。結了婚又會怎樣？無窮無盡的晚宴聚會，不久就是一大堆混血孩子的哭叫？那時她依然會是我愛的女人嗎？

莉蓓卡小巧的裸腳在他腳邊像個驚嘆號。

車窗外，雲像舞伴迅速聚集。在沙漠上空它們變得又黑又大，最後是雷的嚎叫和第一個閃電，比落下的雨純潔。保羅到大馬士革去的路上遇到的不就是這種閃電？

莉蓓卡動了一下，馬上醒了過來。「我睡著了多久？」

雨猛烈地傾向乾裂的土地。

「噢，好幾個小時了，」他說。

趙毅衡譯

Lab Ky Mo

Dining Alone at Wong Kee Restaurant with Seven Men

Knowing none of the names of the seven Chinese waiters on the ground floor, I feel there is a need for a system through which they can be differentiated. Now of the seven, two are distinctly taller than the others though none of the seven can be considered tall relative to the Western man, than whom they are a half-foot or more shorter. But for practical reasons, I will upgrade the two who are of average height (on a par with the Westerner) to the more elevated status of being the "Tall" ones; consequently, the other five waiters assume the role of being of "Average" height (despite their being short). One of these five is in fact distinctly shorter than the rest (very, very short in Western terms). I will henceforth call him the "Short" one.

Of the two Tall men, the one who's youthful and thin will be called the "Handsome" one, as he is not as displeasing in appearance as the other, a larger, bespectacled man of more advanced years - the "Fat" man. Of the four who are "Average", any future reference to them will not in fact be to their height (in which they differ only slightly) but rather, they will become the "Angry" one, the "Happy" one, the "Bald" one and the "Evil-looking little" one, respectively.

So there you have it, an introduction to the waitering staff resident (at the time of writing) on the ground floor of Wong Kee Restaurant on Wardour Street in London. These are the nameless men who people our restaurant and cater for our culinary needs. Our problem of distinguishing between them arises not so much from their "inscrutability" as from their all being of roughly the same height, namely short. But fortunately for us, and contrary to popular belief, they do *not* all, in actual fact, look the same, allowing the writer to come up with appropriately differentiative descriptions. Discrepancies in this system of categorisation exist; for example, the Happy man who is a bit on the heavy side is not to be confused with the Fat man, and the Bald man does tend to be rather *angry* quite a lot of the time, but not sufficiently so as to deem him the Angry man, if you see what I mean. There are, of course, many more waiters in the three-tiered structure of Wong Kee's but I prefer to deal only with those seven who work on the ground floor (remember - we are, after all, dining alone). And, anyway, further classification of many more waiters without names would prove somewhat taxing on the finite human brain whose store of adjectives is far from infinite.

Of the Wong Kee customer, there are two types: those who have been before, and secondly, those who haven't. Those who enter the door of Wong Kee's for the first time divide further into those who will come again in the future and those who definitely won't. But whichever category a customer falls into, and despite any further sub-categories he/she may be susceptible to, only a very few, if any, will be unaware of Wong Kee's formidable reputation. Renowned for her cheap food and high turnover of customers and profits (the latter appreciating in direct correlation to the former), Wong Kee is, however, best revered (and feared) for her treatment of customers. Daring, culinary pilgrims from every corner of God's earth come to brave her wrath. Converts of Wong Kee return with almost religious regularity and obedience, whereas those who do not survive their first Wong Kee experience unscathed will never set foot in her lobby again. In Gerrard Street itself, Wong Kee commands an aura of respect from all her neighbouring restaurants for the omnipotent authority which she wields over her customers. The Wong Kee customer is *not* always right; both right and wrong are relative to the prejudices of this establishment.

And what about the customer? Well, those who come to Wong Kee for the first time are almost always brought by a friend who has been before, but one might question if that be a service or disservice. On the other hand, it could be a genuine recommendation by an enthusiastic regular, but more likely than not it falls under the more probable category of a "dare" or an "experience" (i.e. one that does not require itself to be repeated). These so-called friends are easy to spot; they are the ones who enter the restaurant first, confidently, whereas their entourage follow behind tentatively, and expectantly. As soon as a waiter - say, for example, the Evil-looking little one - thrusts an aggressive arm at them, and then in the direction of heaven, simultaneously blaring out the command, "UPSTAIRS," the friend, that confident rascal, turns to his pack with a smug smile as if saying, "You see, didn't I tell you so?" And thus, he ushers his guests into a practical joke in the manner of one guiding another through a door on top of which sits a bucket of water. But let's quickly bypass these people, who are no more respectable nor less common than the dreaded tourist. It is not with these dregs of restaurant society that the writer is concerned here, but rather with that altogether different calibre of customer - the lone diner.

The psyche of those who dine alone has always been an interesting phenomenon, protruding conspicuously from the general landscape of eating out. However, having said this, I have to correct myself and specify that it is only interesting to the extent to which a person chooses *not* to dine with a companion but rather to dine alone; those of us who have no friends, or are generally disliked by prospective eating company and thus have no choice other than to eat alone, are exempt from that category of being "interesting". I concede that one must eat to stay alive but I would suggest that one might, in this case, eat at home!

Of the types who choose to dine alone at Wong Kee, whether interesting or not, there are two White men, one Black man, one Asian man, three Chinese men, and one woman; seven diners in all, one for each of our waiters.

The categorisation of the White men into two types has, in fact, nothing whatsoever to do with class or social standing. There is the White man who comes to Wong Kee to eat Chinese food and the White man who comes to Wong Kee *to show* that he eats Chinese food. The former commands my highest respect whereas the latter is, in my opinion, no better than the tourist and warrants treatment as such, i. e. one should do one's utmost to ignore him. The latter walks into the restaurant and just as soon as he can sit himself down is already insisting on telling his neighbour that he is a regular. The response received largely depends on whether or not this neighbour is one of the three Chinese men, all of whom will acknowledge him but none of whom will indulge him in the form of a conversation, for one of two reasons - the first being, this Chinese man can't speak English and the second, this Chinese man *won't* speak English, not to this man, at any rate. The Asian man, however, can often be persuaded to enter into a conversation with him, and aside from his taste for hot chilli there is nothing more that the writer wishes to say about this man. The man who seeks to be indulged here is, more often than not, a member of the ranks of the lone diner who may be classified (see above) as belonging to the "less interesting" variety, i.e. he is a man who has no one with whom to dine. And this being the case, he seeks to befriend anyone sitting in the immediate vicinity.

Now, fellow benefactors of Wong Kee, do not be fooled by the advances of such a man. This man has two tricks up his sly sleeve with which to feed on his unsuspecting prey. The first is a stalwart and staunch declaration of his support of the restaurant, spear-headed by "I eat here all the time," followed in quick succession by "The food here tastes great - it even *looks* great too. And it's cheap." But beware, for this is a man of self-rhetoric: a man who is keen to converse with himself. This is a man who knows all the answers to all the questions which he asks himself.

His second tactic is far less obvious but all the more deceptive for it. He is well known for preying on those of us who are unfamiliar with this restaurant. He will wait patiently for us until we appear shocked, if only mildly, at the manner in which we are duly treated by any one of our seven waiters. As for example, when the Bald waiter chooses to walk away from you at that precise moment when you are about to order your meal. The Bald one looks to be in a sulk for no apparent reason and appears to be refusing to come back to serve you. At this point, the man of the above-said accusations might turn to you with a consoling, "Don't worry - they treat everyone like that here. You just have to ignore them." Now this might seem like a well-timed, considerate word of consolation and, admittedly, you are currently in a very vulnerable position because, let's face it, you've entered a restaurant and been told to sit down only to have the waiter walk away from you in a sulk! But, despite this, I would urge you to stand your ground and do your best not to enter into conversation with this man. Why? He is a turncoat; although he will readily admit to being a regular, he will also, without hesitation, attack the establishment with much double-faced venom: "Oh, they don't know how to treat customers with respect here. I've been coming here ten years and the service has just got worse and worse!" (Remember, this is someone who calls himself a regular; a man who keeps coming back for more.) More often than not, this man is nothing more than a social outcast - a leech who considers sharing a table with a stranger in a restaurant a social highlight in his pathetic timetable. This is a man with many troughs but few peaks - don't sink so low as to indulge him.

The White man of that altogether different calibre - the man who comes to Wong Kee for no other reason than to eat Chinese food is a man of culinary mettle. His is a style and an air of grace that commands respect from even the waiters themselves. These are men who are capable of ordering a large meal without so much as a brief glance at the menu. These are men, most importantly of all, who know how to eat in silence. But that's not because they are quiet, wimpish, impotent men to whom a command of words is an anathema. No, not by any means. These are men who order their meals articulately and with a voice equal at least in volume and tone of authority to the grunt of those who wait on him. These are men who are of enough substance to be capable to challenge even a waiter - "No, I'm sorry but it was Chicken Curry I ordered - not Chicken Fried Rice." With this, the whole restaurant comes to a standstill; those other White men who insist on talking to themselves are shocked into speechlessness, if only for a moment; the waiter pauses, as if to assess the magnitude of the threat. The waiter - the Evil-looking little one, walks away and returns only to walk away again like some boxer dancing nervously on his feet at the start of a fight.

"Chicken Curry? NOT CHICKEN FRIED RICE?", the Evil-looking waiter is looking very evil indeed and noticeably angrier with it.

"No. Chicken Curry." Where previously lesser men have been broken, this customer stands his ground, and wins. The waiter concedes to his opponent and walks away but not without his honour; he has weighed up his opponent and knows that he has met his match - there is no shame in meeting an equal, only mutual respect.

But that was the White man. The Black man makes an altogether different type of opponent, as we shall now see.

In much the same way that one type of White man has a compelling urge on entering a restaurant to talk to his disinterested neighbour, the Black man walks in well-prepared to engage in social debate of an altogether different kind. The Black man comes in as if with his fists held up in the sparring position, more than ready to defend himself, whether verbally or physically. Remember, this man carries a history of oppression, of slavery and of exploitation on his shoulders. When the Black man stands up, he stands as an ambassador for his whole people.

"LOOK, MAN, I'm not sittin' beside no bin!" the Black man protests to the Handsome waiter. The Handsome one, who is usually quite a mild-mannered man, is slightly taken aback by this statement.

"Look, who do you think I am that you can sit me down beside rubbish? I AIN'T RUBBISH, OK?" the Black man continues.

The Handsome one looks down at the innocent bin and then back up to the Black man, "You sit where everybody sit. OK?" he says, trying hard to keep his patience.

The Black man is offended. Never one to lose a fight, and never one to argue in such a manner so as not to draw the attention of everyone else in the room, he stands up now like Mohammed Ali in a suit, drawing attention to his solitary fight for human rights, and for liberty. The White man shakes his head and sighs as he looks up from his meal, for he knows that, contrary to what the Black man may think and feel, this is not in fact a discussion of humanitarian equality. To this one White man, the issue is very simple indeed: the waiters run this part of the restaurant and, within this context, they can treat anyone how the hell they like. More often than not, all customers, regardless of race, colour or creed, are thrown into that general category of second-class citizens - the customer (subordinate, that is, to the waiters themselves). Thus, all customers are treated the same.

"Look, you can't speak to me like that. I won't let anyone treat me like that, you hear? Give me some respect," the Black man declares as he is moved to a seat a little further away from the bin than the one previously allocated. It is a proud monologue and he speaks it to the whole ground floor; but, more importantly, he represents his whole people and is, in fact, speaking out to the whole world, calling for equality. The Handsome waiter has still not lost his temper and allows him his little speech; some customers you just don't want to mess with, unless you are prepared to MESS them up in the process, because you will know they will never concede.

Watching this little episode resolve itself is our one lady customer dining alone on the ground floor. This woman, who may be White, Indian, Chinese or Japanese (it matters little), is part of a dying breed, not unlike the woman who still feels safe enough to walk home at night after dark. She too has to be on the defensive but, unlike the Black man, she prefers to attract less attention. And whereas the White man, the talkative one, is not particularly discerning as to whom he might target, this woman, on the contrary, can attract conversational overtures from even the most quiet of men and even, at rare times, from one of the three Chinese men. And whereas the talkative White man might enter a conversation with another diner without any preconceived sexual overtones or intentions, it is sad to say that, more likely than not, it is the sexuality of the Woman that attracts the most banal of chat-up lines, such as "What's that you're eating there?" Now depending on how sociable the Woman wants to be at any particular moment, she can reply in one of two ways. The more succinct "Sweet and Sour Pork" reply has been known to terminate more conversations than the more provocative alternative of, "Sweet and Sour Pork. What is yours?"

And thus, the woman who is not unfamiliar with the experience of eating alone in a crowded place (widely known to be significantly safer than walking home alone at night with no one else in sight) learns to gauge the direction in which conversational niceties may swing.

It is true to say that Wong Kee Restaurant survives as one of the last bastions of human society (in Greater London, at least) where complete strangers are known to introduce themselves to one another and thus enter into civil conversation. However, this rare and precious facility has been abused and exploited by those of us (men) who as well as having no men friends with whom to dine, have no women friends either. I feel it my duty to point out that the mere fact of sharing a table with a stranger in a restaurant does not obligate that stranger to become emotionally involved with his/her fellow diner. Now, if some men choose to take advantage of this situation (as they have been known to do) and introduce themselves to anybody in the restaurant then I guess that is outside the jurisdiction of the establishment. This is somewhat unfortunate to the extent that the primary function of this establishment (that of restaurant to serve food to the customer) has been superseded by an altogether different imperative, that of social interaction, whether platonic or not. The writer appreciates that both these instincts (that to eat, and that to socialise) are equally natural and necessary within the make-up of *Homo Sapiens* but I would suggest that the latter be restricted to an arena more suited to it - a discothèque, or a public house, for example.

On this note of social activity within the context of Wong Kee Restaurant, I come to our last diners, our three Chinese men, whose desire (or ability) to socialise goes further than the minimal words necessitated by ordering one's meal. Reputed for his verbal modesty, the Chinese man seeks to express himself in different avenues, namely, those of his hair, as I shall explain in a moment.

Those Chinese who walk through the door of Wong Kee's and yet do not work there as waiters or cooks invariably make up that nucleus and breed of patron to whom the non-Chinese clientèle refers as "they" in the well-worked phrase, "Well, if *they* eat here then the food can't be that bad." *They* do eat at Wong Kee's and *they* do it both frequently and in great numbers. Of our three Chinese customers dining alone on the ground floor, two are bald. Of the two who are bald, only one can be said to be typical of that part of society where this telling human condition is commonly found - namely, the elderly male. And so we have one Bald, Old man, one Slightly-less Bald Young man, and another Young man whose hair still inhabits his scalp. The Young man who has hair on his head is of an advantage over and above those two who are bald, for it is with his hair that he seeks to express himself to the world, and for the duration of this meal, to the rest of his fellow diners at Wong Kee's. This Young man might, if he wished to make a statement of it, use any number of styles to differentiate his black head of hair from any other black head of hair in the restaurant - a noble enough aspiration, for what lies under a head of hair is a head, in which one expects a brain. But I would argue that if one's mouth does not do an adequate enough job in expressing one's thoughts then might one not hope that the hairs wavering on top of one's head would suggest that the brain underneath is neither dormant nor impotent? Consequently, pony-tails, rat-tails, crew-cuts, bowl-cuts, short and long fringes, and side-burns abound as the Chinese man walks in through the lobby of Wong Kee like some Samurai off the street, more than compensating for any deficiency in verbal vocabulary.

However, for the Bald Chinese man no such alternative serves to colour his bleak and silent landscape. For the Bald, Old Chinese man, it is only half as bad since there is an inverse correlation between his hairloss and an accumulation of respect as he ages. The

Old Chinese man (or woman) is part of a valued generation. Theirs is a privilege few of less advanced maturity can obtain; these old folk need merely to step through the door for the whole of the waitering staff almost to fall to their knees in service to them. They command the best tables on the ground floor; they also get the complimentary vegetable dish (that precious commodity envied by lesser diners); the Happy waiter smiles a little more and the Evil-looking little man makes some effort to appear less threatening in such revered company. The words "Thank you" have even been known to escape from the Angry waiter's mouth, which is significantly less foul when serving this customer. Such positive discrimination towards these old gentlemen leads me to assume that they must either be family or share-holders. Whichever the reason may be, theirs is a meal you would not readily wish to disturb.

And there you have it, a brief introduction to the characters who frequent the Wong Kee Restaurant daily. "Poetry in Motion", a friend and fellow enthusiast once described its daily hive of activity. Maybe not poetry, I would add, but certainly there are lessons to be learned from dining alone at Wong Kee's with seven men. Store up enough adjectives so as to be able to differentiate all the different characters, waiters and customers alike; keep well clear of the Talkative White man; order your meal and sit back and enjoy this society within a society.

Our first customer to finish her meal is a Japanese woman who then pays and leaves as one of the waiters, the Handsome one, waves "Sayonara". Those waiters whose command of Japanese exists not are left to look on in silence.

巫立基

在旺記餐館和七位先生獨自進餐

在樓下一層有七位中國侍役,但他們的名字無從知道。我想應有一個方法用來分別他們。現在七位當中,有兩位較高,因此,他們可以稱爲「高」的人。但是,雖然如此,這七位人士無一可以以西方男人的高度來相比,實在,平均上比他們要矮半呎,或以上。然而,爲了分類的實際原因,我將把那兩位平均高度(以西方人水平)的男士提升至較出色的「高」的一項;同樣地,其他那五位較矮的,將入於「平均」之高度(雖然他們算是矮)。現在這五位「平均」高度的當中,有一位實在相當矮(以西方來看,相當矮)。這較小的一位從今起會被稱爲「矮」的一名。

在兩位高的男士中,一位較年青和略瘦的將被類爲「英俊」一級,因爲他在外貌上較另一位好看;那位身形較寬,架著眼鏡,年紀較大的一是爲「胖子」。在那四位平均高度的男士中,將不會以他們的高度來分類(四位差不多高度),而是,他們將成爲「生氣的」,「愉快的」,「光頭的」和「兇惡細小」的類別來分辨。

你看,這就是倫敦 Wardour Street 旺記餐館樓下侍役們(寫時)的寫照。他們就是在餐館招呼和爲我們預備菜餚的無名人士。要分辨的困難不是因爲他們「神秘莫測」,而是在於他們的高度大致相同,即矮小。幸好(雖然一般人不贊成這樣說),我們看出他們並非每位樣貌相似,因此作者能夠以足夠和適當的方法來描述。但當然這分類的方法矛盾仍在;例如,那位愉快的人,身材較大,不要和「胖子」混淆;而那光頭的有時候也會生氣,但又不如另一位那樣「生氣」,你明白我說的嗎。當然,在這旺記三層高的餐館,侍役多著,但作者寧願和樓下做事的七位交易(記著,我們,都是獨自吃飯的)。而且,再把那些無名侍者繼續分類,這對人類有限的腦袋,藏不了無限的形容詞來說,似乎過份。

在旺記的顧客中，有兩種類－一是老顧客，另一是新的。於是再繼續分支類別中，包括那些剛來光顧的顧客－將來會再來的，和那些將不會再來。但無論怎樣分辨顧客，和雖然再繼續把他／她分類，其中只有很少清楚旺記的聲譽。旺記是以她的價低、客多和利多而著名（最後一項和前者有直接關係）；但是旺記最使人敬重的（懼怕的）是對顧客的態度。勇敢的，愛吃的顧客從上帝每一角落來朝聖，歸依旺記如宗教般定期地和服從地回來，但一些受不起第一次旺記經驗的，將永不再踏足餐館前。在 Gerrard St. 來說，由於旺記能支配其顧客的權威，招來鄰近餐館對她的敬意。旺記的顧客不一定是對的；對和不對都是對這生意的偏見有關。

顧客又怎樣呢？唔，那些初來旺記的人大多是由光顧過的朋友帶去，但你會問該朋友所介紹的是生意還是搞蛋生意。一些來說，多是由一位熱心的老主顧推薦；但大多歸入到另一類「膽敢」或「嘗試」（例如，一次過，不再光臨）。這些所謂「朋友」，很容易辨認；他們多是那些很有信心地首先踏進店子的，然後他們的伴友跟著怯怯的走進來，當一位侍者，例如，那位兇惡矮小的一位，走前伸出那來意不良的手，向上一指天堂，大聲地向他們喊著「樓上」時；那夠膽頑皮的一位，便會向他的同伴作一個會心的微笑，好像在說：「你看，是否如我所說的？」然後，他就帶著朋友以似乎在水桶機關的門下驚恐地走過的態度上樓去。雖然他們引起不少人注目，但且讓我們快快繞過這些既非上流又非流氓之輩的人士，去談別的。寫這篇文章的主要目並非要講這些無聊的餐館社會，而是集中於那些單身的食客，因為這情況是出外吃飯有趣又而觸目的現象。但是，我應在這裡指正一下，有趣的只是限於那些寧願自己進食，而不願與朋友一起的人；而非我們這些沒有朋友，或被所有高尚的朋友討厭一起吃飯而才在此獨自進食的人，都不入於「有趣」的範圍內。我承認人必需吃來生存，但我會認為，在這情況下，在家吃飯最佳！

在旺記獨自吃飯的客人當中，且不論有趣與否，他們是兩位白人，一位黑人，一位印度人，三位華人，和一位華婦；總共七位，正好和侍者一對一。

白人裡，有兩類形。類別與身份和社會階級無關，分別是：來旺記吃中國菜的白人和來這裡表現自己會吃中國菜的白人。前者獲得我最高的敬意，但後者，在我來說，比不上遊客，更不應接受如此的招待；最好，盡可能避開他。後者走進餐館後，一坐下來便堅持要告訴鄰桌，他，事實上，是位老主顧。那鄰桌的反應要看那人是否三位華人之一，他或會和他打個招呼，但沒有一位會和他談起來。其中理由有二：第一，那位華人不會說英語，第二，他無論如何都不肯和這白人說英語。而那亞洲人，卻可以被誘交談，除了他喜歡吃辣的食物外，作者找不到什麼可以拿來談。這位被人拉著談話的，多是獨自吃飯的顧客中被劃為「不大有趣」的一員，例如，他或找不到朋友一起吃飯。因此，他希望和鄰近的食客交友。

現在，旺記的朋友和受益者，一定不可被這種人的熱情所欺騙。這人意圖不利，正在等那些無戒心的人上釣。他首先是熱烈地宣佈「我時常來這用飯」來表示對這餐館的忠誠支持，然後會跟著說「這裡的食物眞好吃－又好看，又便宜。」你要小心，這種人會用花言巧語，他喜歡自言自語，他會自己問自己問題，然後自己來答。

他的第二個手段沒有這樣明顯卻是騙人的陷阱。他素來喜歡騙不熟悉這餐館的人，他會忍耐地等，直到我們被這七位侍役中之一的態度震驚，或略帶震驚。譬如，當那光頭的侍役在你剛要叫菜時，特意背你而去。那光頭的一位看起來不知為何生氣，亦拒絕再轉頭接待你。在這時候，那上面提到的人會轉過來向你安慰：「沒關係，他們對人是這樣的。你不需理會他們。」他說的安慰說話看來似乎時間恰當，又關懷似的，而且說真的，你的處境實在可憐，剛踏進餐館，被人叫你坐下，然後那侍者生氣地走了去！但，雖然如此，我仍舊勸你不要和這人說話。為什麼？這人是兩頭蛇，雖然，他盡在說是位老主顧，但，他可以轉過頭，毫無遲疑地說這餐館的閒話，「哼，他們不知道如何接待顧客的，我來這裡有十年了，這兒的服務變得越來越糟！」但是不要忘記，這人稱自己是常客，但又不斷地回來吃飯。看起來，這人不會比社會的小人物好多少－在他看來，和一位陌生人同分一飯桌是他那枯燥生活中的高潮。

這人在社會上失敗的時候多－不要和這種人打交道。

另一位白人卻是完全不同的類別－這位來旺記只為吃中國菜的是一位熱衷吃的藝術的人，他的態度和優雅的風度，就是侍役們都對他另眼相看。這些人可以不用看菜單而叫菜，他們，最重要的，就是可以在沉默中吃飯。但並非指他們只是沉靜，怕事，無男人氣概，容易被命令而驚怕的人。不，不是那回事。這些人知道如何訂菜，而且聲音帶有權威，比得上侍役們的無病呻吟。這些人夠穩重，甚至敢向侍者挑戰，「不，我叫的是咖喱雞－不是雞炒飯。」這話一出，全餐館霎時停頓；連白人都嚇得話都說不出來；那侍者頓了一頓，好像在看這威脅是否嚴重，那位兇惡細小的侍者，走過去又走過來，有如將要上陣的拳師緊張地舞動其腳一樣。

「咖喱雞？不是雞炒飯？」那位兇惡樣子的人樣子更兇起來，看來是越來越生氣了。

「不，是咖喱雞。」如果是較軟弱的人早就倒了，但這顧客站穩立場，勝了。侍者知道失敗，向裡面走去，但心裡對他不無敬意－強敵當頭，雙方都因對方的條件而互相尊重。但這只是那位白人的情況。黑人卻是完全不同的對手，且看下文分解。

白人，在進餐館時有一種和鄰桌的人打交道的想法，黑人則完全不同，他在進去前，已作好心理和生理上應戰的準備。他進去時，猶如手握拳頭保衛自己，記著，這人的肩膊負著被壓迫，奴隸和剝削的歷史。當黑人站起來時，儼如其民族的發言人。

「喂，你看，我不要坐在垃圾桶旁！」黑人向侍者抗議。那位英俊的侍者一向溫和，被這憤言嚇了一跳。

「喂，你以為我是誰，可以任你把我放在垃圾堆旁？我並非垃圾，知道嗎？」那黑人繼續說。英俊的看看那桶子，再看著那位黑人：「你就坐其他人坐的地方，知道嗎？」他強壓著自己的不耐。

黑人怒了，他從不愛輸，也從來不愛在吵架時無人觀戰，於是他站起來猶如毛罕墨・亞李般，要引人注意，爲全人權，和自由而獨自應戰。那位白人，抬起頭，搖搖頭嘆息，因爲他知道那黑人想法錯誤，這不是一個人類平等的爭論。他知道這問題非常簡單：這些侍役只遵從一方法：就是他們可以任意地對待任何人。很常見的，在這餐館裡，無論何種民族，顏色或宗派，都被列入第二級市民－顧客們（第二類，低於侍者們）。因此，所有顧客都視同一致。

「喂，你不能夠這樣子向我說話。我不可以讓任何人這樣對待我的，你聽到嗎？你要尊敬我。」黑人一面說一面坐在離垃圾桶遠些的位置。他說的很有尊嚴，同時他是向全樓下的人說話，而且更重要的是，他代表他的全民族，向全世界提出平等的問題。那英俊的侍者仍未發怒，由得他去說；有些顧客，除非你有準備，否則最好不要撩他們，因爲他們從不低頭。

在旁邊觀戰的有一位樓下獨吃的女客。她可能是白人，印度人，華人或日本人（無甚關係），屬於將絕種的一類，如同邪些夜間仍舊獨自步行回家的女士們。她算是歸於自衛的一類，但與黑人的不同，她不喜歡惹事生非。另一位愛說話的白人，不大著重與誰說話；但這婦人，相反地，可以和最沉靜的人打開話匣子，有時，甚至吸引到三位華人中一位和她談話。當愛說話的白人和另一食客談話時，沒有包括任何的性別方面的言外之意，但，可惜地，亦很可能地，是因爲這婦人的性別而能吸引到最枯燥的話題，例如「你吃的是什麼？」。現在要看該婦人在該時間是否愛談，她可以有兩種回答的方法。第一，較明簡的「甜酸肉。」可以截斷繼續的談話，或欲繼續談下去的「甜酸肉，你呢？」

因此，這位熟悉在擠迫地方獨自吃飯的婦人（比在晚間獨自走路更爲安全）學會如何控制談話的走向。

老實說，旺記餐館是人類社會（大倫敦）剩下來最後的一個堡壘，在那裡陌生人可以互相自行介紹，而進入談話。但是，這種少而又高貴的品質被我們（男人）污染和剝削，我們沒有男的或女的朋友可以同進餐。我認爲是我的責任指出，在餐館裡和陌生人同分一桌,並不意味著他/她之間有任何情緒上的交節。現在,如果有些男士想利用這機會(曾有這些例子)介紹自己,這我想是在餐館的法例以外。這是可惜的,餐館的主要作用(提供菜餚)漸被社會的不全而取代,無論是否柏拉圖式的純精神的戀情。筆者認爲這種意圖(吃,然後社交)對陌生人都是自然而必須的,但我提議社交方面可以到一個較適當的地方,例如,的士高,或是酒吧內。

在旺記內的社交場面內,我談到最後的食客了,我們這三位中國男士。他們的社交的意欲(或能力)不多於叫菜的那幾個字。一向以少說話爲稱譽,華人以其他方法來表達自己,例如,他的頭髮。

那些踏進旺記的中國人,除了侍者或大廚外,形成餐館內的主要分子,促使其他非華人稱呼爲「他們」,以及著名的說話「唔,如果他們都來這兒吃,這裡的食物不會壞到那裡。」。「他們」是來旺記吃飯,時刻而且來用膳數目頂多。在樓下獨吃的我們這三位華人食客中,兩位是禿髮的,第三位不是。兩位禿髮的,只有一位可以附屬於領導階層的類別－男性和年長。因此我們有一位禿頭的老人,一位快光頂的年輕人,和另一位頭上仍有頭髮的青年。那位有頭髮的年青人比其他兩位條件有利,因爲他能以頭髮向世界,和吃飯期間,向其他吃飯的人表達自己。這青年可以,如果他要宣佈什麼的話,隨意梳一個和餐館內任何黑髮人不同的髮型。這是個高貴的想法,來表達在那束頭髮內,是一個頭,裡面大家都知道是個腦袋。但我以爲,如果人的嘴巴不能足夠地表達人的思想,那頭上飛舞的黑髮不一定可以表示那裡面的腦袋既非死寂亦非無能?因此,當梳馬尾,鼠尾,平頭,蓋頭,短和長的散髮,和臉旁短髮的中國男人走進旺記來猶如街上來的劍客,足夠有餘地補充那口才上的短缺。

然而,禿頂的華人,無其他方法可以使那頭頂增色;但禿頂的老華人卻可因失髮而獲得別人的尊敬;中國的老人(或女人)是被尊敬重視的一代。這是未成長一代所不能得到的;這些老長者只須踏進門檻,所有的侍役們會衝前鞠躬地服侍。他們可以得到全層最好的檯子；他們還得到餐館送的齋菜（其他得不到的在垂涎三尺）；那位愉快的侍者笑得還更多，而那兇惡細小夥記盡力在那長者面前表現恭敬。連那位生氣的夥記都說「多謝」，很明顯地沒有那樣臭脾氣。這種對老長者的偏見態度，使我估計他們可能是自己家人，餐館的股東。無論什麼理由，你最好不要去打擾他老人家用膳。

你看，這就是每日旺記餐館顧客性格的簡描。一位朋友曾一度描寫這每日活動的程序是「活動的詩篇」；或許不是詩篇，但，我可以補充，在旺記和七位食客獨個兒吃飯確可以學到不少。貯起足夠的形容詞來分辨所有不同的性格，侍役和顧客等；儘可能不要理會那位多嘴的白人；叫好菜後坐下來享受這社會中的社會。

我們第一位吃完飯的是一位日本女士，她結了帳後離開時，那位英俊的夥記用日文說「再見」；那些不能說日文的，站著靜默地觀看。

吳何一明　譯

柳揚

江湖故事

那些喬裝的臥底都回來
江湖上沒有蓮花的消息
風依然高，月依然黑
俠隱混跡於市井
在人來人往的客店給五陵少年牽馬
眼睛永遠低垂
破帽簷壓住能能燙傷人的光芒
擦去油膩的午後
酒保把瓦背望了又望
又把抹過整個夏天的抹布洗了又洗
所有的人都說
失落的秘密依然被風塵遮隔
識風水的人流落於海外
有的看相，有的賣藥
而那早早成熟的少年人
收起了青澀狂亂的刀法
睜眼，等待黧夜而來的刺客

Liu Yang

Travellers' Tales

Those undercover agents in their disguises all come back
No news of lotus blooms in the travellers' domain
The wind still fierce, the moon still dark
Chivalrously lying low, taking up humble posts at the marketplace
Tending to the horses of young noble lords at the bustling inn
Eyes forever downcast
Their ragged brims block the scalding sun
Wiping away the greasy afternoons
The bartender looks and looks again at the roof tiles
Then washes over and over the rag that's scrubbed away the whole summer

Everyone says
Lost secrets are still concealed by hardship
Those who can divine roam across the seas
Some tell fortunes, some hawk medicines
While those youngsters who matured early
Have packed up their wild, raw swordmanship
And opened their eyes, waiting for the assasin
to come with the dead of the night

translated by Peng Wenlan

柳揚

流水帳

所有的事情都是不同的事情
他們來了,他們走了
他們趕到時史書已經殺青
頭頂象石,軀體散出燐光
他們血流盡只剩下懷念的權力
流落各朝,不知所終
所有的事情只是一件事情
你的戰爭毫無結果
你的情人卻太認真
你詛咒父親,帶著父親的氣味
梳頭時,落下一地的雞毛
伸出手,你握到了斷臂人的衣袖
只有心跳
只有心跳
是與黑暗的一次爭辯

Liu Yang

Daily Account

All things are different things
They come, they go
By the time they arrive, the history books are nearly complete
Heads like stone, bodies emitting phosphorescence
Their blood runs dry, leaving just the power to remember
Roaming through the ages, not knowing where the end lies

All things are but one thing
Your battle's nowhere near resolved
Your lover though is far too earnest
You curse your father with the bearing of a father
When combing your hair, infant tufts fall to the floor
Hold out your hand, you're shaking the sleeve of an armless man

Just palpitations
Just palpitations
It's an argument with darkness

translated by Peng Wenlan

劉索拉

吃餃子歌

(正月裡來又是一春,那流浪的人湊在一起吃得開心,趁熱吃吧您哪,吃餃子吃得是個人情,抹抹嘴您還得趕路哪!)

大街上都是不認識的人
眼看著草葉子又泛清
摘下了明月換上霓虹燈
背後聽見爹娘的呼聲緊

慢回首,回頭路難走

(耳邊響起自古的話:)

「走路要挑大路走
坐船子要坐船頭
長歇腳　飯要熱」
哎呀我的爹
哎呀我的娘
說乾了嘴　愁白了頭
老爹老娘呀

熱風冷雨它由不得人
老天爺轉陰又變晴
世上有數不清的大小路

船頭船尾好透風

正月裡來又是一春
遠方我拜拜的我老雙親
自古的話的不是不聽
嘴巴一閉我還得趕路程

Liu Sola

The Dumpling Song

With the first month comes another spring. Wanderers get together for a hearty meal. Eat while it's hot! Eating dumplings is a social event. But wipe your mouths now. You must get on the road.

> Streets are filled with unknown faces
> Soon grass and leaves will turn green
> Take down the moon and change it for neon lights
> Behind I hear my folks' pressing cries
>
> Don't turn back. Turn back and the road'll be rough
>
> (My ears sound with words from the past:)
>
> "Take the main road if you're going on foot
> Sit at the stern if you're travelling by boat
> Take long rests, eat hot meals"
> Oh, my dear ma
> Oh, my dear pa
> Their mouths dry from talking, their hair white with worry
>
> But ma, pa
>
> Rain or shine, it's not up to me
> The heavens grow gloomy and then they turn clear
> The world has countless roads big and small
> Stern or bow, you get air at both ends
>
> With the first month comes another spring
> From afar I bow to my old folks
> It's not that I don't heed those words from the past
> But once they're said, I must get on the road.

translated by Peng Wenlan

劉索拉

人堆人（摘錄）

我住的這個公寓在倫敦市中心，裡面住的人多了去。到底多少我也不清楚，只是把全世界各國怪物都集中在這兒了，沒有一個是好東西，一看他們我就對世界悲觀。醫生說我是個「仇恨心裡變態狂」患者，仇恨加變態，還有什麼活頭。每次一犯病，連出太陽我都恨。一天到晚拉緊窗簾我坐在房間裡構思，把那些招我恨的事全——想一遍。除了每天去學校上課增加警察局給我延長簽証的理由，或是做點兒臨時性工作爲了糊口及交學費之外，餘下的所有時間我都是在拉緊窗簾的黑房間裡想可氣的事。如果不是因爲樓下新搬來那家天天不停地放同一首歌，我當然一輩子不會去認識我的那幾家鄰居。

樓下新搬來的那人每天早晨八點開始大聲放音樂一直放到夜裡，老是放那一首歌，來回地唱："My postcard....."。這首歌乍一聽還行，挺熱鬧也挺感人，可越聽越可恨。尤其是在每天早晨八點我正好作夢的時候。別管我的夢好壞，到底一天一個樣，可每天這時候，它們就被"My postcard...."打斷了，氣得我在床上翻跟頭，「仇恨」病頓時發作。還以爲離開了軍隊式的學生生活後一生都太平了，沒想到在歐洲這個「自由世界」每天早晨八點有一首歌專爲了叫我起床！唉呀我太想念「街道家屬委員會」了，只有她們能阻止這個混蛋鄰居。他不僅把音樂放得比「義勇軍行曲」聲音更大，而且一放就是一天，沒完沒了，來來回回，就是這一首歌。如果我在這兒要住上十年，會聽它十年，一天不會少。如果依著我，他該被判刑，但這是個自由的國家，誰想幹什麼，就可以幹什麼。

仇恨中我只好找最近的鄰居商量對策。他們是一對中年夫婦，也從大陸來。門打開，是那個老公，穿著筆挺地正要出去，老婆坐在桌前，穿一件麻袋色的大毛衣，乍看像一堆麻袋。我打招呼，老公點頭，老婆抬頭。老公長得憨厚，老婆長得好看。問他們怎麼對付樓下的音樂，老公說：「反正我要出門。」老婆說:「走到哪裡都一樣。」然後老公對老婆說:「你真的不出去走一走?不寂寞?當然,外面很冷。」

「回來時帶棵大白菜就行。」老婆說。

「你看起來真年輕。」老公說。

「買棵大點兒的白菜。」老婆說。

「如果不是去教課我一定不出去。」老公說。

「帶上包口香糖,你剛吃完生蔥大蒜,要不嚼嚼茶葉?」老婆說。

「記住了。」老公說。

「帶上把傘。」老婆說。

「記住了。」老公說。

「廁所的門怎麼沒關?」老婆說。

「我忘了。」老公說。

「你這人沒記性。」老婆說。

老公呵呵笑著走了,留下我站在門口。

我湊過去看看老婆,她正往一個鴨蛋殼上畫眼睛。她家屋裡到處掛的一串串鴨蛋殼上全是眼睛。和她聊了一會兒,知道我們從一個城裡來,她來了一年還不知倫敦的東南西北,問她為什麼不出去走走,回答是「鬼地方」。

她肯定也有病。我知道我那個城市的歷史。

一看過她，我倒病好多了，也學會了怎麼從"My postcard"中驚醒再怎麼在"My postcard"中接著和我媽媽一起吃花生米的夢。日子一長，它倒成了好催眠曲，崩崩喳喳很有規律。再醒來後，跟著那節奏起床穿衣，出門回家，做飯燒水，"My postcard"在耳邊轟轟，挺好。

剛剛習慣了，一天夜裡就發生了戰爭。那天"My postcard"一氣唱到半夜，樓上的鄰居「呼」地打開窗戶大聲說：「嘿，請注意點兒別人的休息！」說話的人口氣像美國之音播音員似的，我當然沒有見過他。

「我他媽想幹嘛就幹嘛，這是個自由的國家，你有你的生活，我有我的生活！」樓下的人大叫，他口音也不像英國人，嗓子粗啞，好像四十來歲。

「你他媽有完沒完，就他媽這首破歌你是不是要一直聽到死！」樓上又出來了女人聲音，倒是英國口音，像英國胡同串子。

這下可好玩了，終於有了「街道積極分子」，我就愛聽吵架，反正人全是混蛋。

「我們也有我們的生活，我們的生活不需要你的音樂是不是？」樓上的那美國人既禮貌又傲慢地說。

「我這輩子沒聽過這麼難聽的歌！」樓上的胡同串子女人說。

「操你！」樓下的那歌主人喊。

「住口！」樓上的美國人喊。

「呼！」不知從哪個方向飛來的大石頭一下把我的窗戶砸破了。

「呵！」我衝著外面大叫，「誰幹的？」

誰他媽都沒聲兒了。

只有 "My postcard" 還在唱，它唱了整整一夜。

我在紙上寫了「仇恨」二字，把紙釘在牆上，發愣。

第二天早上音樂停了，可能全樓的人這才都睡。傍晚有人敲我的門，打開門見個漂亮俗男人，聽說話聲是昨晚參戰的那個樓上美國人。

「真對不起，你的窗戶是我的女朋友打破的，她的天性太勇敢，像個戰士，但是我必須賠你。」他的確有禮貌地往外吐深沉的句子，因為他戴墨鏡，看不見他的眼睛。
「你最好給我裝上，我根本不懂這個。」我不客氣地說。

「好好好，我裝我裝，一切我包了。」他拍拍胸，又突然像跳舞似地扭。

「太謝謝了。」我仍舊沒笑臉兒。他那身打扮讓我一看就犯病，穿得跟最沒勁的那種劣等西部片裡的人一樣，渾身帶穗兒，還戴著帽子和墨鏡站在我的黑屋子裡，好像我這兒有攝影機等著他似的。

「那兩個字是什麼？」他指著我寫的中國字「仇恨」。

「仇恨！」我說。

「哦！」他做出理解狀。

為了那扇窗戶，他又請我去樓上喝酒，我這才知道他叫羅蘭多，而他的女朋友是個英國「藝術家」。他們在喝酒前要按印第安人的儀式又往頭上撒土又往臉上噴煙，還嘰哩咕嚕唸好多「咒語」，但羅蘭多從不摘那個大墨鏡，不知是不是印第安人的習俗，喝酒時羅蘭多說他在寫一個關於印第安人的劇本，因此他每天按印第安人的方式生活。

「在倫敦！」我故意問。

「唉，人類。」他不回答，只是戲劇地跪下一條腿把酒灑在一堆煙灰上。

「羅蘭多不喜歡美國，那兒太俗。」他的女朋友過去抱住他。

「你是有靈感的戰士。」羅蘭多可能在深情地看她，我看不見，他有墨鏡。

這他媽就是「印第安式」的生活方式，往煙灰上灑威士忌，戴著墨鏡求愛。

我在紙上寫了「裝孫子」三個字交給羅蘭多。

他捧在手上問：「是什麼意思？」

「文化。」我起身告辭。

「我一定把它貼在牆上。」他深沉地說。

沒想到第二天他就約我合作寫個劇本，要關於中國的。當然不能少了灑土噴煙之類的風俗，可以賺大錢。

我把自己關在黑屋子裡一天，想出一個大綱來：

仇恨

我老家那個城亦可是又大又透著文明，在中國以「禮儀之鄉」著稱。我小時候的一天，就在全城的人都點頭哈腰互相客氣時候，不知打那兒來了個肚子裡帶氣的外地遊客，背著黑塑料挎包，一嘴黃牙。他「叭」地一口濃痰吐在地上，「哼」地一把鼻涕抹在電線杆上，然後大搖大擺地朝前走。後面有個本地孩子看見了，也學著吐了口唾沫在地上，抹把鼻涕在電線杆上，見沒有人管，又好玩兒，回家後就告訴別的小孩兒說有了新游戲，大家一試，還算好玩。

Liu Sola

From *The People Pile*

The central London apartment block where I lived was home to a great number of people. Exactly how many, I was never quite sure, but it seemed to be a gathering point for the world's weirdest people. There was not a single trustworthy one among them. As soon as I set eyes on them, my outlook on the world darkened. My doctor had told me that I was psychologically unstable and that I suffered from a hate complex. Was there any reason for me to go on living? When I was having one of my turns, even the sun would arouse my contempt. For days and nights, I would sit in my curtained room going over in my mind everything that I hated, again and again. Apart from attending school to provide the police with a reason to extend my visa and doing odd jobs to pay my living expenses and school fees, I spent my time in a dark room with the curtains drawn tight, analysing the things that had annoyed me. Had it not been for the new family that moved in downstairs and played the same song over and over, I certainly would never have got to know my neighbours.

The newcomer would begin playing his music at eight o' clock in the morning and would go on playing it very loudly until late in the evening. It was always the same song with the same repetitive refrain: "My postcard..." It wasn't too bad in the beginning - it was quite catchy and rather endearing. But the more I was forced to listen to it, the more I hated it, especially at eight in the morning when I was in the middle of my dreams. Sometimes my dreams were good, sometimes they were bad, but at least they varied from day to day. Yet at the same time each morning they were cut short by "My postcard..." It made me so mad I would turn somersaults of rage on the bed and my hate complex would come surging back. I had hoped that I would find some peace and quiet after all the regimentation of student life. I had never imagined that in this "free society" in Europe there would be songs especially designed to wake you up in the morning. Oh! How I missed the "Community

Neighbourhood Committee"! Those women would soon have silenced the bastard! Not only did he play his music more loudly than the proverbial "March of Volunteers", but he played the same thing over and over again unrelentingly from morning to night. If I had lived there for ten years, I would have had to listen to it for ten years and not a day less. If I had had my way, he would have been put away, but this is a free country and people can do as they please.

Driven by hatred, I decided to seek the support of my neighbours in initiating counter measures. They were a middle-aged couple also from the Mainland. When the door opened I saw the husband in a very smart suit on his way out. His wife was sitting at the table wearing a large woolly jumper. Its earthy colour reminded me of a hempen sack. When I said hello, the husband nodded and the wife looked up. He had a down-to-earth look about him and she was pretty. When I asked them how they were coping with the music, the husband replied that he was hardly ever around, whilst the wife said that it was the same everywhere. Then he asked his wife:

"Are you really not going out for a walk? Won't you get lonely? It's quite cold outside of course."

"Pick up a Chinese cabbage on your way back, would you. That'll do me," she said.

"You look so young," he said.

"Buy quite a large one won't you," she said.

"If it weren't for my teaching, I'd never go out," he added.

"Take some chewing gum with you. You've been eating garlic. Or chew some tea leaves," she said.

"Yes, I know," he said.

"And don't forget your umbrella," she said.

"I know," he said.

"Why is the toilet door open?" she asked.

"I forgot to close it," he replied.

"You never fucking remember anything," she said.

The husband chuckled and walked away, leaving me standing at the door.

I moved closer to see what the wife was doing. She was painting an eye on a duck's egg. The room was festooned with strings of eggs all decorated with eyes. We chatted for a while and discovered that we were from the same town. She'd been in London for a year but still didn't know her way around. When I asked her why she hadn't been out exploring, she said that it was a "hell hole".

I could see that she was sick too. I was all too familiar with the history of our hometown in China.

Having seen her, I began to feel much better. I learned how to go back to sleep after "My postcard" had woken me up and how to get back to my dream of eating peanuts with my mother. As time went on, its regular rhythms became my lullaby. When I got up, I'd get dressed to its tune. I enjoyed coming in and going out, cooking and making my hot drinks with the sound of "My postcard" ringing in my ears.

Then, just as I was starting to get used to things, war broke out. It was the middle of the night and "My postcard" was still going strong. My neighbour upstairs banged open his window:

"Hey! Do you mind! Some of us are trying to sleep!" He sounded like an announcer from Voice of America. I'd never met him of course.

"Mind your own bloody business. It's a free country isn't it? Just get on with your own life and leave me to get on with mine!" the downstairs neighbour rebutted. His accent was not British and he had a hoarse voice. He sounded about forty.

"Haven't you had enough of this crap? Are you going to go on playing that bloody song till the day you die?" pealed a woman's voice from upstairs. It was British and reminiscent of some character from a TV soap.

Now the fun was really starting. Here were our local "community activists". I love observing arguments and they were all bastards anyway.

"We have our own lives too you know and we can do without your music thank you very much!" said the American upstairs, politely but haughtily.

"I've never heard such an irritating song in all my life," interjected the soap actress upstairs.

"Fuck you!" bawled the owner of the song.

"Shut up!" screamed the American upstairs.

"Crash!" An enormous stone came hurtling down from one of the battlefronts upstairs and in through my window.

"Oi!" I called up. "Who threw that?"

Silence.

Only "My postcard" played on and on throughout the night.

I wrote the word "Hate" on a piece of paper, pinned it on the wall, then stared at it blankly.

None of us got any sleep until the following morning when the music finally stopped. In the evening there was a knock at my door. A handsome, but vulgar man - who sounded like the American from the previous night's battle - was standing on my doorstep.

"I'm so sorry. I'm afraid my girlfriend broke your window - she's a bit of an adventurist, a born soldier. But I must pay you for it." He was all politeness, saying all the right things, but I couldn't see his eyes for his dark glasses.

"I'd rather you fixed it for me. I have no idea how to go about such things," I replied ungraciously.

"Sure, leave it to me," he said. He drummed his chest then twisted suddenly as if dancing.

"That's very kind, thank you," I said, my face as sullen as ever. He was wearing the most nauseating clothes; all fringes, like some commonplace character from a cheap western. He kept his hat and sunglasses on even in my dark room, as if on a film set.

"What do those characters mean?" he said, pointing at my "Hate" sign.

"Hate."

"I see," he said, as if he understood.

Because of the window incident, I was invited upstairs for a drink. I discovered that he was called Orlando and his girlfriend was a British "artist". Before we had our drinks, they performed an American Indian ceremony, sprinkling earth over their heads and puffing smoke in each other's faces while mumbling "incantations". Orlando never once removed his sunglasses and I wondered whether this was an Indian custom too. Over drinks, Orlando told me that he was writing a play about Indians and consequently was trying to live in the Indian style.

"In London?" I asked pointedly.

"That's human nature for you." He didn't answer my question, but knelt down on one knee and sprinkled alcohol over the ashes.

"Orlando doesn't like the States. It's too vulgar," his girlfriend added, going over to embrace him.

"You're a soldier with a soul," Orlando said, probably gazing lovingly into her eyes. I had no way of telling of course because his eyes were hidden behind his dark glasses.

So this was his so-called "Indian way of life" - sprinkling whisky over ashes and making eyes behind dark glasses.

I wrote down three Chinese characters meaning "Phoney Innocence" on a piece of paper and gave it to Orlando.

He held it in his hands. "What does it mean?"

"Culture." I stood up to go.

"I'll put it on my wall," he said seriously.

Quite unexpectedly, the next day he asked me to co-write a play about China. Of course, we would have to keep up the earth-sprinkling and the smoke-puffing, as these were guaranteed money-spinners.

I shut myself away in a dark room for a whole day and eventually came up with an outline:

Hatred

My native city is a huge, highly cultured place. In China it is regarded as the "home of etiquette". One day, when I was a child, a stranger seething with rage came to the city. The local people were going about their daily round of sycophantic bowing and scraping. The stranger had a plastic satchel on his back and a mouth full of smoky teeth. "Pah!" He gobbed on the ground. "Heng!" He smeared his snot on a lamp post. Then he strutted off. One of the local children saw this. He too began to spit on the ground and smear his snivel on the lamp posts. As it was fun and no one told him off, he told the other children at home that he had found a new game. They all joined in and were greatly amused.

translated by Jenny Putin and Wu Daming

虹 影

鴿子廣場

(中篇小說縮寫)

認識維維安是在那個中午。她頭枕兩本厚書,自個兒躺著,一會兒就半睡半醒了。她聽見草地上有腳步聲走近自己。對任何聲音的靠近,她都本能地警覺。

陽光溫暖地撫摸著霧都大學校園草坪和草坪上的每一個人,像溢出的酒那麼柔軟。

走了整個上午,她一無所獲,找不到一個工作,無論洗盤子,賣水果,上貨架,都人滿為患。

在「匡記」餐館,她生硬地說了幾句拾來的廣東話。老闆似乎有點「唐人」少有的幽默感,笑了起來。她趕緊用英語接上,說她需要一份可以吃飯的工作就行了。

沈每天給華文報紙譯點東西,稿酬之少,只夠他抽煙。

她轉過身,背對沈遠,免得延續至今未停的爭吵。已經全攤牌了,她想。你妻子不是因為知道了我們的事,才提出與你分手。而你正是知道她想和自己的英國老闆結婚,所以慢慢拖著,逼她每月付你生活費,直到你拿到學位,找到工作拿到綠卡為止。

「那麼說,你讓我到英國來讀書,是讓我一起來吃軟飯的囉?」她轉身嚷了起來,甩出一直在她腦中旋轉的粗俗話。

「不不,你吃的是硬的,」沈遠說,臉上畫出一個笑容。

她楞了一下。她要喊「無恥!」但她止住了自己。她將門「匡噹」一聲拉上了,蹬蹬蹬跑下樓去。

沈遠並沒有追上來,他知道她又和以前一樣會回到這個讓她瞧不起的破房子。龐大無比的倫敦,竟沒有她安身之地,僅僅一晚上也沒有。

她穿著綠緞子旗袍，那旗袍開叉很高，露出她尚算豐腴的大腿，她的長髮高高地挽在腦後。幾天下來，她已經渡過了最腰酸背痛難熬的日子。

她終日微笑，這是職業要求。她和同室的二位廣東人沒任何話可說，她們只講廣東話。她默默聽著，聽懂的，學幾句，想到自己到英國後還學廣東話，心裡生出難言的悲哀。

上小學前，母親常把她關在屋頂下的小黑屋裡。家裡閣樓的天窗邊掛了個大竹籠，養了一群鴿子。下雨時，鴿子往家裡飛。木地板有漏縫，可以窺視下面房間裡的一切。那個南方城市，太陽很少出來，陰雨綿綿不斷。

名義上是哥哥餵養鴿子，實際照管的卻是母親。她原在一個小學工作，是一名不錯的教師。某次運動，父親坦白曾被國民黨部隊拉過壯丁，於是父親成了歷史反革命，母親也成了反革命家屬，被學校勒令放下教鞭，回家去，她到處求人找臨時工。

那間小黑屋使她過於緊張而快速地度過了毫無柔情的童年。她如願以償考上大學。從此她很少回家，就出國前回去過一次，然後她走得更遠，到了西歐。

出了圖書館，她走在兩幢大樓相交處的通道裡，沈遠快步跟了上來。

「今天我在圖書館等了你整天，你就這麼對待我？」

「回到你妻子那兒去吧，沒準她不會踢開你，只做那英國佬的情婦，那樣你的軟飯可以一直吃下去。」她只顧自己說，也不看沈遠的臉，逕直朝最底樓地下室的學校學生酒吧走去。裡面鬧哄哄的，酒氣、煙氣使空氣混濁，難以呼吸。

他壓低了聲音，靠著她的耳朵說，他早就知道她想嫁給老外，他不過是她的一個橋而已。

「我嫁人不嫁人與你無關。」

「你和我老婆其實沒有什麼不同，是一路貨。」

杯裡的啤酒泡沫未消散，她盯著一口也沒喝的啤酒，突然抬起手來，迎頭蓋臉朝沈遠潑了過去。

酒吧裡所有的目光都望著他們，好幾個男孩打起口哨，他轉身就朝外走，維維安的眼光盯住他，充滿了欽佩。

「小姐，不舒服？」客人在關切地問她。

她感激地笑笑說沒事，她拿起菜單往櫃檯走去，身體搖晃，她扶住一把椅子，坐下。

第四天中午時分，她已可以上樓下樓，燒開水喝。這場病來得快，去得慢。倫敦，這座迷宮般的城市逗弄了她，刺傷了她，掀倒了她。該是另想生存辦法的時候了。

這個美麗而寧靜的住宅區，讓她感到溫暖的顫動。維維安說這裡一週三十鎊房租，一月只要一百二十鎊？比她現在與人合居一室還便宜。為什麼不答應維維安呢？可是維維安為何只要我那麼一點錢呢？她一邊推開白色柵欄的門。那麼維維安為何有必要多要一些呢，如果她喜歡我留在這兒的話。

維維安的全名叫維維安‧德蒙特。她很喜歡這帶貴族氣的姓，說寧可不嫁人也不能換掉這個姓。她喜歡倫敦，不喜歡北愛爾蘭家鄉的外省氣氛。待她遊歷了世界眾多城市之後，越發對倫敦感情深厚。她好像有很多男女朋友，也有很多衣服，她很少看見她重複過朋友和衣服。

維維安說，如果你教我中文，每天半小時，我們就把那三十鎊頂學費吧。

她看得出來，維維安並不太快樂，她需要男人，是為了忘了他們。但奇怪的是她的男友被她扔了之後，沒有一個跟她翻臉為仇，仍是好朋友，她不得不佩服西方人在性關係上之大度。

她想掀開閣樓門，門很重，拉不開。閣樓上的鴿子撲閃著純潔的翅膀，互相摩擦著身體，它們的眼睛轉動著，一閃一閃，像在嘲笑她，讓人害怕。

「哈囉！」她剛準備問對方是誰，但一聽聲音就明白誰打電話上門來，「你好！」她改用中文和沈遠的妻子說話。

沈遠的妻子仍用她漂亮的英文，聲音慢慢的，聽起來不僅悅耳，而且愜意。你有眼光，我見過維維安，她就是有點怪癖，喜新厭舊。

「這不是你等待之中的事嗎？」

她繼續對她說：「維維安不錯，不錯。」

「這不關你的事！」

「沈遠可痛苦了，陪了夫人又折了情人，但他畢竟還是我的沈啊！我們感情深，別人沒法理解！」

她清醒過來，這個女人不只是來報復幾句，或許有其他用心，是因爲沈遠沒在離婚書上簽字，所以來挑動她，回到沈遠那兒去。

沈遠妻子說，她不會輕易放過沈遠，當然她得養他，這點不矛盾，她也有可能折磨他到發瘋爲止。

維維安似乎在廚房的冰箱裡取什麼東西，大聲唱著一支歌。她聽不清楚。這時，鴿子結伴飛進花園去啄食房東老人扔在花園草坪上的花生，她突然明白，她想吃鴿肉。

她告訴維維安，可維維安卻說：你神經是不是出岔子了。

「你們洋人不屑把鴿子視爲寵物，而我們中國人寵物也可以是食物。」她說。

挺著大乳房的鴿子在人前傲氣十足，不時擦過人的身體騰起，它們顯然活得比這個城市裡的許多人還輕鬆，自然。它們舒展翅膀從高處俯瞰這些不能飛的動物，不時發出一兩聲悅耳的咕咕聲。

母親打開籠蓋，抓起一只灰鴿的翅膀，把它提了出來。她用切菜刀在鴿子的脖頸上割了一個小口，血流進盛有清水、鹽的碗裡。籠中的鴿子在叫，驚恐地打轉。母親不在乎，她在鴿籠前完成殺鴿、扒毛、剖腹、取內臟的全過程，沾滿血跡的手理著內臟，找一小丁點的鴿膽。

父親每次與母親吵鬧總要提到一個男人。母親低低的哭泣似乎充滿了委屈。

她看見那個男人坐在工廠大辦公桌的一張籐椅上，他的肚子已微微腆起，滿臉紅光，母親像不認識他一樣和他說話，求他辦一件什麼事。他不願多說話，打著官腔，說要等黨委研究研究。

白天在比薩餅店打工，將當天賣不完的餅帶回來作為晚飯。這是在那兒工作的好處。她早已吃膩了，但吃這種餅省事又省錢，還有營養。以致於維維安埋怨她不動冰箱裡的食品。

維維安躺在浴缸裡說，你快點完成那倒霉的論文吧，去西班牙，呵，去地中海！她翻動水，嘩嘩地響，「直布羅陀，真是太美了，你難以想象那種美。」她著迷地回憶第一次她在地中海的陽光下裸泳。

一旦返回自然，你總想生活得更自然。

維維安走到她的房間門口，手裡拿著一條浴巾在擦濕髮。她裸露的身體，皮膚並不白晰，她站在那兒，比她穿上衣服自得、大方，維維安身材很美，遠遠超過她的想像。

母親半夜回來。門吱嘎一聲開了，又吱嘎一聲關上了。她站在五抽櫃上的小圓鏡前整理頭髮，她的背上有一道道傷痕。她的頭蜷縮在被子裡偷看母親，母親像累得背都彎了。她當時怎麼就沒有想到母親作出的犧牲是為了自己？後來她才有些明白，母親唯有在她身上才能稍稍渲泄一下壓抑的痛苦，比如把她關進小黑屋。

她套上耳機看電視，免得打擾維維安。下學期的獎金泡湯了。不是她不夠格，成績不拔尖，運氣糟。學校裁員，經濟衰退也影響了大學，縮減了資助。你摘下一顆星，這顆星不會留在枕邊閃爍，你醒來什麼都不存在了。

維維安坐在椅子上，叉著手指說，算了沒了就沒了。邀些朋友來玩玩，你的論文報告也作過了。這樣美好的週末，該輕輕鬆鬆，對不？

不等她答應，維維安便跳起來去打電話，她在這個時候能找到什麼樣的朋友來？

她看了看錶，已快七點了。

她趕緊去洗澡。推開泡沫，雙腿伸直，正好抵到浴缸那頭。她想把自己裡外洗淨。對面的鏡子模模糊糊，被水蒸氣遮住。她坐了起來，抹去鏡子上的水氣，鏡子裡出現一個眉清目秀，黑髮掛著水珠的典型東方美女。第一次對自己容貌如此關注,她呆呆地看著鏡子。她從水中站了起來,鏡子映出她修長的腿,挺直的背,背脊上的溝痕,臀部上兩個深深的酒窩。她轉過頭,維維安在門旁一盆剛萌發小蓓蕾的熱帶植物旁,她可能已經站在那裡一會兒了。

隔著門,維維安叫道,全到齊了,快來!

她打開門,燈突然熄滅了,維維安在嚷,都戴上面具。

有人遞到她手裡一個塑料殼,叫她戴在臉上,露出眼睛和鼻孔,在嘴的位置有活動的口。

有人打開了壁燈,燈光調得很弱,但可以看見各種各樣奇怪的面孔,狗臉,貓臉,狐狸,一律白色,房間裡每個人說話聲調都有意改變。

「你怎麼不鳴叫啊,可愛的鳥兒?」一頭牛對她說,打量她的旗袍,「你從中國飛來找誰呢?」她靠近牆上的鏡子,看見自己竟是一只鳥,嚇了一跳。人們胡亂拿的面具,她怎會是一只鳥?一只手在她腿上拍了拍,低頭一看,一只狐狸遞給她一支煙,她接過來吸了一口,吸第二口時,她明白了,他們在抽大麻。難怪房間裡有一種奇特的香味,叫人聞後骨頭微微地顫動,身體變得酥軟,而心裡卻非常輕鬆無憂。旁邊的老鼠叫她遞過去,音樂響起,是成人模仿兒童的輕聲哼唱的曲子,節奏很和緩。

搖晃著和自己臉不相稱的身體抱在一起跳舞。她被一只虎抱在懷裡。突然大家呆住了,門開了,莊嚴地進來一條帶人臉的狗。是樓下老人的丘比特。肯定是維維安想的絕招。丘比特撒歡地吠叫,滿地打滾。

她的臉緋紅,身體在慢慢散架,快成一堆隨時會因風起而紛飛的羽毛。我真要成為一只鳥?幹嗎不呢?她問自己。她被一只貓一把搶過來,那雙手極熟悉,柔軟而帶點潮濕,那灰藍的眼睛,紅色的頭髮還會是別人?

她不知怎麼掙脫了那只貓的懷抱,晃悠悠地從人堆中跨出去。她躺倒在自己的床上。你手伸過去,摸到那扇舊木門,門邊皂桶樹,桑葉相擁,你抓住母親的手,她輕輕撫摸你的臉。門外低低流淌的旋律裡,鼓聲輕瀉進來。但腳步聲從她床頭退去,門被輕輕關上,她為什麼不來?她想。

難道維維安有意不理她,讓她一人呆在黑暗裡。維維安早已忘了她的存在？隔壁房間裡濺起一片歡鬧聲，她驚異地發現自己嫉妒起來。

你若今晚不來我這兒，我就死給你看。」沈遠忽然打電話來，冒頭就是一句。「不信，是不是，我會死給你看的。」他激動得語無倫次，說話顛三倒四，「我不信你真是同性戀。」

她盡量控制住自己，不去回答他的挑撥，她只是輕聲緩氣地說：「你說要死，就像個人樣死給我看。你算什麼男人，只不過身上多了一塊像橡皮糖似的東西而已。」

她從床上猛地坐起，渾身冷汗，想著沈遠那個電話，越來越不安。最後輕腳輕手推開已睡覺的維維安的房門，拿了她放在桌上的車鑰匙。

在一個上坡處，她往右轉彎，進了四層樓高的一幢破舊房子前的小街。雨下了起來。

房間裡靜悄悄的，一片漆黑。她打開燈。

沈遠仰臥在床裡側，手上都是血，血濺到牆上，床單上。

她緊緊地閉上眼睛，用左手指甲掐右手的虎口，直到痛了起來，然後重新睜開眼睛，推開浴室的門。

浴缸的帘子垂在地上，她拉亮了燈，打開窗子。她站在那兒，不敢瞧那一池血水。一個人飄在滿滿一池水的浴缸裡，水是鮮紅的，淹沒了全身。

她後退一步。那一池水清澈透底，沒有可怕的紅色，沈遠蒼白的臉斜露在水上。她走上前去，搖沈遠的肩膀。沈遠一下從浴缸裡坐起，雙手掩面。

「我沒有死，你很失望，對嗎？」好一陣，他才開始說話。「難道我這輩子真差個手捧鮮花的黑衣寡婦在墳前假惺惺哭泣？」他一把將帘子扯下來，光著身子從浴缸邁到地上。他站在那兒，不知是冷還是激動，渾身直哆嗦，而那個器官縮得象根小蟲，可憐又可笑地吊在腿間。

她抹了抹濺在她臉上的幾點水珠，一字一句地說：「沈遠，我真的受不了，不是對你，而是對自己厭惡到極點。」她使勁抓住門把，「我此生此世再也不想見到你。」

沈遠呆看著地上的塑料帘子，像個公雞拔了毛洗得渾身蒼白。她心軟了一些，動了動身體，想向他靠近。但她的雙腳定在那兒了。她問自己，為何不趕快逃開？她不明白自己在等待什麼。

駛回那幢熟悉的房子，沒想到，維維安披了件風衣坐在路旁石階上，抽著煙，明顯在等她回來。

「他死了？」維維安問了一句。

「你別問了，好嗎？」她幾乎是在哀求。

雨早停了。漆黑的街道，路燈照著仍然濕漉漉的路面。她背靠著車座閉上眼睛，隔了一會，說，「他要是死了，可能我就不會離開他了。」

「那麼你跟他上床了？這麼長的時間。」維維安尖刻地問，扔掉了手裡的煙。維維安你問得太多了點。維維安沒有再說話，示意她往左邊移一下，讓她坐上駕駛座。她猛地發動，嗖的一下用大油門衝了出去，開上半夜無人的道路。

車子駛去一個圓形馬路，轉著圈。尖頂，斜頂的建築陰森可怕地注視著這輛彷彿沒人駕駛的車。地鐵標誌閃著亮光，連一個醉鬼也沒有。越過泰晤士河，穿過廣場，穿過那些古色古香宮殿式的建築，穿過那最後一批盛開的康乃馨花。整個倫敦冷漠地聳立在四週，毫無表情地注視著他們幾個人在發瘋。

她感到臉上流下滾燙黏濕的液體。她想，那可能是眼淚。

虹影

最後的情節

對面的人小心打開窗戶,忽又
猛地關上。他捂住嘴,喉嚨裡怪聲地響

那扇窗離地面有兩米高,枯黃的草
在幾層寒霜中搖曳。而暗紅的牆上
有個蝎子幾次三番想攀進窗

那人張嘴呵氣,鼻子壓平在玻璃上。然後又在屋裡
走動,他抛出整齊的煙圈,身上的白衣
使他的臉像缺乏營養的灰色石塊

他拿著一件兇器,這麼那麼比劃
隨時可能擊破玻璃,蹦進這白光扎眼的世界
抓住鮮血循環的軌跡,可是他不

而且我們不會去認識他,這層層加厚的寒霜
把我們也關在窗後。真的,誰
有興趣看他一眼?蝎子,或是‧‧‧‧

Hong Ying

The Last Episode

The man opposite opens the window carefully, only to
Shut it suddenly, his hands covering his mouth to stop a strange grunt.

The window is two metres high. The sallow dry grass
Waves in several layers of frost, and on the dark red wall
A scorpion tries several times to climb into the window.

The man breathes out a mist, and flattens his nose on the glass, then
Walks around his room. He tosses up tidy smoke rings. His white jacket
Makes his face a malnourished lime-pale.

He has a weapon in hand and points to this and that, as if he may
Shatter the glass at any time and jump into the glaring daylight world
And seize the trace of the blood circle. But he doesn't.

What is more, we shall try to know him. The thickening frost
Shuts us behind our windows too. Who indeed is
Interested to look at him? The scorpion, or...

translated by Jenny Putin

虹影

情書

信不讓我作最後的決定,它瞪著眼,然後
斜擦過我的頭頂,好像灰貓
激動的一剎那

喋喋不休的朋友,你追著我旅行
在我面前塗一片緊張不安的黃色
你讓我醒著,一直觀看你的獻舞;
說是我必有壞名聲

是的,信推擠我到壞名聲上,輕輕哼兩聲
還剔了一下手指甲!壞名聲令人想入非非

如聳在高地上的塔。而觀塔的人越離越遠
決非我一意孤行
目標正確:塔尖撐著雲端。它保証

我將成為它的同伙,長出一張
嶄新的臉,讀秒倒數,等著——

Hong Ying

The Love Letter

The letter allows me no final decision. It gazes at me, then
Flies tangentially over my head like a grey cat
In an agitated moment.

My babbling friend, you chase me in my journey
And dab an unnerved yellow before my eyes.
You force me to stay awake to watch your dance:
    You indicate nothing but that I shall have a bad reputation.

Yes, the letter pushes me towards a bad reputation, snorting lightly
Even picking its fingernails! But a bad reputation is
    An incitement to sin

Like the tower perched high on the hill. But the spectators move
further and further away.
It's not that I'm headstrong,
My aim is exact: the spire props up the clouds. It ensures

That I shall be one like it, showing a
Fresh new face, counting down, waiting...

translated by Jenny Putin

Maria Lin Wong

Shadows

She was lying amidst the fluff-balls on the bedroom floor. Above her she could see the bed-springs of the old iron bedstead; beneath her the bare wooden floorboards where the linoleum didn't reach. Through the bed-springs she saw the striped ticking of the old lumpy mattress, and contemplated the diamond-shaped bubbles where it pushed through the springs. If she tilted her head backwards and to the right she could see the other bed in the room and wondered whether, beneath it, the view would be the same. Her mind returned to the space she occupied and she questioned the presence of the fluff-balls and the thin layer of dust. Her eyes moved quickly from one corner of the space to the other and then settled on the bedroom door with its coating of shit-brown paint. Quickly she withdrew her attention from the door, lest looking at it too hard brought her mother up the stairs and into the room. She turned her head to the left and looked instead at the window. It was still light outside, although here beneath the bed it was dark - the blankets hung over the edge of the bed and partly shut out the light. But her eyes were again drawn to the door and the shaft of light at the bottom.

She could hear her mother, downstairs, talking to Aunt Esther. They were good friends. Aunt Esther came quite often when her father was away and when she didn't come here, Mother went to Aunt Esther's house. Uncle Piper, Aunt Esther's husband, was always smiling. He was a huge man. Very tall and broad. He might have been fat but not in the same way as her mother and Aunt Esther. His fat seemed hard and unyielding. But her mother's and Esther's fat was soft and fleshy and warm, and it wrapped itself around her on the now rare occasions when she was given a hug.

Aunt Esther had two daughters, Doreen and Thelma. She liked Doreen. Doreen didn't treat her like she was a child. She talked to her quite often about grown-up things. Thelma, though, didn't have time for small people. Aunt Esther also had three sons, who did have time for small people, sometimes too much time. One of them was almost a man, a boy-man, but the others were still boys. She didn't like the time she was forced to spend with the boy-man and one of his brothers.

She tried hard not to look at the door. She knew if her mother came in and found her underneath the bed, lying in the fluff and dust, she would be cross. She'd been told many times not to go under the beds. But today she had on a clean cotton frock, which would make her mother doubly cross. She'd been told often that she didn't realise how much work her mother put into washing and ironing her frocks, her brother's shirts and trousers, and the new baby's clothes. Her mother didn't have a washing machine and the wash-house was a long walk away, up near Ninnie's house. Ninnie was her grandmother. She, too, was fat - the same warm and comfortable fat as her mother - and she had a ganglion on her right arm, just near her elbow. It was a strange and fascinating thing that ganglion. It sort of hung there, and wobbled when her grandmother was busy doing things. The child wondered if it was held on by an elastic thread.

She was careful to keep the front of her dress from getting creased and dirty so that her mother wouldn't be cross.

"What are you doing up there?" her mother called. But not in an angry voice, more impatient than anything. Like when she called several times and no one answered. Or when she felt she had to say something and it didn't really matter what, so long as it came out fast.

"Shh," said the boy-man, "don't answer." But she thought she must answer before her mother came up the stairs and opened the shit-brown door and found her amidst the fluff-balls. She wished her mother *would* come up and make the boy-man stop what he was doing to her. And then she hoped that her mother would not come up and find her playing where she was not supposed to play. Both these thoughts rushed around inside her head, chasing each other, and then tied themselves into knots in her stomach.

"I hope you're not under those beds!" her mother shouted. The boy-man put his hand over her mouth.

"Move over, let me in before she comes upstairs," the boy-man's brother whispered. She felt sick, but she didn't know why.

She had already told them that it hurt her but they wouldn't listen. They told her it was all right, that she wasn't bleeding or anything and tomorrow the pain would be gone anyway. She tried not to think about it and thought instead about how she liked the feel of her freshly laundered cotton frock and her new white three-quarter-length socks. She didn't understand why they were called three-quarter-length socks but liked the sound the name made. Three-quarter-length socks. It was more musical than ankle socks. Her mother said she would need three-quarter-length socks for school, so she had more than one pair.

When the family Piper had gone home, the table was made ready for tea. The same shit-brown paint covered the lower half of the walls in the back room downstairs, just as it did in the hall and on the walls of the stairwell. The top half of these walls were a sort of creamy beige and the two were separated by a strip of paper about an inch wide. The corporation came every few years to paint over the shit-brown paint with yet another coating of the same colour.

No one knew what the house had been used for before but in the far corner of the back room, on the left hand side as you came in the door, there were three wooden steps leading up to a raised wooden platform. Built into the inglenook was a cupboard with glass doors, framed by dark-stained wood. Inside this cupboard her mother kept her dishes - the Chinese dinner service brought by some little known and seldom seen "uncle" (the term used when addressing her father's countrymen.) This dinner service was never used. The plates, cups, saucers and teapot were a sort of grey-blue-white colour, with a brown dragon sprawled across each piece, and a thin gold line around the perimeter of the plates and saucers. Despite the dark colours, you could almost see through the fine china. Her mother was very proud of her real Chinese china. Next to this were kept the everyday dishes and plates: the rice bowls her father used and the different sized dinner plates, none of which matched.

She sat at the table with her big brother (who wasn't really any bigger than she but was eleven months older so deserved the title) and her little sister (who wasn't much smaller but was fifteen months younger, so deserved her title). She didn't know where her baby brother was. She hadn't seen him since the day she had tried to wake him and he had lain there, not moving, not breathing, not anything, but with his eyes wide open. She remembered the panic in her mother's eyes, and her mother's screams when the men in the dark grey van came and took her brother away, cot and all. Mother had cried for days afterwards and had screamed at her father when he arrived home from sea, just in time for the funeral.

Her mother was out in the tiny kitchen now, no more than a passageway really, between the door to the cellar and the door to the back yard. There was just enough room to move between the cooker and the old sink which was big enough, still, for the children to have a bath. There might have been some cupboards too.

The back room was dark, being lit only by four gas mantles, two on either side of the main walls. Just next to the three wooden steps was an old black fireplace with a hob on either side of the grate. When the fire was lit, the hobs would be used to warm the plates and keep the food warm. It was a good place for her father to steam his rice.

When Father was away at sea Mother did the cooking. She cooked simple dishes; they tasted good but not as good as the food her father cooked, and her mother never cooked rice. Her favourite "mother" meal was bacon and tomatoes, except when they had to mop up the juice of the tomatoes with bread. She didn't like soggy bread. Today her mother was cooking bacon and tomatoes. She could smell them

- first both together, then each smell came through from the kitchen separately. There was a large plate full of bread in the centre of the table, surrounded by the crumbs that had fallen as her mother had carefully cut each slice. Soon everything would be ready and they would begin to eat.

Her mother never sat down to eat with the children. At least, the child didn't remember her ever having done so. When her mother emerged from the kitchen the child realised that she still felt sick and told her mother she couldn't eat.
"But it's your favourite."
"I know but I don't want any."
"Well, you'd better eat something now, there's nothing else."

She could see her mother was getting angry, so put a spoonful of the tomatoes slowly into her mouth and held it there for a few seconds before she could swallow it. Her brother and sister were already dipping their bread in the tomato juice. She felt her stomach begin to move upward, toward her throat and swallowed hard to make it go back down. She took another spoonful of the tomato and squashed it against the roof of her mouth with her tongue. But again she felt her stomach trying to crawl up her insides towards her throat, leaving a burning trail behind.

"Are you eating in there?" her mother called from the front room. She couldn't answer. She was busy holding the squashed tomato with her tongue and wishing her stomach back to its rightful place. Eventually she managed to swallow and began to cut a piece of bacon from the rasher on her plate.

"You have to eat it all before you move from that table." Her mother was still shouting. By now she knew she was losing the fight with her stomach. Her throat began to burn but she wasn't sure if that was the tomato or if her stomach had actually reached the end of its journey.

"Do you hear me?" Her mother was coming back into the room. The child looked around quickly, wondering what she should do next - sit where she was and hope her stomach would stop running up and down her insides, or run to the toilet? But she'd been criticised so many times for going to the toilet in the middle of her meal. She'd just decided to risk another telling-off when her stomach raced so fast towards her throat she could do nothing about it and everyting she'd eaten that day came rushing out. Luckily for her big brother and littler sister, she was facing away from the table and the whole soggy mess went flying across the platform and landed with a splat on the three wooden stairs. Her mother said something as she moved from the door to the platform but whatever it was was drowned out by the ensuing *splat, splat, splat* of vomit landing on wood.

She was picked up and rushed out, past the cellar door, into the kitchen, and out through the back door to the toilet in the yard where she was left to "finish it off" while her mother went to clean up the mess. She stood looking down the toilet.

She hated this toilet. Every time she sat on its wooden seat she imagined that the rats with their long tails were going to come up through the water and bite the cheeks of her bum as they dangled over the vast bowl. Or that giant- sized serpents would come snaking around the bend at the back and swallow her up, whole. She couldn't empty her stomach in there; it would only entice the rats and the serpents. If they knew there was food in there they'd follow the smell until they found it. So she swallowed her stomach four or five times and waited for her mother to come back.

That night, while she slept, someone climbed up to her window. She didn't know who he was or what he was doing there. Nor did she know how he got there. The window was very high off the ground. She could only see it from the outside if she stood in the middle of the back yard and tilted her head backwards until it touched the space between her shoulder blades. But then she was only small. Maybe he climbed up the huge beam of wood that was fastened to the wall to stop it from falling down. But he couldn't have because it was holding up the back yard wall, not the wall where her window was. He was a big man. She knew he was big because his hands were resting on the top panes of glass. There were eight altogether and if she stood on the bedroom floor on tiptoes she could just reach the wood in between the bottom two and the next two. But he was standing on the window ledge outside and he'd jammed his feet against the wall on either side of the window.

She didn't like this sleep-visitor. He frightened her and no matter what she did he would not go away. She tried shutting her eyes tightly for a long time and then opening them again, but he was still there. Then she turned her back on him. But when she turned her head around again, there he was. And he spoke to her in a rasping whisper, like the noise of new paper bags being rubbed together. "I'm coming to get you and there's nothing you can do to stop me."

She tried shouting for her mother but he had stolen her voice. When she opened her mouth nothing came out, no matter how hard she strained. He must have gone away at some point, though, because when she got out of bed the next morning there was no sign of him having been there. No handprint on the window, no footprint on the ledge. Nothing.

She started school on the same day as her big brother and they were put into the same classroom. Their teacher was a tall, slim woman who had no fat but who was warm. The child loved the smell inside the school. And as she got to know them she separated the smell of powder paints from the smell of chalk dust and the smell of the duplicator which was in a room just down the corridor. The smell of fresh paint faded as the year wore on but, following the summer break, she recognised it as soon as she walked in.

The first few weeks of school mother met the child and her brother outside the school gates. Sometimes they were given pennies to buy sweets or ice-lollies. But then their mother began to grow with yet another baby and it was arranged that the boy-man and his brother would bring them home. Her mother had no idea why the child didn't want the boy-man to bring her home from school but said it was naughty of her to cry just because mother wouldn't be there.

On the way home from school they passed through Sun Street and Moon Street before crossing Brownlow Hill and walking down Mount Pleasant. Between Sun Street and Moon Street were some other streets but she didn't know their names, she couldn't read that well yet. In these unnamed streets there were strange buildings. Just one room with a flat roof and doorways but no doors, and gaps for windows but no glass or frame. Nobody lived in there. Her mother told her they were shelters left over from the war and would soon be knocked down so that the corporation could build some new houses. Her mother told her not to go in there.

When the boy-man met her at the school gate she thought perhaps it was all right to go home with him since her mother had told her so. So she walked behind him or in front of him but never with him. As they passed the strange building with no doors and windows her big brother ran off with the boy-man's brother, across the main road. She couldn't go after them because she'd been told not to cross the road by herself. The boy-man had gone into the doorless, windowless house.

"Look what I've found," he called to her. She didn't want to go inside, her mother had told her not to. "Come and see!"
"Bring it out here."
"I can't, you'll have to come in here." She could hear his voice bouncing off the bare walls.

She stood at the doorless doorway. There were old newspapers scattered on the floor, and lots of bricks inside. Nothing else. The doorless, windowless house smelled like the toilet smelled sometimes. A mixture of damp newspaper, piss and shit that had not been flushed away properly. She didn't want to go in because it did not smell nice and because her mother had told her not to. And, anyway, it was dark in there.

"It's OK, you're with me. Your mother won't know, unless you tell her. If you're afraid of her, don't tell her." He was standing in the corner, leaning against the brick wall. He stretched out his hand and took hold of hers and pulled her inside the doorless, windowless house.

"What have you found?"

"Nothing. I just wanted you to come in here with me." He fiddled with the front of his trousers for a while and then put her hand there. She pulled it away but he took hold of it again and put something long and hot into it. She didn't want this thing that he'd found, it didn't feel very nice. The back of her neck felt strange and her stomach began crawling its way up her insides. She withdrew her hand quickly, expecting the thing to fall to the floor, but it didn't. It just hung there, balanced on the seam of his trousers.

"Go on, touch it! It won't hurt you." But she didn't want to touch it. She clenched her fists, kept her arms close to her sides and bit down hard on her lower lip.

He took her hand again and rested it on top of the thing, then slid his hand up inside her navy-blue gym slip. She felt her blood drain away as his fingers fiddled with the elastic on the leg of her navy-blue knickers. Then he began pulling them down. She wanted to pee, and cry, and run away, and be sick, all at the same time, but she was petrified. Her hand fell off the thing hanging from his trousers and she stood staring at the brick walls of the doorless, windowless house. Then she felt the long hot thing being pushed against her leg and towards the place where her pee came from.

"Don't tell your mum, will you? I won't hurt you, but don't tell anyone. If you tell your mum she'll know you've been in the shelters and she'll give you a hiding." She stared at the walls and made the building disappear.

That night the sleep-visitor came again. He blocked out the light from the street lamp in the back alley as he stood against the outside of her window. His great baggy trousers hung in wrinkles around his knees and his toes poked out from the front of his shoes. His eyes were dark and menacing and he told her, once again, that he was coming to get her and there was nothing she could do to stop him. She screwed her eyes up tight so that she couldn't see him, but she knew he was there. His long, bony fingers scratched at the glass as he tried to open her window, and she could hear and smell his foul breath even though he was outside.

"I'm coming in to get you. It won't be long now, you'll see. You can't get away from me." She turned her back away from the window and pulled the blankets over her head until he went away.

The sleep visitor came every time the boy-man brought her home from school, and every time he visited he managed to get closer and closer to her bed. She asked her mother if she could put the bed that she shared with her big brother and little sister into another room but her mother said no. The only other room big enough was the one that her mother shared with her father, when he was home from the sea, and her new baby brother. She asked her mother if she could sleep beside her in her father's place, but her mother said she was too old to do that now and that place was not for big girls who went to school. She tried to tell her mother about the sleep-visitor but she didn't have the words.

Her mother said it was a dream and would not hurt her. "If he comes again, you just shout for me. He'll soon go away."

Then she tried to explain about the boy-man and the windowless, doorless house but as soon as her mother heard where she had been she got cross and slapped her legs. Then she stopped trying to say anything because she had broken her promise and made her mother angry.

The last time she saw the sleep-visitor he had managed to get in through her bedroom window without her knowing and when she opened her eyes he was standing beside her bed. He held a huge axe poised above his head ready to bring it down upon hers. She opened her mouth to scream and felt her throat tighten, but no sound came out. She kicked her legs out but her mother had tucked the blankets underneath the striped mattress so that she would not fall out of bed in the night. All that happened when she kicked was a big gust of air as the blankets rose and fell back again. She carried on kicking until she had worked the blankets free but her feet hit nothing. He was there and yet he was not. She could see him and yet he had no substance. She saw his arms move forward and knew that soon her head, arms and other bits of her small five year old body would be lying on the floor. She could see the blood spattered on the walls and the threadbare carpet. She could feel and smell its warm stickiness all around her, the sheets felt damp already. In desperation she tried to scream once more for her mother. She opened her mouth, squeezed her eyes shut to give her more power, and put as much pressure as she could on her vocal chords. All that came out was a deep low groan. When she opened her eyes again all she could see through the fuzziness created by her tears was the darkness.

Shortly after this visit from the sleep-visitor the Piper family moved to a New House in a New Town. That particular sleep-visitor did not come to her again. But then her mother took her and her brothers to see the New House in the New Town. At first she cried because she didn't want to go, but her mother convinced her that Doreen was missing her and waiting for them to arrive. So she washed her face, like her mother told her, changed into the new dress that Ninnie had bought her, and kept her fingers crossed that the boy-man would not be there.

That night, the child had a new sleep visitor, more hideous, more frightening than the one before.

浴缸

餓的故事

輪船失事,我是唯一的生還者,抓著浮木,載浮載沉到一個面積不到三十公尺的荒島。這島其實只是海礁的突出部份,寸草不生也沒有水鳥停駐,我更沒有辦法捉魚,雖然偶爾會看到大白鯊耀武揚威游過,背鰭在烈日下閃閃發光。那天浪潮送來一個瓶子,似乎有些東西,令我欣喜若狂,敲破瓶子一看,只是一封信,是《讀者文摘》的好消息,我只有把好消息吃下肚。

過不了三天,又餓又渴,癱在地上,閉眼看見牛頭馬面朝我走來,高興得掙扎著起身撲上去,嚇得他們狼狽而逃。

後來又後來,我餓得神志不清了,我發狂了,就咬了一口手上的肉,吞下肚去,還喝了點血,總算恢復了元氣,我的肉還不算難吃。再過幾個小時,又餓了,於是繼續吃我的手臂。儘管我非常省吃儉用,不到四天,我就把兩條手臂都解決了,包括手掌。我把皮肉都吃得乾乾淨淨,骨頭也舔得發亮,我吃東西從未如此徹底。然後我開始吃小腿,其實應該先吃這個部位,因為肉質最精美。然後我又吃大腿,也非常可口,小腿,大腿,讓我挨過了十三天左右。

我本來該把屁股也吃掉,但我暫時還想坐得舒服一點;至於生殖器官那個部位,太多毛,我嫌清理麻煩,而且我想保留我男性最後的雄風,逼不得已才動口。所以我開始吃我身上的皮肉,我曾經有肚腩,現在殘存的脂肪組織,很難吃,但很耐飽。前胸及背部的肉不算多,而且依附在肋骨上,吃的時候要很小心。

大約十天,我解決了上半身,不到兩天,我把頭部及頸部的皮肉也解決了。很遺憾,耳朵及鼻子不夠一餐,若我鼻子有成龍的大可能飽一點,現在胃還是很空虛。既然消耗了大部分的皮肉,我目前樣子,差不多就是一副骷髏。現在我開始吃內臟,在吃肝的時候，發現有硬化的跡象，可能我酗酒過度，現在發現是遲是早？我慶幸自己很少抽煙，所以肺的情況很好，能夠下嚥。大腸小腸，要整個翻過來清洗一番，略嫌麻煩，但蠻可口，值得推薦。胃的內部有黏膜，也要刮乾淨，才能吃出它的原本味道。

我把胃吃掉後三天，還是一點也不覺得餓，這時我才省起，應該一開始就把胃解決掉，消除飢意，這樣我就不用犧牲身體其他部分，不用把自己吃得那麼乾淨！我很懊悔，我犯了難以挽救的錯誤。

「我真笨！」我大力敲我的頭，由於頸部沒有皮肉相連，我的頭顱與身體銜接得不太安穩，這一敲就像球一樣飛到丈外遠。

Bathtub

The Hunger Story

I was the only survivor of the steamer accident. Clutching a piece of driftwood, I half-floated, half-sank to a desolate island measuring less than 30 metres square. Actually, this island was only a protruding piece of reef. There were no signs of vegetation, and waterbirds never came to rest. Although I sometimes saw large white sharks swimming by threateningly, their backfins glinting in the light of the fierce sun, I had no way of catching fish.

That day the tide brought a bottle to shore; it seemed to contain something. The anticipation made me delirious with excitement. After breaking the bottle, I found only a letter inside: the *Readers Digest's* good news. I did the only thing I could do, I ate the news.

After less than three days, I was hungry and thirsty and lay around almost paralysed on the ground. Closing my eyes, I saw messengers from hell - men with cows' heads and horses' faces - coming towards me. I happily struggled to my feet and rushed towards them, but they became frightened and scattered in disarray.

Later and still later, I was so hungry my mind was not clear. I went crazy and bit a piece of flesh from my arm and swallowed it, even drank a little blood. My flesh didn't taste bad and at least I felt I recovered some energy.

After a few more hours I was hungry again, so I continued eating my arm. Despite being extremely economical, in less than four days my two arms had gone, including the palms. I ate the skin and the meat clean to the bones, which I licked till they shone. I'd never eaten anything so thoroughly before. Then I started eating my calf. In fact, I should have eaten this part first. The quality of the meat was the finest. I went on to eat my thigh, that was also delicious. The calves and thighs let me endure about thirteen days. I was going to eat my buttocks, but for the time being I wanted to sit comfortably. As for my reproductive organ, there were too many hairs around that part.

I didn't want the trouble of cleaning it; moreover, I wanted to preserve to the last the magnificent symbol of my manhood. I wouldn't touch it unless it became absolutely necessary.

So I started eating the flesh on my body. I've had a beer belly before. Now the remaining fatty tissue, though it tasted awful, was very filling. The quantity of meat from my chest and back was not much, and as it was attached to the ribs I had to be careful while eating.

Within a period of ten days, I had disposed of the top half of my body, and after another two days, the skin and flesh from my head and neck were also finished off. Regrettably, my ears and nose didn't even make up a meal. If my nose had been bigger, perhaps I would be fuller. Now my stomach still felt very empty. Since I had consumed most of my skin and flesh, my present appearance was almost that of a skeleton.

Now I started eating my innards. While eating my liver, I discovered traces of its hardening. Perhaps I'd drunk too much. Has this realisation come too early or too late? The condition of my lungs was excellent and they were easy to swallow down. I congratulated myself on being a rare smoker. The large and small intestines had to be turned inside out and washed clean, which was rather troublesome. Nevertheless, they were quite tasty, worth recommending. The stomach's inner part had sticky membranes which had to be scraped clean; its true flavour could be appreciated then.

Three days after I'd eaten my stomach I still didn't feel the slightest bit hungry. It was only then that I realised I should have eaten my stomach first and dispelled the feelings of hunger from the start. This way, I needn't have sacrificed the other parts of my body, I needn't have eaten myself so clean! I felt very regretful, I had made an irreparable mistake.

"I'm really stupid!" I hit my head. Because there was no connecting skin and flesh on my neck, my head was joined precariously to the body. With this knock, my head was sent flying through the air like a ball.

translated by Oliver Lim Bunnin

浴缸

敦倫記（摘錄）

你為什麼來英國？打算逗留多久？你身上有多少錢？你在你的國家從事什麼？薪水多少？折算英鎊是多少？給我看看你的機票。你在英國有沒有朋友？這個地址是什麼地方？你喝咖啡加多少茶匙的糖？你先穿左腳還是右腳的鞋？你喜歡那件格子絨的襯衫嗎？你記不記得是誰送給你的？你早上散步嗎？你用什麼方法來叫醒自己？你做夢嗎？

對答如流，把關婆娘橫我一眼，狐疑一番，決定放我生路，護照上一蓋，於是，倫敦我來啦！

巴士進城，突然我明白了，我明白啦！旅行了兩個月歐洲，也當了兩個月的瞎子，現在我知道了這個那個廣告說的是：「阿妹，為何如此憂鬱？」「澳洲佬不會為任何東西放棄XXXX」「黑的現在也供應白」，「扔掉那死爐子！」「我長大後要成為一隻貓」，「園裡的白蓮都盛開了，但你找得到嗎？」「敬啟者…」，「關於這女人，你媽警告過你…」，「為了地鐵的清潔及安全，請你把垃圾帶回家。」

後來我注意到倫敦的地鐵大多是找不到垃圾桶的，也沒有廁所。這是為了防止北愛爾蘭共和軍隨處扔炸彈。如果你在地鐵站看見無人認領的包裹行李，不要貪心撿回家，知道嗎？你應該保持冷靜，扶牆（這是防止自己昏倒），慢慢朝緊急出口走去，如果不會語無倫次，就通知地鐵職員。

我們去找阿猛阿嚇，他們從窗口探出身時，令我們都吃了一驚，闊別一載，倫敦嗇吝的陽光，使兩人都變成白雪公主。他們住在閣樓，樓下住的是老太婆，走廊有花屍混合貓尿的怪味。老太婆幾乎是精神衰弱的同義詞，所以我們要像賊一樣走路。幾日後發覺自己在公共場所也是躡手躡腳的。

阿猛阿嚇帶我們到唐人街吃東西，侍者端來一碟又一碟的味精，我們一邊吃得津津有味，一邊撿起紛紛掉落的頭髮。不遠處坐著西奈噢可奴，她放下筷子，撫撫自己的光頭，深情地望著面前的空碟，雙眸含淚唱說：「你無可比擬…。」

我們到海德公園看巴伐羅帝的露天演唱會，因為是免費的，很多人來執死雞。我們也不必辨方向，就跟著人潮走，天灰灰的下著雨，許多人都撐著傘穿著雨衣，好像送殯的行列。在倫敦一下雨就像辦喪事。

終於看見舞台了，拚命向前擠，仍然是可望不可及，只見台上一個揚著白手絹的大胖子，五宮也看不清楚，他唱得好極了，竟然和錄音機唱的一模一樣呢！

後來他唱的一首歌，說是獻給一位美麗的女士，我才知道戴安娜也在場。晚上電視看到新聞報道，夏日最後一場淫雨，淋得她花容失色，仍堅持到完場。因為她為藝術的犧牲精神，因為那場雨和海德公園傘的世界，使巴伐羅帝那場演唱會成為一個傳奇。而我該感恩的是，地球那麼大，我曾經和兩個偶像那麼接近－兩百碼而已。

有一回倫敦舉行大日本文化節海德公園升起一長串的蜈蚣風箏，煞是壯觀。有擊鼓表演（我沒看），還有近百檔的東洋食品，人頭湧湧，只見人頭，賣什麼都看不到，只好當是賣人頭。阿猛阿嚇工作的日本餐館也有擺檔。他們說顧客太多，最後什麼炒麵炒飯也上，不管什麼傳不傳統了。

阿猛阿嚇現在已變成日本人了，你說奇怪不？在倫敦變成日本人！阿猛還取日本名字，叫冼大雞，意思是多茹，這是配合她的髮型。阿嚇已沒有了昨年的戾氣，變得溫文爾雅，而且很有耐心，能花幾小時弄壽司給我們。這是自己弄也很貴的食品，必須好吃。阿猛口味也變得很素，不喜歡雞啊鴨啊，唯一例外是帶血的牛扒。兩人的樂趣就是找一間間裝璜特別的餐廳飽食一頓，探險一樣。我介紹他們到全世界最老的人人戲院的地下室餐廳去，我極喜歡它的簡單優雅，阿猛卻不以為然，不過她瘋狂地愛上了那裡的牛扒，說是全世界最好的，以後常去鋸。由於我對牛本身興趣較濃，所以不以為然。

倫敦人也不介意用二手貨，什麼保護動物協會，癌症研究協會、老人協會、盲人協會、非盲人協會等機構都有專店售賣收來的舊衣物，倒不乏顧客，全都穿出一身陳舊感。我有樣學樣，身上只有內褲是新的，毛衣本來也是新的，交給洗衣機打兩次後，也舊了。又買了一件長外套，三鎊，送去乾洗的費用，六鎊。

倫敦的男人在地鐵一坐下就把頭埋進報紙，以為他們看到世界，世界卻看不到他們。女人不是讀磚頭小說，就是玩填字遊戲。英國人對填字遊戲有特殊癖好，我想主要是他們不會方塊字，所以對格子有強烈需求，這也是所以他們會寫一個「米」字，就很高興地寫在國旗上。

倫敦治安不算差，但經常這裡那裡炸彈驚魂，生命有些朝不保夕的感覺。地鐵常因保安問題停駛，也沒人怨聲載道。但有一回地鐵大打形象廣告，說什麼「在未來的日子裡，我們接到的投訴只會來自我們自己」。我非常生氣，這太無恥了，竟然剝奪搭客放屁的權利。

倫敦有很多露宿街頭者，多數是年輕人，在橋頭或地鐵出入口，手持紙皮一張，上書「餓、冷、無家可歸」。有時路上會有沒破沒爛的彪形大漢向我討錢，感覺總是怪怪的，也有清秀的少女，帶著狗呢。我偶爾也當善長仁翁。有一份專為宿露街頭者而辦的雙週報，叫「大派發」，我對這課題非常關心，時常買來讀，但還是不很明白，只知年老的很多是退役軍人或精神病患。年輕的多是離家出走者。阿嚇說那些都是好吃懶做的傢伙，但我覺得寒風寒雨在戶外蹲一整天，再勤勞的人也吃不消。阿猛說很多年輕人一成年就被父母趕出家門，但很多還沒有自立能力，只好睡街，我還是不很明白。

後來我在一家馬來西亞餐廳工作。老闆是印裔前護士，朋友讚她菜煮得好，於是開業。但經濟不景，有時一晚才兩三桌客人，她於是向我訴苦，用兩千五百字刻劃一名女性在婚姻及事業上心力交瘁的奮鬥歷程。我一邊聽一邊以淚洗臉－剝著洋蔥的關係。

深夜我窩在床上看電視,廣告竟然比正片好看。飄飄然的麥片,會踢足球的乳牛,推銷巧克力也像賣化裝品一樣華麗。某一回清談節目,幾個人在罵一些無聊的書,但那些書眞是無聊。「如何自言自語」、「如何在夢中發達」,又有一回的課題是討論塑膠聖誕樹的存在意義,一個說沒關係,反正它只是一個象徵。另一個說不是眞的聖誕樹會影響孩子的童年,我的天,竟然可以這麼無聊!我於是無聊地看下去。

日子後來過得白開水一樣,精彩的情節全發生在電影裡,生活中唯一的高潮是夾克被人偷掉,懸案一宗,是在自己房裡不見的,但沒有其他財物損失(房間太亂,可能有我也不知道),後來逛舊貨市場買了一件軍用夾克,好像是蘇聯的,喜歡它的土黃色,貪它口袋多,方便偷雞摸狗。

回去後在口袋裡發現一枚子彈。

Bathtub

From *Notes from London*

"Why have you come to the UK?"
"How long are you going to stay?"
"How much money have you got on you?"
"What do you do in your own country?"
"How much do you earn? How much is that in sterling?"
"Show me your air-ticket."
"Have you got any friends in the UK?"
"What's this address?"
"How much sugar do you take in your coffee?"
"Which shoe do you put on first, the left one or the right one?"
"Do you like that checked shirt? Who gave it to you?"
"Do you take walks in the morning?"
"How do you wake yourself in the morning?"
"Do you have dreams ?"

All these questions were impeccably answered. The woman immigration officer cast a suspicious look on me but after a moment of hesitation, she decided to give me a chance. A stamp on my passport and London, here I come!

As the bus entered central London, I suddenly realised that I might as well have been blind for the last two months when I was travelling on the continent. Now I could understand all these advertisements.

"Sis, why so blue?"
"Australians won't give xxxx for anything else."
"Black now also available in white."
"Drop the Dead Donkey."
"I want to be a cat when I grow up."
"White lilies are in full bloom but can you find them?"
"Dear..."
"Your mother has warned you of this woman."

"For a safe and clean environment please take your rubbish home with you."

Later, I noticed that you couldn't find any dustbins in the London underground, nor any toilets, in case the IRA decided to plant a bomb in them. Be warned, if you see any baggage or parcel lying around unattended in the underground, don't be greedy and take them home. You should keep calm and while holding on to the wall (to prevent your falling over in a faint), move slowly towards the emergency exit. If you can still make yourself understood, report it to the staff.

We went to see Ah Shek and Ah Mui. When they leaned out of their window, we were surprised to see that a year of living in London without any sunshine had turned them into two "Snow Whites". They lived in an attic room above an old lady. The hall smelt of dead plants and cat piss. We had to move stealthily like burglars because the old lady was a bit neurotic. After a while, we caught ourselves walking on tiptoes even in public places.

Ah Mui and Ah Shek took us to China Town for dinner. The waiter brought us plate after plate of monosodium glutamate. We stuffed ourselves while picking up our fallen hair. Sinead O'Connor happened to be sitting a few tables away. She put down her chopsticks and stroked her shaven head. Then staring passionately at the empty plate in front of her and with tears in her eyes, she started singing, "Nothing compares to you..."

We went to Hyde Park for Pavarotti's open air concert. Because it was free, millions of people turned up. We just followed the crowd. The sky was grey and rain drizzled down. Many people had their raincoats on and their umbrellas open. The scene looked like a funeral procession. In London, whenever it rains, it feels like a funeral.

At last we could make out where the stage was. We pushed and shoved but got nowhere near it. All we could see was a blurred image of a fat man waving a white silk handkerchief. He sang beautifully and it sounded as real as if it had come out of our tape-recorder!

At the end, he dedicated a song to a beautiful lady. Only then did we realise that Princess Diana was in the audience. That evening, the television news reported that Diana, though apparently distressed by the last of the summer rainstorm, had remained until the end of the concert. Because of Diana's dedication to the arts, the rainstorm and the myriad of umbrellas in Hyde Park, that particular concert of Pavarotti's became a legend.

I should be thankful. The world may be very big but I was only a couple of hundred yards from two idols.

Hyde Park was also the setting for a Japanese cultural festival. The sight of a long winding centipede kite flying high in the sky was spectacular. There was a drum performance (which I missed) and nearly a hundred Japanese food stalls. Hundreds of heads bobbing up and down in front of these stalls made it impossible to see what was on offer. It looked as if human heads were on sale. The Japanese restaurant where Ah Shek and Ah Mui worked had a stall there. They told me that there were so many customers that they had to forget about authenticity and started selling Chinese fried noodles and fried rice.

By now, Ah Mui and Ah Shek had turned Japanese. How strange that they should turn Japanese in London! Ah Mui had also acquired a Japanese name "Shitake", meaning mushroom; the name went well with her latest hairstyle. Ah Shek had lost his arrogance, becoming more demure and patient. He would spend hours preparing sushi for us. This was very expensive even when prepared at home, so it must be delicious. Ah Mui had become almost a vegetarian and lost interest in eating chicken and duck. The only exception was beef steak dripping with blood. Their major interest in life was to go to a restaurant with unusual decor to have a good meal. They regarded it as an adventure. I recommended the underground cafe in Everyman cinema to them. I liked its simplicity and serenity. An Mui didn't think much of its setting though she was mad about the steak there, considering it the best in the world. She often went there. Personally, I think the cow itself is more desirable.

Londoners don't mind second-hand goods. There are numerous charity shops run by various institutions specialising in animal protection, cancer research, helping the old, the blind and the non-blind. And they never lack customers, who are all dressed in things from an old wardrobe. I have followed their example, wearing nothing new except my underwear. My jumper was brand new, but it has been inside a washing machine twice so it's old now. I once bought a long jacket for three pounds and spent six pounds to have it dry-cleaned.

On the London underground, men bury their heads in the newspapers as soon as they sit down, thinking that they are observing the world and the world can't see them. Women, on the other hand, either read novels shaped like bricks, or fill in crossword puzzles. The English are particularly addicted to crossword puzzles. Perhaps it's because they don't know square-shaped writing, like Chinese, so they have a strong desire for squares. This must be the reason that, knowing one square-shaped word ※, the Chinese character for rice, they have happily written it on the Union Jack.

On the whole, London is not a dangerous place to live in. However, the frequent bomb scares, all over the place, make people feel that their lives are constantly being threatened. The underground often stops because of security but no one complains. Once, the underground had put up billboards saying: "In future, the only complaints we receive will come from ourselves." I was really angry, they were so shameless, even depriving passengers of their right to let off steam.

There are a lot of homeless people in London. Most of them are young people.

They hold a piece of paper saying "hungry, cold and homeless" under bridges or at tube entrances. I'm not used to being asked for money by well-clad, able-bodied men or nice girls with dogs. Sometimes, when I do feel charitable, I give them some money. There is a bi-weekly paper published in aid of the homeless called *The Big Issue*. I often buy this paper because I'm very concerned with this problem, which I don't understand. The only thing I know is that the elderly ones are mainly veterans and mental patients, while the younger ones have run away from home. Ah Shek said that they are all lazy-bones. But I think that even the hardest-working people can't stand being exposed to the elements all day long. Ah Mui told me that quite a lot of young people are kicked out of their home by their parents once they have grown up. However, they can't support themselves so they have to sleep on the street. There are many things that I can't understand.

Once, I worked in a Malaysian restaurant. The owner was Indian and used to be a nurse. She started the restaurant because her friends always praised her culinary skills. But the business was not good; often only two or three tables were occupied in the evening. She confided her troubles to me, using 2,500 words to describe the experience of a mentally and physically wrecked woman struggling between marriage and career. I listened with tears rolling down my cheeks - I was peeling onions at the time.

Late at night, I curled up in my cosy bed watching the television, the adverts are even better than the main features - there are images of cereal floating about and cows kicking footballs. Chocolate adverts are as beautifully filmed as adverts for cosmetics. On one talk show, the panel were criticising some boring books. And these books were really boring: *How to Talk to Yourself; How to Be Successful in Your Dreams*. On another talk show some people were discussing the meaning of the existence of plastic Christmas trees. Someone said it didn't matter since the Christmas tree is a symbol anyway. Another person argued that if the tree was not real it would affect one's childhood. Good heavens, things can be so absurd! Still, absurdly, I carried on watching.

Time passed as blandly as the taste of boiling water. Drama only occurs in films. The only real-life climax happened when my jacket was stolen. A mysterious case which happened in my own room. Nothing else was missing (in fact, my room was too chaotic for me to detect any other loss). Afterwards, I bought a Russian military jacket in a jumble sale. I liked its earthy yellow colour and also the fact that it had many pockets - handy for stealing.

When I got home, I found a bullet in one of the pockets.

translated by Ni Yi Bin

劉洪彬

詞語

我活在詞語裡
為意念找衣服
詞語是房主
我出賣自己
然後付他房租

我活在詞語裡
我說不出話想逃出時
詞語是看守
他硬把自己的詞語塞進我腦袋
我抵抗的是無孔不入的聲音

我活在詞語裡
詞語賴在我的腦袋裡
我不想跟他性交時
他硬強姦了我
在榮耀和邪惡中跳起了舞
聲音的塵土飛揚

我活在詞語裡
詞語游進我的腦袋裡
我懷著復仇的心要毀滅詞語這房屋時
他卻變得友善起來
我們成了朋友
一起逃進另一個房屋

他還想做房主？

Liu Hongbin

Words

I live within words
looking for ways to clothe ideas
Words are a landlord
I sell myself to
and pay him rent

I live within words
Where words fail me
Words are a jailer
Who forces himself on me
I am fighting a voice in every pore

I live within words
words loiter inside my head
When I don't feel like sleeping with them
They rape me,
They dance in glory and in malice
kicking up the dust of voices

I live within words
words swim into my head
When, out for revenge
I try to destroy this house of words
Suddenly it turns amiable
and makes friends with me
we run away together to another house

Does my landlord still want me as his tenant?

translated by Peter Porter

劉洪彬

你是誰

我是早產的嬰兒
我是夭折的天才
我是避孕術發明前無奈生下的孩子

我是熱愛父母卻被父母拋棄的孩子
我是珍重貞操卻被強姦的少女
我是青春漾溢卻被閹割的男子
我是忠於愛情卻被背叛的情人
我是倒在觀眾讚譽聲中的拳擊手
我是昏倚在月光照耀下現實之牆的流浪漢
我是厭惡虛偽而被虛偽猥褻的詩人
我是崇尚高尚卻被高尚埋葬的殉道者
我是目光呆滯　孤獨地凝視著夕陽的老人
我是從人體內溢出的美麗的血
我偶然地從生走來
向必然的死走去

我是被割掉卻在聆聽福音的耳朵
我是想發泄痛苦卻被牆一樣的手堵住的口
我是遭剮刑卻想聞玫瑰的鼻子
我是想表達愛情卻被割掉舌頭的苦戀者
我是擁抱著愛人手指殘缺的雙手
我是忍著骨折劇痛在雪原中向前挪動的雙腿
我是身患霍亂把自己焚燒的焦屍
我是燃過而被扔掉的火柴桿

我是被醉漢摔碎的酒杯
我是人們眼中向高空升起的氣球
我是清潔夫討厭的玩童燃放過的鞭炮的屍體
我是為判定輸贏在人們腳下痛滾的足球
我是被盜賊搶走的 情人互贈的信物
我是救過主人命卻死在主人槍口下的獵狗
我是狐狸摘不下的酸葡萄釀成的憤怒的酒
我是遭人詛咒卻降下及時雨的烏雲
我是落在集市人群裡的兀鷹
我是扛著鐵軌使列車通過的臂膀
我是永恆空間的普通裝飾
我是時間的殉葬品

我是拉船而蹦斷的被縴夫詛咒的繩索
我是負載溺水人繼而被遺棄在海灘上的船板
我是因帆的愛戀而折斷的桅桿
我是海嘯與船上水手對話發出的聲音
我是被挖空而吹出漁歌的螺號

你是誰
我是我
你到底是誰
我就是我
我不是甚麼
我是我
我就是我

Liu Hongbin

Who are you?

I am a baby of premature delivery
I am a genius who died before the age of thirty
I am a child born inadvertently before the invention of contraception

I am a child loving my parents dearly now abandoned
I am a young girl cherishing my virginity but raped
I am a virile young man now castrated
I am a loyal lover now betrayed
I am the boxer pole-axed to the cheers of the spectators
I am a vagrant leaning under moonlight against reality's wall
I am a poet who detests hypocrisy now slandered by it
I am a martyr adoring the sublime now buried by it
I am a senile man, alone, staring with dull eyes at
a setting sun
I am beautiful blood gushing out from a body
I come from contingent birth
walking towards inevitable death

I am severed ears still wanting to listen to good news
I am a mouth venting suffering but gagged by wall-like hand
I am a severed nose still wanting to smell roses
I am an unrequited lover expressing love with a torn-out tongue
I am a pair of hands with amputated fingers holding my beloved
I am legs trudging across snow enduring fractured bones
I am a corpse that burned itself because it contracted cholera

I am a matchstick struck then thrown away
I am a liqueur glass shattered by a drunk
I am a balloon rising over people's staring heads
I am the remains of firecrackers lit by children, hated by streetsweepers
I am a football writhing in pain under a player's foot

used to decide who wins or who loses
I am a lover's token taken by a thief
I am a dog who saved his master's life dying from his gun
I am a wrath's wine, sour grapes that foxes could not reach
I am a condemned cloud giving timely rain
I am an albatross fallen among the crowds of the marketplace
I am the shoulders holding up the railway so that trains may pass
I am the ordinary decorations of eternal space
I am the grave goods of time

I am a frayed rope, cursed by people who used it to tow their boat
I am a piece of wreckage on the beach to which the drowning clung
I am a mast broken by sail's love
I am the conversation between sailors and tidal wave
I am the conch shell, innards scooped out, now blowing a fisherman's song

Who are you?
I am I
I am exactly what I am
I am I
I am just the thing I am
I am I

translated by Peter Porter, Jason Brooks and Liu Hongbin

喬林

蛻變

當我想到綠葉
我變作冬蟬
喊不出來

當我想起星球
我變作乒乓
彈出宇宙

想起他
見到一隻不長尾巴的蟾蜍

口吐金針　鑽入針眼
縮成童年的小仙子
在森林的通風口珍藏一張張小紙條

警報四處游蕩
尖尖的蚊嘴
刺破一個充血的夏天

於黑色的泥沼中
繼續召喚潔白的失眠

一想起陽光
立即變成一扇生鏽的窗

Chiao Ling

Metamorphosis

When I think about green leaves
I turn into a winter cicada
Unable to shout out

When I think about planets
I turn into a ping-pong ball
Catapulting out of the universe

When I think about him
I see a tail-less toad

Spitting out golden needles   Piercing the needles' eyes
Shrinking into a childhood fairy
Secreting paper messages in the windy openings in the forest

Alarm loiters at every corner
Mosquitos' spiky mouths
Prick a summer congested with blood

On the black marsh
I call and call the pure white insomnia

When I think about the sun's rays
I instantly turn into a rusty window

translated by Chiao Ling

Lili Man

A Batty Metamorphosis

The story

She woke up one grey morning, glanced at the mirror and discovered that she was no longer Chinese. She had acquired - overnight - blond hair, blue eyes and a big nose. Many mirrors later she had to accept that she no longer looked oriental. *Well, I thought I had a cultural identity problem before ... now I'll really need help.* Blank mind, confusion and racing thoughts. How, why and was this permanent? But that is so mundane. Let us be philosophical and look at the implications my dear - how do you feel now that you are white? *Oh, my God - I'm white! But I was just getting used to being Chinese. I'm not sure I'll be able to deal with not looking different.* But how you look is sooo superficial, my dear. Yes, I am still me. The inside me and the outside me are maybe not so different now. I grew up with Britain, Smash and Coronation Street. I will go out and look like Britain, Smash and Coronation Street now. Fuck it, the now is the now. Right...I'm getting ready and I will go to meet the world. I think I need a drink - the pub. See - am I even thinking like a Chinese person? Have I ever? What is a Chinese person? She fell back to sleep, having exhausted her brain cells.

She dreamt of black, black seas taking her boat to rocks and smashing it against them. She turned into a bird and became part of the design on a blue-and-white China plate. She was being peered at through the Smash and sausages - a fork being waggled in her direction. "Those two birds on that plate are luvvers, innit Bert...that's a willow pattern or somefink, innit?" She hurls the plate - *I will not be part of the willow pattern . I am blond and white now.*

Time to get up. *Yup...I'm still unChinese.* Out to the pub. *A pint of cider, please.* Hello, luv, don't I know you from somewhere? *I don't think so.* Retreat to the toilet. Shock again as she passes the mirror. *Good grief - that's me! But it's not. How are people looking at me? Are they looking at me?* Twitch, twitch, twitch goes the nerve at the corner of her mouth. This isn't a game. This is life. And you might think this is great...but is it?

Her father used to give long repetitive rants about white imperialism. She still feels the need today to enlighten people about the Opium Wars. Those "white bastards". *Oh...but...well, so what if I am white? I always knew some of us were OK(?!)*

She did not phone her friends, her mother, or anyone at all. The only person she might have gone to was her Dad. He was on another planet anyway and would have appreciated the oddity and humour of the situation. *I miss the sanity of his madness. Metamorphosis - one of his favourite stories, about the man who wakes up in bed one morning to find he has been transformed into an enormous beetle. At least I can still feed myself. Better a blond than a beetle - that's what I always say.*

She could see herself, white, walking the streets like a raving Sinofile...practising Taichi, reciting poetry about the moon and her homeland, and inviting people home for a stir-fry. *Wok would you like to eat? No. 46? It's OK, I'm just practising being mad in case I become so. You might too if you were Chinese one minute and then Anglo-Saxon the next. And - sudden thought - just imagine if you, Anglo-Saxon suddenly looked Chinese? Hey up! What a turnabout, eh?!*

Instead, she hibernated. She unplugged the phone, ignored the door bell and only went out to the shops, hurriedly, resisting the impulse to wear a paper bag over her head. All the time thinking but not thinking. *What shall I do? Who am I? I am invisible - nobody knows me now.* You are nothing if you are not reflected in the eyes or heard in the voice of others close to you. She consulted the *I Ching* repeatedly, with a clink, clink of coins and a furrowed brow of concentration, and ...became more confused - but then that often happened. Night-time was her world now - awake and strumming the guitar to strange melodies and awful depressing lyrics. She couldn't play the guitar anyway. Asleep she was told by a jumble of faces that she was adopted, that she was dead, or they ignored her

- family and friends drifted along past her unaware.

A week later she cracked and headed for the phone. Her first chosen victim was Tommy, a fine young man - staunch in his help, practical advice and decadent drinking. *Hi, Tommy! Hi Lisa! How's it going? Fine (but let's get to the point, shall we?)...listen, Tommy, I need to see you, but...I have to tell you something first. Imagine I've dyed my hair blond, I'm wearing blue contact lenses and I've had a nose job. I don't look like me anymore - OK?...(chuckling)...You're having me on, aren't you? NHS, was it?...(ho ho ho)...Well, not exactly...*

Finally he arrived at her door, looked over her shoulder to find her, then remembered and focused back on her. He did his goldfish impersonation, came in, sat down, then commenced questioning. It could have been worse. His mind was broad enough (or had lost enough brain cells) to stretch and accept the ridiculous - though his chuckles and jokes were a bit much really. *You're looking a bit off-colour, indeed! I mean, really - this is serious!* Something that had been nagging at her insides for years was threatening to break out. *You don't understand. You didn't then and you don't now. I am a bloody wanderer in life - no real home, never at rest - always alien and careful, always in the company of strangers. Yes, I can cope of course - be practical, laugh, adapt. But now what? Where do I belong now? You go ahead and let me know! At least, before, I belonged to not belonging. Aaaaaargh.*

Luckily, Tommy had brought some cider. She allowed the soft buzz of alcohol to envelop and comfort her and restrained herself from vocalising her anger and frustration. Phew. That was close. *Calling sense of humour, earth calling sense of humour...please come in.*

At least her "me" was now reconfirmed by Tommy's presence. They talked and laughed about (*always look on the bright side of life...da dum...da dum da dum da dum...*) the probable and improbable consequences of her metamorphosis: numerous identification problems, rejection by her family, scientific experimentation (*block out the images of those scalpels, steel-rimmed glasses and white coats*), confusions just waiting to crop up...

But nothing toooo insurmountable - no need to panic, my dear. I am strong. I am me ... I think.

The interview

(*two months later*)

Interviewer: So you claim to have previously been Chinese but to have woken up one morning to find yourself transformed into how you now look: a rather attractive, if I may say so, young Anglo-Saxon woman.

Ex-Chinese: I am Chinese - I just don't look it any more.

Interviewer: Indeed - although you obviously have a British accent and seem very British to me. Tell me, how has your life changed since your metamorphosis?

Ex-Chinese: Hmm...my family and friends have been very supportive, though it obviously took some of them awhile to accept that I was me. I do find it interesting how people's reactions towards me, or perhaps my own reactions, have changed.

Interviewer: And how have these changed?

Ex-Chinese: Well, a lot of people think I'm mad, but in general I get a feeling - sometimes good but sometimes uncomfortable - of equality with the powerful, which does make me wonder whether I'm still Chinese.

Interviewer: You've said that you are Chinese and yet that you also wonder whether you are - do you think you will eventually come to some conclusion regarding this?

Ex-Chinese: No - perhaps it doesn't matter anyway.

The poem

When dawn is breaking
and the light shines on your night before
When you are alive with...
Don't tell me it matters what you are
or who
We are all very small...
Listen to Johnny Cash
and laugh.

The beginning

喬林

心經

當玲聲不再響起
第一回,我很快忘了這件事
第二回,我替你找了一個好理由
當一句接受把拒絕包括進去
第三回,我按下高高彈起的耐心
當親暱的詞成了客套
當信賴需要眼神的保證
第四回,我不知道該盯住什麼
是時候了
雨點不必等待風起便往下落
當胳臂不再往裡彎仍扎出了血
當我笑出了哽咽
當一覺睡到失眠
當...
最後一回
我聽見有人在胸膛內使勁摔門

Chiao Ling

Sutra of the Heart

When the door bell no longer rang
The first time I forgot about it quickly
The second time I made excuses for you
When a sentence of acceptance included a refusal
The third time I suppressed my bursting impatience
When intimate words became a formality
When trust demanded the eye's confirmation
The fourth time I did not know what needed to be watched
Now is the time
The rainfall no longer waits for the wind to blow before it falls
When arms, still smarting with blood, no longer folded inwards
When my laughter turned to choking sobs
When sleep became sleeplessness
When ...

The last time
I heard someone slam the door inside my chest

translated by Chiao Ling and Jenny Putin

B. Y. H. Guild

A Late Mixed Marriage

I was at the point in my life when I no longer wanted to be doing the same work I had been doing for the last five years. There was nothing else that I particularly wanted to do except to stop working altogether and to travel. I had saved enough to make this possible and I just had to be brave (or stupid) enough to relinquish my job when people around me were losing theirs. My parents, as always, were very supportive, offering me advice and setting aside a contingency fund. (I discovered later that they were terribly worried about my grand plans to travel around the world alone, but they hid this from me.)

Several weeks before I set off on my long journey, I fell in love - with someone I had known for years. I had taken stock of my life and set about changing it but I did not expect anything to happen before I had even left these shores. It was a crazy time. I was making frantic preparations to leave London for a year - packing up my flat ready for the tenants, moving all my belongings to my parents' home for storage, having farewell dinners with friends, giving instructions to the managing agents, the bank, etc. I was also torn, trying to spend as much time as possible with him and with my parents respectively. I had not yet told them about him as I felt it was not the appropriate time.

So I left for Canada where I was to start my year off with a "holiday" staying with my aunt and her family. It was good to have a base for a few weeks, somewhere I could be reached. The first phone call from London came the day after I arrived. It was totally unexpected. We had been so "sensible" about our relationship, realising that we were to be separated for a whole twelve months. We had said that we could meet in six months' time in Malaysia if we still felt the same way; that we really should not make any commitments to each other given the circumstances. I was thrilled to hear his voice. I had already missed him so much. We arranged there and then to meet in New York in three months' time - his period of notice at work.

Those were the longest three months of my life. There was I, on the trip of a lifetime, travelling across Canada and America and pining for my loved one left behind. It was even worse for him, he did not have the daily distractions of new places and new discoveries. We wrote to each other every day and phone calls were many and sometimes very fraught. These modes of communication were a poor substitute for visual and physical contact, but his letters were wonderful and kept me going. (We marvelled at the international postal service, something I had always taken for granted and never really appreciated before.)

Then came November and New York ... we could barely speak at Kennedy Airport. Words failed us as we clung on to each other desperately as if our lives depended on it. We had poured out so many words into our letters that it was no longer necessary to speak. We were reunited at last. We spent two glorious months touring America, trying not to think about the time when we would have to say goodbye again; trying not to speak of it because it was too unbearable. It was difficult, but we planned our next reunion while managing to avoid mentioning the separation that must precede it.

We talked about the future. We discussed the possibility of curtailing my travels so that we could be together but we both knew that this was not the answer and neither of us wanted it. We decided that when we were finally reunited again in London we would live together. This would be a very big step for me to take, never having lived with anyone before, and I knew my parents would not be happy about it and I was a little apprehensive about breaking it to them. I had, of course, written to my folks about him by that time and they were happy for me; but living together - that would be something else. We talked about his pending trip to Malaysia and meeting my parents and how they would react to him. I knew my parents had always had big expectations of my boyfriend, I suppose all parents do, and no one would be good enough for their "little girl". I hoped that they had realised that after all my years in

England, the chances of my ending up with a Chinese boyfriend were quite low. We talked about how his parents would react to me; after all, resistance to cohabitation with an unmarried partner of a different race is not confined to the Chinese!

An agonisingly tearful farewell followed on the last day of that year, ending the two-month reunion. I continued on my journey around the world and he returned to New York. The next two months were worse than the first three. I was on the move a lot more and communication was extremely difficult. We had to make do with reading and re-reading old letters until the next one arrived. In the southern hemisphere the postal service was not so brilliant any more and each day brought its disappointment upon the depressing discovery that there was no letter - though I never doubted that he had written.

My parents welcomed him to their home in Malaysia and respected my wish to meet him at the airport alone. I had been gently interrogated the day before he arrived (I made sure I had been home a good week before he came) about the seriousness of our relationship, his prospects, etc. My mother was worried because he was a lot younger than me.

He asked me to marry him the day after he arrived and again he took me by surprise. It may seem strange that he did not do it on the very first day, but his proposal had been designed in a crossword clue complete with red herrings (we had spent our time on American trains doing *Guardian* crosswords) and it was a wonderful feeling to know that he must have been working on it for some time. I think my parents were pleased; it was about time, I was already thirty-seven. I think they too were taken by surprise given the circumstances of our relationship and the fact that I was in the middle of my round-the-world holiday. We set the date for an October wedding, which would enable me to complete my journey and return in time to finalise arrangements for the day. We had protracted discussions with my parents about the reception and the guest list. I felt guilty about the timing - my father had just retired, and a Chinese father should not be having to worry about the financial implications of his daughter's wedding, only his son's.

There was more agonising about the reality of finishing my trip. Our engagement had effectively changed the situation for me and I felt the responsibility of my commitment. When the depression of impending separation overshadowed the celebration of climbing Kinabalu, the highest mountain in South-east Asia, I knew that day that I had to make a decision about whether to continue or not. By this time a girlfriend had also joined us and she and I were to continue from here on and travel to Thailand, India, Nepal, Hong Kong and China together. This we had planned a while ago and circumstances prevented my fiancé from coming with us. I decided what I must do.

It was a bleak day, one of the worst days I have ever experienced. My girlfriend took it very badly and was extremely upset; my mother thought it was a terrible decision and one I would regret; she thought I was letting my friend down and was worried about her travelling alone. I was in terrible turmoil. My loyalties were torn and I no longer knew what I wanted to do and what was going to hurt whom less, and what about me? My fiancé was not looking forward to another period of prolonged separation, neither was he happy with the prospect of my abandoning my trip altogether. After a lot of tension, argument and painful soul-searching I finally compromised. I would continue with my travel but would return to London a month earlier than originally scheduled.

We travelled to Kuala Lumpur where followed another parting, more painful than the last - yet this was to be the last time we would have to do it. He flew to London and I returned to Kota Kinabalu to spend some time with my parents. We had had no time together since the others had arrived and I thought that everything had happened so fast it would be good to have some quiet time together. I was also very conscious of the fact that this would probably be my last visit there. I visited the graves of my grandparents, baby brother and uncles, and I took photographs of their gravestones, aware that

I would not be able to tend them again.

I flew to Thailand and met up with my girlfriend. It was exceedingly hot in Bangkok and I could not believe that we were actually sightseeing in the midday sun - it was madness. When we left Bangkok we headed for the international telephones at the airport. The timing was right to phone England. He had just awoken...

I was not looking forward to her reaction when I told her a second time that I had decided to terminate my journey. However, she must have expected it because she took it very well and understood what I was going through. Thus, before I had even arrived in Bombay I had already arranged to depart. This time there was an inner peace with the decision to stop travelling and go home. It was right and I felt ready for it and content to return. I did not want to see any more places without him and I was looking forward to the day when he and I would complete this journey together.

So I arrived home two months ahead of time for our final reunion. It had been a difficult period for us both and now it was behind us. Ahead of us were all the arrangements to be made for the wedding and it was just as well that I came back when I did as there was much to be done.

Meeting my future in-laws was a strange experience since I was already his fiancée and we were presenting them with a fait accompli. Obviously I hoped that they would like and accept me but I was not going to allow it to affect us if they did not. I realised that so much of my life had been spent unconsciously doing what would please my parents. I think I had always been looking for someone whom I thought they would like. It finally dawned on me that my marriage partnership had to be with someone for me and not for my parents or his. I was very aware of being Chinese at this time, and that his parents had not had much contact with Chinese people, but I think they approved of me.

I have always been proud of being Chinese but I have never had to think about what it really means to me until my marriage to a *gweilo*. I did not hesitate in accepting his marriage proposal. Later I had to deal with changing my name and I was concerned about the loss of my Chinese identity through adopting his name but it is good that a Chinese wife retains her Chinese maiden name. When we returned from our honeymoon, my parents were concerned about how they would be addressed by their Scottish son-in-law. They wanted him to call them "Mum" and "Dad" as I did. I was unsure how he would react to this but was really pleased when he consented. His parents had asked me to call them by their first names shortly after I first met them - as had happened with their sons-in-law. Had I married a Chinese man, there would have been no question about my calling his parents "Mama" and "Baba". I am not completely comfortable calling my in-laws by their names as I feel they deserve the respect of their generation. I tell myself that it is not the custom here and, besides, they probably do not want me to address them as their son does. I do ask myself, however, whether I would feel just as awkward calling them "Mummy" and "Daddy".

Anna Chen

The Next Wave Home

I was shoving the whites into the machine when a great wave of grief engulfed me. For no reason at all, I started to cry. I looked down and saw that I was holding a pair of Alex's tiny cotton briefs, stained with the faintest shadow of blood, which resolutely refused to budge despite a thorough soak. Maybe my period had synchronised with my daughter's and this was simply irrational pre-menstrual tension signalling the onset of my own bleeding. With the machine spluttering into action behind me, I carried the customary mug of Earl Grey through the long white corridor of our north London flat and stopped at the door pinned with a garish hand-painted sign:

GENIUS AT WORK
WRINKLIES KEEP OUT

I ignored the warning and stepped into the room, picking my way through the usual teenage obstacle course of comics, skates and multi-coloured felt-tips which threatened to leak indelibly on to the carpet. Half the contents of her wardrobe lay where they had been tugged off the night before. Tangled heaps of vivid limes, turquoises and clashing hues of red marked out a path across the floor, impossible to miss in the half-light. Alex, at thirteen, was passing through that retina-searing stage of fashion sense prior to the discovery of colour coordination. But I found her clothes irresistibly attractive in the way that they affirmed life; a far cry from my relentless blacks and greys at the same age.

And there she was - my beautiful daughter, fast asleep. Her lean, supple limbs flopped at haphazard angles; her breath popping from her delicate pink mouth in a little "kah". I placed the steaming mug next to the clutter of beads and bangles, worn religiously ever since her progression from pop idols Bros to Madonna, and bent down.

I always loved this quiet moment when I could drink in her loveliness to my heart's content. I never ceased to be amazed that I had borne this creature: stardust put together to divine specifications according to Rick's and my genetic blueprint; a never-ending spark of life passed down through the aeons and expressed in this perfect form. Her expression was one of bliss. What could she be dreaming? Something wonderful, I bet. I took a deep breath of her delicious scent and gently shook her into consciousness.

Her sweet smile of sleep turned downward and her brows furrowed. With a groan she heaved the duvet over her head. I hoisted up the blind, allowing the sunlight to stream in, and yanked the duvet off her.

"Come on, luvvy, school."

"Oh, no. I'm ill," she whined.

"Alex, don't be such a wimp, it's only a period."

"Yeah, sure. Your only daughter's losing umpteen pints of blood and that's not serious, is it?"

"Surliness will get you nowhere. Now get up or it's the cold sponge."

"Oh, major threat!"

I willed hard for something, I'm not sure what.

At last, she opened her eyes and screwed them up against the light. She made an almighty effort to haul herself up and reach for the tea, and, with each successive sip, her eyes brightened into the sharpness of a child raring to engage in life. She returned my smile with a broad beam that radiated an inner light and she gave me a warm hug.

"Thanks, Mum," she said, grateful for the tea.

Satisfied that there would be no slip back into blissful sleep, I returned to the kitchen and prepared breakfast.

The two of us sat facing each other, me nibbling my grapefruit and crispbread in a perennial battle with what I had finally ceased to call puppy-fat only a few years earlier; Alex tucking into the latest craze in breakfast cereals, a porridgy concoction liberally laced with poisonous levels of sugar.

"But the packet says 'Natural', Mum." She poured fresh orange juice into her Dan Dare mug, her sole concession to my demands for a healthy diet. Rule of the house: no cola drinks before 5 o'clock tea.

The awareness that something was missing dawned slowly. Something comfortingly commonplace without which the easy familiarity of this daily scene seemed to slip out of sync with itself. What was it? I pressed my lids together and concentrated. Hard. I opened my eyes and looked at her bare wrists.

"Hey, I thought it seemed quiet. What's happened to the hardware?"

"No one's wearing that stuff now. Only little kids like Madonna. Everyone's playing Janis Joplin." Her first bra and period, and now Janis. All within two years.

"That must be the third time around. At least," I continued, playing the experienced oldie to the hilt. "When I was your age, I broke in my voice to 'Cry Baby'. Of course, that was pre-punk when we took the revolutionary step of deconstructing the melody." Alex made dramatic barfing noises right on cue. We were a great double-act.

"Punk's ancient," she pronounced with all the authority of a veteran music pundit.

1977, the year she was born, was too recent for Punk to have been endowed with nostalgia value and respectability. Give it maybe another five years for its inevitable second cycle of popularity and then you'd see serious interest from Alex and her peers. But for now, she was happy to tease me for having been a seventeen-year-old punk, and I was happy to collaborate in her search for identity and pride.

And then the crying started. I was struck in the pit of my stomach by the same wave of grief and helplessness as earlier. A great amorphous blackness reared up out of the deepest recesses of my psyche and shook me in its jaws. Alex looked scared and rushed to comfort me.

"Mum. What's the matter?" For a moment I didn't know. I merely wept and dodged the fear. And then the blackness took on shape. It all came flooding back into view.

"It was a dream. An awful dream - about you. I dreamt I'd lost you." With that last thought, my blubbing intensified. Alex pulled up her chair and sat cradling me, stroking my hair with firm, capable hands.

"Tell me. Tell me from the beginning," she cooed softly in my ear.

"Remember I told you how, when I got pregnant, Gran sent me off to some agency to arrange an abortion?"

"Yeah, but at the last minute you realised how much you loved me and you defied everyone so you could have me." She faked light-heartedness like a consummate actress, but I knew she was feeling my distress as her own. Of course I knew; wasn't she my own flesh and blood?

"That's right. Well, in this dream, everything started off the same as that day. I took the bus to Streatham - three changes - because I didn't know anyone who had a car. I walked up the overgrown gravel driveway of a huge old Victorian house, which had been converted into a private clinic. In the lobby, about a dozen women, ranging from other teenagers to a couple of mature women of about forty, sat or stood dumbly around their overnight bags. They were all accompanied by husbands or boyfriends. Or parents."

I remembered how I had felt the odd one out, standing there in the middle on my own, almost foolish; the local Jezebel who had neglected to bring her own partner to the Church Hall dance. Although these women had fallen about as low as one could in those days - but not as low as those who would follow a few years later, darting within spitting distance past outraged latter-day Madames Defarges who would have seen such matters resolved with the knitting needle - their eyes told me that, unlike myself, they hadn't completely slipped through the invisible safety net of kith and kin.

I sipped my tea and glanced over at the snapshots lovingly selected and tacked to the cork noticeboard in a proud display to the world: of Alex mid-romp with her friends; Alex with Rick on the waterslide at some theme park or other; Alex, Rick and myself swaddled in matching snowgear, straight off the Austrian piste, a ball of snow in Alex's hand in the moment before it was shoved down Rick's neck. Such a happy, secure child surrounded by the smiling faces of those who loved her. I shuddered at the thought of her ever going through an experience like mine. That would happen over my dead body.

I went on. "I was led into a room - white, cold, clinical - not a scuff mark on the skirting-board, not a single streak on the gleaming steel taps. Sterile. I undressed and pulled on the scratchy green paper robe laid out on the bed, the only colour in the room. I was being given priority treatment because of the lateness of the pregnancy. Oh, God, they were going to whip you out double quick. Twenty-one weeks - just within the limit. You'd been kicking for ages, letting me know you were there. *Alive* and kicking."

Alex interjected: "But why did you and Gran wait so long?"

"I couldn't believe this could be happening to me. I wouldn't believe it. Plus, two hours of yoga a day had given me stomach muscles flatter than beer the morning after. Even the Harley Street doctor was amazed at how flat I was. I ignored all the signs. I thought my new larger breasts were a last-minute gift from God."

"A nurse came in and gave me the pre-med. It was going to be easy, she said, telling me nothing I didn't already know. Like having a tooth pulled. I'd wake up and it would be over. Ha!" I gave a sharp snort as I remembered the nurse's well-meaning but automatic assurances, no doubt laid on for every miserable girl who, betrayed by her own body, tramped up that driveway. Did she really believe what she was saying? Could she possibly have been as much in the dark as this confused seventeen-year-old?

"I got drowsy. They laid me on a gurney and wheeled me down the long echoing corridors to the theatre. Fluorescent strips of light strobed past on the ceiling as we thunked through door after door. And suddenly, I don't exactly know when, I was overwhelmed by the most incredible feeling that I had ever experienced. It was as if I was at the centre of a vast, rolling universe, a quiet, endless power I had accessed. Despite everything else that was going on, I felt at peace. And you were at the heart of that peace. I knew I loved someone beyond myself for the first time ever." Alex's eyes widened into deep pools I could happily have drowned in. "I realised it was probably the maternal instinct that people go on about. But it was a new one on me."

"Yeah, I remember this bit."

"That's the point when it all changed. I was watching myself in the dream, expecting to do the same as I'd done in life. But this time I didn't do it. I didn't call it off. I didn't shout and struggle when the matron told me to pull myself together. I wanted to but it was as if I was gagged. Or stupefied. They wheeled me into the theatre and the anaesthetist came at me with the needle. And instead of knocking it out of his hand or doing something, anything, I just ..."

A fresh bout of sobbing interrupted the tale. Alex squeezed me tightly.

"I let him stick the needle in my arm, right into the vein. I felt ice-water pouring into me while I counted to twenty-eight. And when I woke up... you were... you were gone." I couldn't stand the memory of the dream. Its vividness had spilled over from sleep to wakefulness, bringing with it all those little deaths, the attendant gut-wrenching emotions of loss.

"But, Mummy, it was only a dream. Look, I'm here now." She tore a sheet from the kitchen-roll and dabbed my eyes. "It's all right. Shush."

I was so proud of her; she was exactly the compassionate young woman I'd hoped to raise.

"I know. I'm just crying with relief. Oh, Alex, I don't know what I'd have done without you. Who would I have been? Just some half-dead thing."

"Maybe you would have had other kids."

"Hmm. Maybe. But not in this dream. There's more. I dreamt a whole different life for myself. I just went to pieces after I'd had you ... "I spluttered for the word.

"... aborted," she spoke the word clearly and without my fear of it. We often finished each other's sentences for each other but I flinched at the power given to this word merely by its utterance.

"I lost all my emotions. I couldn't feel a thing. It was weird, the complete opposite of what I'd felt on the gurney. I was now cut off from all that quiet power. The power that had made me feel more real than at any other time. Now, nothing mattered. Objects were just objects and nothing more, including myself."

Alex looked perplexed. This was too abstract for her.

"Gran and Grandad didn't want anything more to do with me. None of the family could understand my erratic mood-swings and I couldn't give in to self-pity. So I learnt to keep my anger, my fear, my loss to myself. Years passed. I couldn't hold down a job or keep a relationship going. It was horrific - the numbness. Nothing mattered to me. Nothing meant anything." I slumped on the table, my shoulders heaving under Alex's warm caress.

"When you went, a whole, vital lump of me went with you. I was lost. For ever." Then, quite without warning, Alex's cool words sliced through.

"Mum, how would they have done it at twenty-one weeks?"

The question startled me. But then I suppose every thirteen-year-old has a gory curiosity which, once on track, supersedes all other considerations. If you are open with children, you stand a chance of removing some of life's fears. I wanted Alex fully equipped in order to deal with her own life traumas, if and when they pounced, so I controlled my emotions and gave an honest answer.

"Well, I suppose if it's not performed as a Caesarean, which they said wasn't necessary in this case, they would go in through the cervix and get the foetus out that way."

Alex had stopped hugging me to concentrate on this information. She was finding it compulsive listening.

"But a twenty-one-week-old foetus must be pretty big. How can they get it out?" Her questioning seemed to be for my benefit, as if this thirteen-year-old was playing therapist with me, trying to get me to face up to forgotten fears. It was irritating.

"Well, if they can't... then they'd have to... " What was that droning? A low hum like an unearthed electrical appliance.

"Mummy?" she insisted.

"If you want to remove a large object through a small opening, you either make the hole bigger, or the object smaller." I felt uneasy. I wanted her to drop the subject but she continued in what was beginning to feel like an interrogation.

"Snip."

"What?"

"Snip. Cut up the baby into little pieces and pull them out one by one."

"Perhaps."

"How small?" The question was abnormally ghoulish, even for a curious child.

"Not necessary, Alex."

She changed tack. "What about Daddy? Wasn't he there to save me?"

"He must have been there. Somewhere." I broke off. The drone. I couldn't get the drone out of my head and it was driving me crazy.

"I can't remember anything about Rick. I don't know why he wasn't with me in the clinic. But he came up trumps afterwards, didn't he?" My voice tailed off as I struggled to remember shadows. Exploring the Marianas Trench with a pen-light would have been easier.

Alex disengaged her arms from me and sat fixing my eyes with a stare eerily penetrating for a child. For a long time we said nothing. The drone grew louder, threatening to engulf me. I felt faint. Then Alex spoke.

"Mum. Dad was a methodone addict you'd known less than a month. You can't even remember his name." I pulled up sharply. My own daughter was beginning to scare me.

"Daddy's in Manchester for a week. Working. Alex, come on, this isn't my idea of humour." But she persisted, oblivious to my unease. Or welcoming it.

"You went through it on your own. No one thought it was important at all. You even had to go into work the very next day. Remember?"

"No, darling, I had Gran and Grandad. Without their help I'd never have coped."

Alex ignored my protestation and came out with another odd piece of fantasy plucked from Lord knows where.

"Gran and Grandad lived with you in a one-bedroom council flat. They couldn't have helped you even if they'd wanted to. Which they didn't."

How stupid and selfish of me to burden her with my problems. She had a vivid imagination and my nightmare had invoked some ugly demons which I had better neutralise fast.

"They took one look at you and they were smitten. You were a gorgeous baby." But Alex was, by now, too immersed in her fantasy to hear me.

"Mum, Granny didn't like you."

"No. We had our problems, like any family, but we pulled together in a crisis."

"Grandad doesn't know to this day what happened 'cause you were scared he'd beat hell's bells out of you."

"They loved you from day one. They were tremendously supportive." I searched her face for a sign of what she might be driving at.

"Why are you saying all this, Alex?"

Alex didn't answer my question. Instead, she relaxed back into her chair. She looked at me with huge brown eyes filled with hurt and betrayal.

"Why didn't you do it, Mum? Why didn't you save me? We could have managed."

"Alex, sweetheart, it was only a dream. I jumped the gurney in the nick of time."

A long silence. Except for the drone.

"Didn't I? Alex?" Something shifted in the back of my head; the cold crunch of worlds colliding.

After a long pause she spoke with clinical precision.

"No. No, Mummy. I don't think you did." My eyes darted around the kitchen, mapping out the room with her landmarks; the cereal box, her Dan Dare birthday mug, the snapshots on the noticeboard, all juddering in and out of focus.

Alex stared at me, stared right into me, and although we were close enough to touch, she seemed to hover at the far end of a long tunnel. I called her name, over and over, but she didn't say a word, just stared at me. Tears welled in those innocent eyes that, under my care and protection, had known no real traumatic pain in any of her thirteen years since birth.

I thought I could make out the white tiles on the wall behind her. Directly behind her. She picked up her mandarin nylon carrier with the lime zipper and slowly heaved it on to her shoulder.

"I'm off to school now, Mummy. I'll see you in a little bit." Her voice was faint and tinny under the drone, like a bad recording from the

1920s. I tried to hold on to her but her ethereal hands slipped from my grasp.

So it was time. I'd stretched it out longer than usual due to my growing ability to plug those sticky moments when everything can unravel in an instant. I choked down the lump in my throat and waved goodbye as she backed down the corridor.

"I love you, sweetheart."

"I love you, Mum."

"Take care now, darling. I'll be thinking of you."

She was drifting away, far away. She opened the front door into blinding sunlight, as bright as a bursting star. I froze the sight in my mind's eye, trying to drag out the final moment for eternity; my last glimpse of Alex in silhouette at the end of the corridor. And then she was gone.

I was overwhelmed by the drone, loud and maddening; an unbearable grating as worlds slipped out of sync, one sliding into oblivion while the other, the one where the black amorphous shadow swam, took on a stark and terrifying clarity.

The machine crashes to its climax. The locking mechanism clicks off and I open the door. The blood-soiled cotton briefs - my cotton briefs - fall to the floor. I straighten up, my vision rippled by tears and a head splitting with a pain that can find no outlet. A row of china teacups stands next to various health foods. The notice-board contains the odd list, mini-cab cards and a couple of photos of myself. My breath erupts in shallow, fitful bursts of terror and I wander through the flat like one of the undead. Gone is the handpainted sign. A blank expanse of white wall stares back where once there had been a door.

I stretch out my hands and my heart into a great nothing. Objects are objects and not much more. A scan of the cheerless sitting-room (to call it a living-room would be a lie) reveals a single photo of myself, alone, brooding and disquieted - sole proof to me of my own existence. There is a space where the framed photo of a happy family group - Rick, Alex and myself - had stood. There are no coloured felt-tip pens, left lidless on the floor for me to nag about; no teen comics, with the girls' names as titles, for me to condemn for their frivolity; none of my precious record collection peeks out from bent covers. Instead, I pace up and down the tidy room and weep.

When it gets like this I just have to wait until the next wave picks me up and drops me back into the real world to join Alex who should have been, but isn't. The universe has been split in two and I have been chosen to occupy this version. But, very occasionally, for a few minutes only, I can live out a lifetime as it was destined, as mother to a fine and wonderful daughter who waits for me even now. In the small hours I often hear her sobbing on the other side, missing me as much as I miss her. So I fill my hours with unimportant chores and doodlings I try to transform into work and wait to catch the next wave home.

顏展民

點點溫馨

他們沒有甚麼好交談的,卻能意會彼此的心意:大家履行著在生活的職責就是了,不必期望甚麼。不知不覺間,把飯菜預備妥當,她拉直嗓門催他,他卻貪婪地看報,懶於站起。她就頻頻催他,催到他很不悅。

他最後不得不費點神吃,拿著碗飯,慢慢細嚼,總覺得有點東西入口已很不錯。碗碟底下的舊報紙,是她事先放上去的。他就把碗碟攏放得更近些,不時細看報紙上的新聞,哪裡再去管甚麼?她在旁侍候,享受著是次慇懃帶來點點溫馨。轉眼,坐下來吃,於是,把一碗一碗粥填滿口腔,顯出十分滿足的樣子。他無心管她吃甚麼。吃,這一個動作,她很在行。

吃罷,他並不在意將桌上的殘羹料理,只管施施然走開去,沒有甚麼事情可做。低頭又見不堪入目的殘羹。想來過意不去,便趨前拿起碗碟送進廚房裡。她要為他代勞,忙從廚房走出來瞧。他卻走快兩步,將殘渣堆疊在舊報紙上,並且一手把它裹起,然後,擲往露台的垃圾桶裡,一了百了。洗碗這一撈什子,他從不過問,彷彿向來也毋須如此。

此刻,無無聊聊的,在客廳裡逛。她從廚房裡探頭出來,遙指桌上的紅蘋果,遠遠地。蘋果傻兮兮地發著羞澀的微笑,彷彿招惹他來吃。不吃,可能會令她不悅,還是吃好。他大搖大擺、大口大口地吃起來,她忙嚷:「要煲三蘇熟地嗎?」「要。」這總教她神氣半天。瞬間,他在雪櫃面前停下,或往廚房那邊走去,眼見石油氣爐和火水爐都點燃起來,分別承起水煲和沙煲。她沒等他吩咐,為他煮水。漸漸,她呆在廳裡不知幹甚麼,而他漫不在意地說:「魚很鮮美。」當然,很不錯,她還解釋曾挑揀過,價錢也很相宜。總之,要指出好到不能再好,只有她方才能夠弄到。念叨念叨,還重溫是次佳績。

水騰起來,她第一時間向他報訊,從廚房走出來嚷:「水滾啦!」聲音尖利,刺得他心頭很不舒服。他正翻閱報紙,一旦坐下來便賴著不走,早已受到甚麼奇聞逸事吸引,再也聽不見她叫嚷。幾分鐘後,總不能呆坐,得「死死氣氣」走去。旋即,來回已將熱水倒在大面盆上,但走回客廳裡取內衣時,不期然瞥見石油氣爐仍在點燃,上面放了一個水煲,於是說:「沒有甚麼就別亮著火,要不然,很容易忘記關掉。」「但水燒起來,隨時可拿來用。」人在,火就亮起,其實,這已見怪不怪了。

Helen Soo

Rosie

Rosie tossed back her raven hair and roared. The dawn sky was shimmering flashes of vivid light: shooting stars of fuchsia, indigo, and turquoise. A neon sign loomed large above her head. She looked up to see the fat body of the Pepsi bottle bulge and ripple, and the more she concentrated on it, the more it pulsated. All down Sunset Strip she watched the brightly-lit signs from the shabby nightclubs leap and tremour. It was a typical night. Rosie and Leo had taken two aeroplanes each and now wandered aimlessly. They had just stumbled in and out of The Catclub; five minutes of thrashing drumbeats, hot sticky bodies and garish leopard skin, had been enough.

Tears of mirth rolled down her cheeks, smudging her heavy mascara and crusted eyeliner. She wore a short, lowcut dress which stretched tautly across her breasts. They heaved as her heart pumped at giddying speed. She tottered on her scuffed heels, swayed and grabbed Leo's sleeve.

Leo had torn his jacket. His hair, once neatly braided, was now an eruption of frenzied dreads. He still had the black porcelain skin of youth. Only his glassy eyes, with their deeply etched shadows, revealed years misspent. He gave a throaty chuckle did a quick spin, and sent them both crashing to the slippery sidewalk. The traffic loomed near - approaching spacecraft in the dark of the night. They dazzled their lights before speeding off down the wide avenue. Rosie and Leo were oblivious to the vehicles, the cold breeze, the slight drizzle of rain. The ground was soft, a cushion in their heady euphoria.

"Hey, Rosie, you look like a clown," chuckled Leo as he tenderly dabbed her face with his grubby sleeve. He sounded close yet so far away.

"You're the clown! Look what you've done!"

He looked down to see two bony knees protruding through her torn stockings. They both stared momentarily before bursting into another torrent of laughter.

"Hey, Rosie, didn't I tell you to stay away from that punk?" Rosie prickled at the rasping voice. She looked up to see familiar grey eyes set in a craggy, whiskered face. A face that tonight loomed close and even more menacing. She could smell the stale whiskey on his breath. Everyone was a bit scared of Slacker, whether they cared to admit it or not. No one knew how many people he had killed, but he wrenched out a tooth for every victim, a macabre souvenir. His weak spot, as with all men, was women, and he had never hidden his lust for her.

"Fuck you. Leo's my friend," she hissed contemptuously.

He stiffened. "No one talks to Slacker like that. Not even a pretty pussy like you."

He moved closer until she could see the blackheads and pustules on his nose. They oozed and jumped with volcanic energy.

"You're breathing my air, asshole," she said, refusing to be intimidated.

"Say that again?" He grabbed her jacket and pulled her so near she could taste his pungent breath.

"Hey, hands off the lady!" cried Leo indignantly.

He tried to push Slacker away, but he didn't budge. Slacker loosened his grip on Rosie and stood up. Leo stood up to face him, but he strained to look up to the tall figure.

There was a moment's pause. The air cracked. Then a woman's long piercing scream echoed down the street. The punches began. They were clean and swift, the kicks hard and accurate. Then the sound of splintering bone.

Leo groaned from a pain deep in his gut. Rosie's eyes were fixed and wide. Cold terror rooted her feet to the spot. Leo was now curled into a ball and Slacker was kicking like a machine that could not stop. A few drops of thick scarlet spotted Rosie's dress. She looked down in horror. As she looked back at Leo, his face was fast disappearing beneath the rivers of red that streamed from his ears, his eyes, his nostrils, his lips. She convinced herself it wasn't really him any more.

She felt the warm, metallic taste of blood in her mouth and instinctively retched. Brushing her wet cheek with her palm, she looked down to see watery scarlet. Turning, she ran as fast as her shaking legs would go. The tears streamed so heavily she could barely see through their glistening haze. On and on she pounded through the dark streets until her lungs heaved and moaned in pain.

She stopped and realised she no longer knew where she was. She saw boarded shopfronts. Graffiti-covered walls. Battered vehicles. A few tramps paused to give her a cursory glance, contemplating the request for a dime before shuffling on. She rounded a corner and sank into a stream of molten traffic. A limousine screeched to a halt inches from her face. She looked on, dazed.

A glass window slid silently down.

"What the fuck do you think you're doing?" bellowed a voice from inside. She collapsed to the ground weeping.

"Hey... hey... hey!" The voice became low, gentle, comforting. "Sweetheart, what the hell happened to you?"

Before she realised it, she had sunk into one of the brushed-velvet seats and the car had driven on. She was cocooned in its embryonic warmth.

"What's your name?"

"Rosie"

"Where do you live?"

Silence.

"You need money?"

The sobbing stopped.

"That's my girl. Don't you worry. Suli will look after you."

His smooth dusky hand grasped her own. His nails were neatly manicured and a gold ring perched proudly on his third finger. The car swam with his sweet, heady cologne. He excited her.

She woke up to the sound of the early evening traffic. The room was close to the edge of the street and the paper walls shuddered with each vehicle that went by. A stream of grey light filtered through the grimy net. Something scuttled across the bare floor. She sighed. She thought she'd got rid of those dammed cockroaches. Suli had promised she would be out of this dump and out of this area soon. She guessed that wouldn't happen now. She turned over on the soiled mattress and spat. A yellow globule sank slowly into the rotting floorboard.

Suli should be round today. Her stocks were getting low.

It was dark and she strained to see. After fumbling for a few seconds she found what she was looking for. She filled the pipe, put it to her quivering lips and lit the end. As she greedily sucked, a smile began to curl the corners of her mouth. She thought about getting up.

She sat back against the peeling, yellowed wallpaper and closed her eyes. Once again, her mother, tiny and wizened from years of labour, appeared at the end of the mattress. She looked just as she had done that last time. She was wearing her old flowery apron, her sleeves were rolled high and her calloused hands were still soapy. A deep sadness hung at her eyes and mouth.

"May Lee. You are going out again ?"

Rosie had hoped to slip out unnoticed. She turned around to see her mother in the hallway and looked down at the floor. She became very conscious of her scant clothes and thick make-up.

"I just can't understand you. Look at your brother and sister. They study hard. Kwok Lee will be going to UCLA. You, you always want to go out and party. Those people you call your friends... always smoking, drinking ... "

"Mum, I like them. They're good fun. Kwok Lee, all he talks about is his grades! I'm not interested."

"How are you going to get a job? I don't want you just to carry on the family business."

"I've no chance of getting a job. We're not in Hong Kong now."

"At least if you study you will have more ... "

Rosie was tired, the words never changed.

"Look at you and father! You came over here with big eyes and big dreams. You work so hard. And for what? For this shack that lets in the draught and the cockroaches? Have you ever stopped to look? You call this living. You have no idea ..."

Rosie stopped and looked straight at her mother. Her eyes sparkled with anger but she bit her lip.

Her mother blinked away tears. "This is my home... *our* home."

Rosie couldn't back down now. "How can I call this home when all I get is constant criticism and nagging? Can't you see I need some space?"

"So where do you go to now? Are you going to be very late?"

"I don't know. I don't know if I'm coming back tonight."

"Well, if you're not back by twelve then don't bother!" her mother cried.

Rosie slammed the door and stormed out into the chilly night. She was unsure of where she was going. She felt excited, terrified and acutely alone. She was sixteen years old.

School bored her. The daily routine. The constant taunts. People always mistook her for her sister. She had begun to skip classes. And the lies got easier and bigger. They had been burgled. She was ill. She had to stay home to take care of her youngest brother.

Out of school she could assume a new identity. She began to hang around Venice Beach. She found it strangely surreal. The whole of humanity had been compressed to its base extremes, then viciously thrown together in the uneasy mix. Celebrities, tramps, street performers, drug pushers, body builders, Hollywood wives, family holiday-makers - all were there. She envied the apparent freedom of the vagabonds and rogues who had nowhere to go and nothing in particular to do. And the girls who just wanted to have a good time. She began a search for the indefinable. That extra kick. To free her subconscious she dabbled. A bit of smoke, a bit of speed, a bit of fun. She roamed the streets wide-eyed and eager. Once relaxed, the uncontrollable urge began to free her body.

She no longer felt an outcast. In fact, she became highly sought. The young men were intrigued by her slight curves, her smooth olive skin, her fathomless dark eyes. She became one of the lone pawns in the human zoo. And it was so easy. The locking of pupils for a second too long. Then the obligatory chit-chat before a flicker of the eyes to indicate a quieter meeting place. The sex was always rough and selfish. She met men on the beach in alleys that stank of urine, in hallways littered with condoms and empty syringes, or, occasionally, in a dingy room with a bed that rustled with underlife. It didn't matter. The more abhorrent the place, the more she felt detached.

She had discovered copulation in biology lessons at twelve. She had been mystified. And she was amazed that all the others already knew. So she pestered to know more.

"May Lee, if you sleep with a man, you will have been bitten by a snake. You will never be free," she was finally told.

From that moment on, she had a perpetual curiosity for the meeting of the flesh. Her mother could not have said anything more tempting. But it was a sweet with a lingering rot. Fat, thin, hairy, smooth, eager, weak. Faceless, always faceless. She indulged in a pleasure and pain that was driven by the hunger to feel desired. And a fascination for the forbidden. She was independent. She was in control. She told herself that by occupying her body she was liberating her soul. But there was always a guilt and hollowness she could never shake.

It was Leo, realising he would never have her to himself, who had called her a cheap tart. Other girls were forced to prostitute themselves. Why should she get nothing in return? She soon realised it was the only way to feed her ever increasing habit. Solvents and powders no longer satisfied. The temporary moment of exhilaration and strength she could get from rocks was of unequalled intensity. She couldn't get enough.

Leo. He had tried so hard but he was always too soft. A lost and loving soul, now dead. Slacker had given him such a thorough beating that night, he had been disfigured beyond all recognition. But by the time Rosie learnt of his death, he was only a vague, warm memory. Suli had seeped into her skin.

It had been several months since they first met, but she still knew very little about him. He was from the Caribbean, of mixed African and Asian descent. He had been in LA for the last fifteen years and, for him, it was a love/hate relationship. LA grips you by the throat and drains you dry, he once declared. He always spoke with calculation, he moved with efficiency and he had a self-assurance that often bordered on arrogance. Rosie had never met anyone quite like him. He had the energy of ten men and she now rarely looked elsewhere. He had found her this room downtown and he gave her rocks. She thought she had found what she needed, but began to spend her days yearning anew. She realised she wanted stability.

She closed her eyes. It was her eighteenth birthday again. They were in a restaurant in Westwood. A mahogany-walled, mirror-lined, hanging-plant place of contrived intimacy for the *nouveaux riches*. Rosie was wearing a dress Suli had bought for her that day, from one of the exclusive boutiques off Pacific Avenue. She was flushed and radiant and drinking the best wine from the restaurant list. Suli sat opposite, in dinner jacket and silk shirt. She smiled at him. He smiled back. That night he took her to one of the most luxurious rooms she had ever seen. They smoked, drank and indulged in abandon. She had never felt more satisfied.

She looked around the shabby walls and laughed a wry, bitter laugh. How she had fed on the ludicrous extravagance ! How did he acquire the constant wad of notes he kept tucked in his jacket? She had her suspicions, but only once had she asked.

"Oh, import/export business, sweetheart. Dull, but pays the rent."

She questioned him further, but he remained vague.

Rosie had ignored all the worse stories about him. She was happy to live in blissful ignorance and decided that they were vicious, jealous girls waiting to pounce. Until, one night, she knew she had to find out the truth.

Suli had popped in earlier that evening. He often dropped by at erratic, unpredictable times, but she would always be waiting for him.

"Hey, sweetheart. you're looking sharp tonight." He was animated, his eyes darted at nineteen to the dozen. His breathing was quick and shallow. Rosie was wearing a dress she had stolen just that day.

"Yeah? So where are you taking me?" She walked up to him and nuzzled his neck.

"Listen, Rosie, I'm gonna be busy for a few hours... "

"But you said we were going out on the town tonight!"

"When did I say that?" he said impatiently, a stranger again.

She looked at him. Her lips pressed tightly together.

"Listen, I've got some business to sort out. Suli can't take Rosie nowhere without the dough, mmmm?" He tipped up her chin to look into her eyes. She looked away.

"Listen, sweetheart. I gotta go. Don't sulk, huh? Look what I got here for you." He pressed a small bundle into her hand. "I'll be back later."

As he strolled out of the room she kicked the door behind him. He could be gone all night. She looked down at the bundle and threw it to the floor.

She decided to hire a cab and tail him.

He went through all the backstreets. Around 5th, 6th, 7th. Stopping to chat to the Latino girls who languished sultry and hard in the early evening warmth, he seemed to know them all. They wore cheap clothes, displayed yards of tanned thigh and sported bright crimson nails. He was taking money off them and he was more intimate with some than with others.

She had even got the cab to wait when he occasionally disappeared upstairs with one or two of them, stroking their hair, fondling their asses, whispering in their ears. He seemed to like them dark and petite. She shuddered, but she was transfixed. She had to know how much time he gave each of them, convincing herself it was never as much time as he gave her. She was also pleased that he had never asked her to work for him. Little did she realise the truth. They must have driven round for hours and hours. It was getting very dark. The cab driver became edgy, convinced she wouldn't pay. She eventually gave him all the money she had, about two hundred dollars, and a blow job he would not forget.

That was two nights ago. She hadn't seen Suli since. The cab had followed at a distance, but she was sure Suli had spotted her. She no longer had any illusions. From that evening on she felt small, insignificant and dirty. She sighed and huddled into a little ball. Tears rolled down her pallid cheeks.

Suddenly she heard the outside door open and bang shut. Heavy footsteps mounted the creaking stairs. She recognised them as Suli's. They were sure and determined ...

曲磊磊

走進威虎山

說的是上山下鄉的事,一晃二十多年,像是昨天的,又恍若隔世。

鄉下的日子,沒有什麼驚天動地的事,都是實實在在的生活,吃飯,幹活。但那是特殊的年代,也叫「戰天斗地」,也叫「五七道路」,也叫「接受再教育」。事實上,最愉快的事莫過於過年吃肉,最痛苦的事是晚上點著油燈聽傳達中央文件。幹了一天活,就想睡覺。

無論如何,我是懷著一顆真誠的心去的農村。這一生中大概很難再找到那種感覺,那種真誠的自我革命,那種無私的奉獻,那種犧牲的愉快,聽起來像是一種宗教迷狂。有人在這種迷狂中喪生,有人在之中成長,我是後者,那是一種珍貴的經驗,走進去又走出來,知道了是怎麼回事,當時年青,火力旺,意氣風發地越窮越革命。而且家遭厄運,天各一方。

那年我十七,正好和我女兒今年一樣大。我父母也正是我現在年齡,他們成了「走資派」,「新資產階級分子」和「反革命修正主義分子」。每天挨鬥,家也被抄了。我走之前,媽媽給我縫了一條厚厚的棉褲。他們熟悉那個地方的一切,他們曾在那一片冰天雪地中度過了一段槍林彈雨的青春歲月。

我是老初二的。那幾屆的中學畢業生,有的去了內蒙、山西,有的去了陝西、雲南、有的去了建設兵團。我則去了東北一個偏遠的小山村。它屬於黑龍江省海林縣;縣城離牡丹江不太遠。從父母角度來說,那是一個很慎重的選擇和安排了。我相信無論任何時候,那兒都是家父的最後一塊「根據地」。就如同薛地之於孟嘗君。他和他的戰友們,是當地人心目中傳奇式的英雄。用不著我多說,只要提一下「曲波」這個名字,男女老少無不立刻肅然起敬。當年他們剿滅了許大馬棒、座山雕這樣的匪幫。楊子榮也犧牲在那兒。早在五十年代末,《林海雪原》成了四大暢銷書之一,家喻戶曉;後來《智取威虎山》改成了樣板戲,海林人就更牛氣了。眞實革命傳統加上傳奇故事,都籠罩了一層神秘浪漫色彩。其實他們並不知道江青竊取了那段故事,又對家父妒恨入骨。海林人以他們擁有的一切而自豪,就連生產的香煙都只有三個牌子,普通人大都抽「林海」牌,有點文化的抽「雪原」牌的,年青人都抽「威虎山」。中國文化和這個民族的心理上,有著崇敬聖賢,懲惡揚善和感恩報德這樣的傳統,即便是在文化革命這樣的特殊條件下,人們可能多少聽說一點我父母正在挨整,但終究改變不了他們習慣上的觀念,加上到底山高皇帝遠,所以,既使有人故意難爲,也會有人出來保護我。

我到的當天便去祭掃烈士陵墓。楊子榮墓座落在縣城東邊,一條長長的上坡路把我引上一片高地,名叫東山。滿山松樹,墓碑和墳冢在山頂。山上很靜,我在那兒待了很久,松濤颯颯。

我最終落戶地方叫「三部落」。眞是一個頗有年代感的名字。我們的三部落處在原始森林和農耕文明交界的地方。從人文角度說,既沒有什麼歷史,也沒有多少文化,有的只是最基本的東西:天地山水,耕種收穫、吃飯以及與此有關的必需的東西－女人養孩子。過去人跡了了。日本開拓團駐過,國軍到過,土匪出沒過,最終共軍平定江山,其中也有老父。他當年率軍追剿,大獲全勝,下山時二十三歲。再以後是人民公社,當地農民有漢族和朝鮮族,也有關裡出來闖關東落了戶的,再往後我們去了,知識青年。就這麼簡單。留下了無數汗水,在那片土地上。我還會再去的,因為那兒實在太美了,無邊無際的森林,數不清,望不盡的荒地,山間清澈激冽的河水,滿山野果子和出沒的飛禽走獸。今天,才覺出有多麼巨大的潛力,當年首要的是革命,為革命種田,糧食為綱,不許搞副業,打場時剛剛接近場院,野雞呼啦啦飛走一大片,不許打,叫防止資本主義。

冬天沒有農活,跟林場定合同,上山伐木;間伐,碗口粗的樹林,因為樹太多,林太密,必須間隔著伐掉一些,大都是柞樹和樺樹，也有松杉之類，根據木材長短大小造材，或做鍬鎬把，或鐵路運輸貨車小杆，或建築用杉篙。冬天通常溫度是零下三十到四十度。晚上睡在靠山崖用樹枝編起又抹上泥的窩棚裡，一覺醒來，嘴邊眉毛上都是冰霜。天不亮就起來上山，白雪覆蓋的大地在黎明前夜空下泛著藍色，星星在凍僵了的夜空中閃著冷光，零下四十度，踩著咯吱咯吱的雪路，心中有一個很強的信念，好像很清楚，但又不具體，只堅信這一切都是必要的。上山時雪深沒膝，有的地方齊腰深。

放倒的樹砍掉枝叉，幾棵一梱拖下山，再上。幹熱了脫下棉襖，渾身冒煙，熱汗蒸汽升騰。大家唱著「吃小米爬大山，反修防修‧‧‧」一天幹下來回到家，棉襖棉褲都刮破了，露棉花。每天晚上補衣服，針線活從小就會，我那條褲子也不知道縫了多少層不同形狀不同顏色的布，真可以送進博物館了。過年回家我也就這麼穿進了北京。我倒還覺得挺光彩。我媽一見眼淚都流下來了。這兒子過得也太苦了，那條褲子我曾保存了好些年。後來被我女兒的媽媽剪了綁拖把了，我還為此發了一頓脾氣。在山裡有的時候暴風雪來，那景象壯麗。風捲刮著漫天的雪橫掃過山嶙，天地茫茫一片。這種時候我常迎著風站在山崗上，心裡頗有種英雄感。我沒對人說過，怕是小資產階級情調。靠的是一股「氣」。我寫過詩，寄給賀敬之。他後來見了我曾興奮地賞識並誇獎了我下鄉後的詩作。他當時還沒有蛻變成極左的官僚，他當時是我崇拜的敬之叔叔，父親的老友，處於困境的大詩人。他以前看過我十五歲下鄉前寫的詩，說我是「典型的資產階級個人奮鬥」。我當時的詩很受郭路生（筆名食指，我最老的朋友）的影響。他是我們這一代人公認的中國新詩運動的盟拓者，才華橫溢，後來精神分裂，長期住在精神病醫院，我想到他，心裡總是很難過。歷史會記下他的名字。若干年以後，我終於發現詩人的桂冠不會屬於我，才斷了當詩人的念頭。可惜那些詩稿都找不著了，這些是題外的話。

我們養了幾十箱蜜蜂，攪蜜的時候，戴著大白紗罩帽子，興奮異常。那年除了賣一些，每人還分了兩斤蜂蜜。用山泉水沖，大約瓊漿玉液就是那個味道。那個長著一對咪咪眼的小伙子喝了三大碗，睡了兩天，我才知道蜂蜜真的能安神。後來在一夜之間被「黑瞎子」（東北黑熊）偷蜜，毀了十幾箱，幾個小姑娘哭了好幾天，不知是心疼蜜蜂還是被熊嚇的。

二賴子是我們部落最混的小子。奇醜。在外張口就罵人，在家抬手就打老婆。他老婆人極老實，不好看，心眼好，埋頭幹活，從不多話。因為二賴子太賴，年底評工時我們給他評了三等，他老婆一等，他當時就蹦起來，爹娘一路罵著出了會場。第二天他老婆臉上青一塊紫一塊，不敢抬頭見人；身上的看不見。就這麼著，孩子一個接一個生，領著一個，抱著一個，還懷著一個。有一天夜裡這女人又哭號不停。第二天，我們幾個人在一個安靜地方堵著了二賴子。他見勢頭不對，蹲在地上抽煙。問他認揍還是認罰，他願認罰。刨樹根去，伙房缺燒柴。他倒是有勁，一氣沒歇，執著鎬頭把一個大樹根刨出來。警告他日後不許打老婆，否則當心老二。

椴樹開花時是採蜜的最好季節，特等椴樹蜜是最上乘的蜂蜜，市場上一般供應都是雜花蜜。那時正是春光明媚，雖然時有俊風寒日，但滿地花都開了所有的顏色。我們上工時，男的女的都隨手採點花，因為實在太好看。也不管是什麼階級的情調了，再說毛主席是讚美「鮮花」的。有一天下工回來，我專採純白的和火紅的，採了一大包，紅的在中間，都給了一個女孩兒。她高個子短頭髮。名字忘了。她像春天一樣明媚。說也奇怪，我在鄉下的整個期間竟沒有跟她說過多少話，我最終離開那兒的那天，她和另外幾個人一直送我上了火車，她竟哭得像個淚人似的。

Qu Leilei

Walking to Tiger Mountain

I will speak of "going up to the mountains and down to the countryside." Twenty years have elapsed since those things happened. It seems like yesterday; it seems like a different world.

There was nothing earthshattering about life in the countryside. It was all day-to-day existence: just eating and working. But this was an exceptional era. It was called "struggling against heaven and earth", "the May 7th Road", and "receiving re-education". Actually, the happiest time was when we could eat meat at New Year, and the most painful was in the evening when we had to light our oil lamps and listen to directives from the Party Central Committee. After a hard day's work, all we wanted to do was sleep.

No matter what actually happened, I went to the countryside with my whole heart. I guess I will never again experience that feeling in my lifetime, that feeling of self-criticism and renewal, that selfless dedication, that ecstasy of self-sacrifice that sounds like a religious delusion. Some people lost their lives amid that delusion, and some people grew up in it. I belonged to the latter kind. It was a precious experience, to go in and to come back out, to know what it was all about. In those years I was young and hot-headed, so high-spirited and enthusiastic that the poorer I was, the more I dedicated myself to the revolution. Moreover, my family was beset with tragedies; and we were all scattered in different directions.

That year I was seventeen, just the age that my daughter is now. And my parents were then the age I am now. They were labelled capitalist roaders, neo-bourgeoisie and counter-revolutionary revisionists. Every day they had to suffer criticisms, and everything in our house was confiscated. Before I left, mother sewed me a pair of thick cotton-padded trousers. My parents knew everything about the place where I was going.

I was in the second year of middle school. Among the secondary school graduates of those years, some were sent to Inner Mongolia or Shanxi, and some to Shaanxi or Yunnan. Others were sent to the construction brigades. I was sent to a remote mountain village in the northeast. It was part of Hailin county in Heilongjiang Province. The county seat was not too far from Peony River.

From my parents' point of view that was a very deliberate arrangement. I believe that, no matter when, that place will always be my father's base of operations, just like the region of Xue was Lord Mengchang's during the Warring States period (463-221 BC). My father and his war buddies became legends to the people of that region. I had only to bring up the name of Qu Po, and men and women, young and old, would immediately feel great respect rising in their hearts. During that year they exterminated Horse Cudgel Xu, Eagle, and bandit gangs of that kind. Yang Zirong, another hero, sacrificed his life there. By the end of the 1950s, Qu Po's *Tracks in the Snowy Forest* (*Linhai Xueyuan*) had become one of the four books in greatest demand and his name was a household word. Later, *Taking Tiger Mountain by Strategy*, based on an incident in the novel, was made into a model revolutionary opera. It combined a true revolutionary tradition with a legendary story and was permeated with a mysterious, romantic flavour. The people of Hailin became sick to death of it. Actually they didn't know that Jiang Qing stole the story for the opera; she felt bitter envy and hatred for my father.

The people of Hailin were proud of what they had. They even produced three different brands of cigarettes. The common people mostly smoked Linhai, those with a little bit of culture smoked Xueyuan, and the young people smoked Tiger Mountain.

In Chinese culture and in the psychology of our people, sages and heroes are revered, and there is a tradition of punishing the evil and raising up the good, rewarding kindness and virtue. Even in the unique situation of the Cultural Revolution, the people's habitual ways of thinking could not be changed. It is really true that "the mountains are high and the Emperor is far away." That is, that the authority of the central government cannot dominate people's thoughts about everything in every corner of the country. Some people probably heard that my parents were being criticised. But even when a person intentionally went out of his way to embarrass me, someone would always come to my aid.

The day I arrived, I went immediately to pay my respects to the graves of the fallen heroes. Yang Zirong's grave was on the eastern side of the county seat. A long road up a long hill led me to a high, flat plateau called Eastern Mountain. The whole hill was covered with pine trees, and the monuments and graves were at the top of the mountain. I stayed there a very long time.

The place I finally settled in was called Three Tribes. The name truly conveys the feeling of the era. Our Three Tribes was located at the junction between the primitive forest and agricultural civilisation. From the viewpoint of human culture, not only was there not much history in that place, but there was also not much culture. There were only the most basic of elements: sky, land, mountains and water. People tilled and harvested the land, the women raised the children, they ate, and their possessions were comprised of necessities for those activities. Every trace of human habitation in the past was well-known. The Japanese troops who had been stationed there had opened up the land; the Nationalist army had been there; bandits had come and gone, and finally, the Communist troops - among them my father - had conquered the rivers and mountains. That year, he led the troops to pursue and destroy the bandits and attained a great victory. When he came back down from the mountain, he was only 23. After that the area became a People's Commune, incorporating the local farmers of both Han and Korean nationalities, as well as others who braved the journey from the interior and made settlements there. We went there after that, we young intellectuals. It was as simple as that. Countless drops of our sweat flowed onto that land.

I will go back to that place again, the place of exceeding beauty - endless forests, trees beyond counting, and a vast wasteland that seemed to go on forever. Clear, icy-cold mountain streams, mountains filled with wild fruit, and birds and animals roaming everywhere. Only now do I realise what great potential it had. That year all I thought of was the revolution. For the revolution I cultivated fields. Producing food was our guiding principle and we were not allowed to engage in sideline activities. At threshing time, as I approached the threshing area, a large flock of pheasants would flap their wings with a whoosh and take flight. We were not allowed to go after them; we had to guard against that blasted capitalism.

In the winter there was no agricultural work, so we made a contract with the forestry centre to go up to the mountains to cut wood. The trees in the forests were as thick as rice bowls, and because of their abundant growth we had to thin them out a bit. Most were sap and birch trees; there were also pines and firs. According to the length and thickness of the trees we made logs, spade or axe handles, railroad poles for freight trains, or beams for construction. In the winter, the temperature was often 30 to 40 degrees below zero. In the evening, we slept in shacks constructed at cliff edges out of branches packed with mud. When we woke up there was frost around our mouths and eyebrows. We got up before daybreak and went into the mountains, and the white, snow-covered, pre-dawn expanse of land looked all blue under the dark sky, with stars twinkling in the icy coldness. It was 40 below and the snow crunched as we walked along the path. In our hearts we had a strong belief that seemed crystal clear - but not at all concrete. As we went up the mountain where the snow was knee-deep, and in places waist-deep, we so firmly believed that this was all necessary.

We had to prune the branches from the trees we had felled, bind them up into bundles and pull them down the mountain. Then we went back up again. When we had worked up a sweat, we took off our jackets and clouds of steam rose from our bodies as the hot sweat condensed in the cold air. Everyone sang, "Eat rice and climb the big mountain, be on guard against revisionism". After a full day's work we came down and went home, our padded jackets and padded trousers all torn and ripped, with cotton padding protruding from the seams. Every evening we mended our clothes - I had been able to do needlework ever since I was little. I don't know how many layers I had sewn on that pair of trousers, all of different types of material and colours. They could very well be sent to a museum. I wore that pair of trousers to Beijing when I went home for the New Year, exuding a sense of pride. As soon as my mother saw them, tears flowed from her eyes - this son of hers had endured so much suffering. I kept that pair of trousers for a number of years. Later they were cut into strips by my wife and made into a mop. I was very angry at her for doing that.

In the mountains there were sometimes violent snowstorms that produced a spectacular sight. The swirling wind filled the whole sky and swept across the hills. Heaven and earth were one great blur. At times like these, I often stood on a hill, facing the wind, and felt rather like a hero in my heart. I had never told anyone about this, fearing it was the emotion of a petty bourgeois. Relying on a bellyfull of high spirit, I wrote poems and sent them to He Jingzhi. When he saw me later, he enthusiastically exalted my poetic accomplishments of this period in the countryside. At that time, he had not yet transformed into an extreme leftist bureaucrat. Then he was my "uncle" whom I greatly admired, my father's old friend, a great poet writing in difficult circumstances. Earlier on, he had seen the poems I had written at the age of fifteen before going to the countryside, and had said I was typical of a capitalist struggling for himself. During that period, my poems were influenced by Guo Lusheng (penname Shizi), my oldest friend. A number of years later I realised that the poet's crown would not belong to me; only then did I give up the thought that I was a poet. Unfortunately, I cannot find any of the drafts of these poems. But this is all beside the point.

We raised several dozen hives of bees, and at honey-collecting time we put on our white mesh bee-keeping suits and were full of excitement. Other than selling a bit, we each took a two *jin* share of honey. We immersed it in spring water and it tasted like nectar and pearly dew. One young boy with greedy eyes drank three big bowls of it and slept for two days. Only then did I realise that honey has such a soporific effect. Late one night a Black Blind Man (Manchurian black bear) came to steal our honey, and destroyed several hives. A few young girls cried for several days. I couldn't figure out if they were sad for the bees, or just frightened to death.

Erlaizi was the most disreputable young man in our tribe. He was exceedingly ugly. Outside the home he would criticise others, and at home he made a habit of beating his wife. His wife was an extremely honest person, not good-looking but good at heart. She would put her head down and work away, never speaking very much. Because Erlaizi was so lazy, at the end of the year when it was time to assess and criticise his work, we gave him a third rank and his wife a first rank. At that moment he jumped up and left the hall, cursing all the way. The next day his wife's face was so covered with black and blue bruises that she would not raise her head to passers-by. We couldn't see the bruises on her body. Be that as it may, she had one child after another - there'd be one by the hand, one in her arms, and one at her breast. Once in the middle of the night she was crying and yelling without stopping. The next day a couple of us intercepted Erlaizi in a quiet place. When he realised the odds were against him, he squatted down on the ground and lit a cigarette. We asked him whether he would prefer a beating or hard labour; he chose hard labour. It was to dig out a tree root for firewood required by the kitchen. He certainly had a lot of strength. In one burst of energy he brandished an axe and extracted a large tree root. We warned him that if he beat his wife again he'd have to watch out for his private parts.

The best season for gathering honey was when the linden blossoms were out. Honey taken solely from the linden tree is of the highest quality. What you get in the market is mostly honey from mixed flowers. Those were the enchanting days of spring. Although some days were windy and cold, the flowers were in bloom everywhere and in all colours. On our way to work, we all - men and women alike - picked as many as we wanted. They were so beautiful. Once when we were coming home from work, I picked just pure white and fiery red ones. I made a big bouquet, with red ones in the middle, and gave them all to a young girl. She was tall with short hair. I've forgotten her name, but she was as enchanting as spring. It seems strange now, but the whole time I was in the countryside I had hardly exchanged more than a few words with her. On the day I left, when she and a few others took me to the train to see me off, she cried so much that I thought she'd never stop.

translated by Sally Church and Mausang Ng

小芸

相親

「好姐姐,陪我一次吧。這可是爸媽迫我的,不是我自己恨嫁呢!」

「死丫頭,你不想,爸媽迫得了你嗎?」玉蓮笑罵道。

「嗯,雖是這樣說,但相親這回事,我不是頭一次,想必是挺好玩的。你整天做呀做呀,就不可以陪我去開開心嗎?說不定那個人會看上你呢。」

玉蓮放下了電話,回味著玉英剛才的話,對掛在牆上的鏡子看看自己的臉容。玉英說得不錯,目前的生活勞勞碌碌,真的缺乏一點情趣。從孩子出生那年跟他父親分開後,千辛萬苦敖過來,一眨眼孩子已有十歲了。這十年來,單身帶著孩子生活,沒有的是時間、金錢、娛樂,有的是困苦中磨出來的自尊、老練。玉蓮在父母跟前從來不說她跟孩子爸爸的事,他們也沒有問過。除了孩子的存在是事實外,好像什麼事情也沒有發生過。前兩年,妹妹玉英也離婚了。小兩歲的玉英人長得漂亮,又拿了博士學位,一向是家中的寵兒。離婚後,父母一直替她著緊。這次經人介紹,去相親一個中國來的青年。由於父親對中國感情濃厚,對這次相親抱很大希望。

星期六的唐人街道上熙來攘往,一些人站在街上溜連張望,希望遇到相知。他們約在爵祿街的龍鳳酒家會面,取那兒吉祥的意頭。到達酒家時,對方已經在座了。見來了姊妹兩個,很詫異。玉蓮父親連忙介紹。那何先生夫婦見玉英長得標緻,十分歡喜。跟著介紹了他們的兒子-何業。何業大約三十出頭,來英才一年,現在正在學英語。他的父母留英公幹,急於在離英前為他安排生活,及替他物色一個有居留的對象。

點過餐點後,何太太首先打開話題:「玉英在哪辦事?多大年紀了？」

「玉英是博士，在大學裡做研究，今年三十歲了。」玉英父親說。

「哎呀，一個女孩子，可眞不容易。」何先生顯得有點兒不自在。

玉蓮父母兒女雖多，但大都是在英國長大，在婚姻上有自己的主意。這樣的場合，他們還是頭一趟，所以覺得很拘謹。

男主角何業一直沒說話。側著頭，不停的挪動身體。點心上桌了，他也不客氣，第一個就起筷。玉英向他瞪瞪眼，又對玉蓮眨眨眼，玉蓮知這門親事不成了。

何太太夾一件點心放在玉英碗裡，滿面堆笑著說：「你平時幹些什麼呢？」

「我？我平時很忙，很多活動呢。」玉英答道。「看戲啦，開party啦，練空手道啦⋯⋯。」

「你喜歡這些玩意嗎？」何先生笑著說，「說到武術這回事，還是我們中國的比較實在些，好像氣功與太極⋯⋯」

「我認爲沒有所謂，中的、西的，反正有趣味就可以。」玉英說：「就好像我交朋友一樣，有英國人啦、非洲人啦、印度人啦、日本人啦⋯⋯」

「你很多朋友呢。」

「對呀，我對上一個男朋友是非洲來的，還教過我弄非洲菜。」玉英眉飛色舞地說。

「女孩子別亂說。」玉英母親向她橫了一眼。不好意思地對何先生夫婦說：「我這個女兒喜歡開玩笑。」

何先生夫婦看看玉英，沒有作聲。各人低下頭吃點心。玉英偷偷對玉蓮擠擠眼，玉蓮忍著笑，差不多要可憐她的父母與那個何業了。

過了一會兒，何太太慢慢放下筷子，移過身向玉蓮說：「玉蓮，你結了婚吧，你丈夫在哪裡工作呢？」

「我沒有丈夫。」玉蓮對她笑笑。

何先生夫婦同時看看玉蓮，彼此交換了一下眼光，對玉蓮父母說：「你們玉蓮雖年紀大一點，人品可不錯呢！斯斯文文的，有找對象嗎？」

玉蓮母親遲疑了一會，搖頭道：「不，玉蓮雖然離了婚，但已有了一個兒子，跟他的爸也還有聯絡的。」

何先生看看他太太一眼，夾一塊點心進口，緩緩地向玉蓮父親說道：「孟先生，我們了解你們是好人家。不過，我們只有這一個兒子，想給他找一個好對象，讓他能夠在英國留下來。這本來是很難。你們玉英條件太優了⋯人也太洋化一點，我覺得彼此都不是太合適。不過，我這有個意見，說出來你們別見怪，我們的意思是⋯⋯不如叫何業跟你們玉蓮結婚，將來等他辦好了居留，如果有不滿意，也可以再離婚；我們也會給你們報酬的。玉蓮的孩子方面，我們也不是嫌她的孩子，只是⋯⋯何業現時還未能養他，不能負起這個責任⋯⋯你看，這會行得通嗎。」

玉蓮父母愕然的望望玉蓮，有點兒不知所措。這個女兒外面沉靜，心中想些什麼，他們卻從來不理解。「玉蓮你怎麼看呢？」玉蓮母親終於低聲向她問道。玉蓮看看他們，又看看何先生夫婦，突然感到很憤怒，拿筷子夾了一只鳳爪放進口中慢慢咀嚼。

「我說，爸爸，嫁出去的女兒是潑出去的水不是？我現在是自己拿主意了，中國人從來把婚姻當買賣，那我就開個價吧。廿千鎊一分錢也不能少，倘要加一個白胖胖的兒子另加十千鎊。

我自己的兒子也這麼大了,證明是生養的,對不對?條件開出來了,你們盡可慢慢地商量,我和玉英先去牛津街看看,看有什麼合意的。二十千鎊可以去買好幾個 Louise Vuitton 袋袋尿片充充呢。」說完拉起玉英便走。

中午的牛津街依舊繁忙,玉英知道這個姐姐的脾性,挽著她的手走進大公司裡的咖啡廳。呷著咖啡,玉蓮的氣也下了,對玉英說:「爸這次可不知怎樣下台了。」

「你也好狠,明知爸爸一向愛面子,你這不是拆他的台麼?你是借題發揮吧!」

「嗯…我其實也不真的惱他們,我知在他們眼中,我的一生是完了。有了孩子的失婚婦人,只能在等待她的命運。前些時,我見過一位在英工作了多年的中醫,他問我在做什麼事?我告訴他我是一邊工作一邊讀書。他說我一把年紀,聲音都轉了,不應還去讀書,應該把時間用來栽培孩子上。我從前聽說在中國,婦女的地位不同了,很多舊的,腐敗的傳統思想都改革過來,我看那只是些表面現象罷了,骨子裡還不是一樣?不論中國、香港、還是海外,時代變了,生活變了,掙錢的方式也不同了,但有些事卻始終都不變。我們婦女的價值是什麼?」

玉英低頭喝著咖啡,默然無語。她自己也不是為了理想而走上離婚的道路嗎?只是離婚後,無牽無掛,上劇院、學語言,倒沒有去想過這些懊惱的問題。

咖啡廳裡來來往往一批批衣著入時,富泰優悠的女客。玉蓮望望那邊幾個日本婦人帶著齊齊整整的小孩,輕談淺笑,面上洋溢著滿足的神情;忽然感到很疲倦,剛才發生的一切都彷彿很遙遠了。明天,明天又要掛起倔強的臉譜,去面對新的一天。

Zibao

A Transcription of Something I Heard

(Jacquard lace nets raised slowly, revealed an unexpected silent-motion picture.)

Though I know that there are people suffering everywhere on the earth, all these had become so boring: loaves of thick cuts, fictions, spring onions and mushrooms on the lawn, daddy-long-legs, aroma of grasses, clocks in slow motion, and broadcasts in alien tongues...

(Trees waved goodbye and the scene faded out as the frost lowered the lace nets. The pebbles and waves overlapped a red carpet. The sunlight curtain hanged from the cloudy sky.)

...and then those breakfast cereals, flickering telly images, those same old chain stores, slams from old train doors, uphill walks, gulls' songs, naughty gales, thunderbolts linking the heaven and the hell, large oily oblong pancake rolls, and nice OAPs...

...those agency consultants are supporters of paper recycling? Oh, no. No wonder my...

(Hence, not another retired.)

At first they had arranged to let me peel vegetables. And then move on to the frying oil and fish. That's fine, at least something new.

(A lay person learning and trying in the catering field?)

"Bullet holes" made by "golden fingers" were just recovered before I brooded over the preparation of mid-year reports of ME for visiting relatives from my origin. I left out any line that might cause embarrassing or scornful response.

(On the covers of the reports there was some graffiti, and some blank sheets inside. Curtains of salty rain, hail and mist lowered, and the scene ended with a breath saying au revoir to the ferries.)

Regretting, idling and dreaming...things passed by so slowly: time passed by so fast...

I had tried hard to hide my little secret dreams of a peaceful/cosy/poetic/exotic future and something new.

(Covering-up or forgetting the past is funny, sometimes.)

...I was supposed to leave something behind, but not everything.

...I miss them, too, those little things, over there, still dancing...in waves of quavers and semi-quavers, treble clef...

("douk-douk-douk-douk-tsang", karaokes, lutes, "ghee-ghee-goo-ghee-ghee", synthesisers, "ghong-tseh-ho-si-sang", city beats etc. make up the unique background music. Interferences in lento, bass clef, flats and occasional thunders roar in ff. Falls and rises, sweetened refrain repeats.)

...round and round and round. All there, just that they no longer dance on my halls of red, blue or green...

Why? I cannot stand seeing what will happen when the clock strikes. You know that. I know. Don't laugh...damn the recurring wish-I-were-there dreams that make my pillow cases damp.

Are you suggesting that I confess about my choice (abandoning the paradise)?

(A camcorder is panning: the clumsily designed and developed webs make these nuts - once brilliant - passively, ignorantly, stupidly rolling. Battered with the mixture of chocolate, tobacco, alcohol, and frying oil, only have some kind of sepsis to live with.)

...they come, just occasionally, to play hopscotch on our twenty-four-hole plan.

Poor, not only them, me too.

...it seems that those with some good grey cells, are never in charge, only shown occasionally, on air or on paper, leaving the webs weaved and the spalled shoddy brick wall repointing actually in trial-and-error, hit-and-miss, touch-and-go ways. Don't you think so?

(Split screen: eight screens of sequential-time-lapse-stills show the close-ups of punch and blow, ricochet, feint and duck, hand-chopper and Tai-Chi push - and then one screen in right bottom corner shows wind flipping through a pocket diary, its white belly like its owner, as a slightly soiled oddment on a shelf, double exposure of a sort of wilderness, light source is somewhere out of touch, out of sight...)

Well, well, well, hibernating here, wincing and wilting, inside pancake sheets, soaked in oil, facing the music and lyrics that rhyme with "dew", "lung", "height" and "duck"...

(A lot of special-chow-mein caterers use the sheets as magic cloths to call forth the appearance of the most practical portraits of the crowned bust.)

...sometimes it's just too hard to stand with the non-sackable, noisy, prolix, ignorant big-headed boss and all those built-in dead-knots. I can't take them anymore.

(This corner of this part of the Thames - probably abandoned by most of the prosperous industries or proper young couples - greets newcomers with magic of dust, of dirt, and of chilly spells.)

Mornings disappeared. Time has been cut up, pasted and patched with pieces from diaries, photos, pancake sheets and Dickens' portraits...

Not everything can be fitted in between the noon-to-two and five-to-midnight slots. These bars are too much for me...jailbird and cage? Well, we are all in some kind of cage. How about you?

(Scenes outside the building: a lot of suicidal, if not murderous, people, aged from ten to seventy, endanger the society by smoking and deliberate self-intoxication: teens are left to keep loitering, littering, spitting, playing and laughing at silly things, leaning, sitting and speaking nonsense and racist language, stealing to buy drinks and fags...grey rain drops and black dots outlined lace nets are hanging there, facing the street of chips-eating city-gulls, dog shit, phlegmy saliva, loiterers...)

How to get rid of recurring nightmares and dreadful memory of some scenes?

(To readers who are psychologists or physicists: when does "slow-motion" become "time-lapse"?)

When my brain is overloaded I tend to compress memory of acquired dogma, tables of unfavourable comparisons and reflections, annoying scenes, etc. into a compound stored in the fourth stomach.

So far, there's just one side-effect: occasional spills of the contents are far more bitter than bile.

I have to use dreams and stories as temporary anaesthetics, light melodies my tranquilliser, stacks of prose and diagrams as pillows. These placebos are not too bad, are they? Do you have any good recommendations?

(How about these: counselling by experts, church-going, fiction-reading and writing, fantasies, physical and psychological stimuli from fast tracks, streets and video games, soaps, whirling clanking and electronic stereo, horse-betting, horse-rocking, intoxicating liquid, nicotine, drugs...)

... monasteries? Death?

Forgetting, dreaming and destroying ... yesterday ... today ...tomorrow ...

(Excuse me, where are we?)

Maybe reflecting, living and hoping would help. Or would this just worsen my problems? Visualise this, a scene that I cannot forget: the pink petals, flying in the breeze, with a little girl climbing up the tree above the green, witnessed by the sun and a turtle...What would you feel about the waiting, the time-lag, between this moment and the future unforseen?

(Messy twisting threads and chains, twining around, snaking, making people the stake of their merry-go-rounds and their bonfire. Far more tears were squeezed out than by splits or pangs. Only the scorched figures of sixty-four ninety-seven help this languished to count the blessings.)

"Get up, you, passive player!"

Me? What player?

"Everyone take Life, the Game, as the constructive lifelong habit for pleasure."

(Hints: the Game Players should keep scrambling and gambling: scooping, collecting, snatching, grabbing, snapping up: manoeuvering and revenging; blending in and serving a coup de grace; scheduling and timeserving ... Not much law or morality in certain levels.)

The fit ones enjoy the pleasure from contesting, parading and exploiting their abilities, captures and captives?

("So-desu-ne." Simulation games of any types are top-sellers - for the majority: the not-so-fit ones.)

Could you tell me who made and who revises the rules? Why must I join and follow them?

"Anyway, just keep playing...just have to carry on playing...better than having nothing to do, isn't it? Try harder. Toolbox and icons are there, buttons to be clicked."

Shall I continue playing the Game as anybody does? But I have lost my bearings and everything...

"D'you understand? Stand there watching others marathoning for the tubes and chasing the buses is not funny, especially helpless when you are thinking whether you should or should not be one of them."

Well, merely watching the huge hour-glass in action is killing me, not time ... I ...

"Come on, rebuilding, refurbishing. and reshelling will make any miniest vehicle a lovely one."

(True, but one has to gather enough batering counters first. Eighteen carats, and "999" always see featherweight nine carats as scorns, and expendable; let alone some other glittering golden pieces or colourful plastic.)

"What's on your score board and your stock list so far?"

I dare not tell anybody about my being nearly ten years behind.

(Poor soul. Languishing for catching up and breakthroughs, which seem too abstract to be grasped, is a tiresome job.)

"You'd better not waste the precious time, power and space - write down something before your crayon of youth is whittled."

(Or the worst scene will be recorded and the whole history will be blackened, all at others' mercy.)

Maybe the making of the chapter at hand itself is enjoyable. Isn't it what people used to say?

(Having found a piece of wood to cling on to on the choppy sea, a dying person would be thankful for that piece, too.)

Well, there must be some other things. The plot is great, but it may have loopholes somewhere.

"No more excuses, please."

(Lullaby is sung by clocks in darkness. Tic toc tic toc tic toc tic...go to the power of n.)

Can anyone foresee the end? My time is dripping away. Is the Game the fun we live for, the reason we exist, the way we stay alive? Tell me ... help me ...

(The murmurer fell back and lay there with a faraway look, possibly will still be there unconscious for some time. IQ test, psychoanalysis, aptitude test, hypnotism diagnoses were suggested. Electric shock therapist standby, please.)

(Check whether your diary is still locked and your place is intact.)

(No comment?)

乞靈

謝佩兒

那日佩兒拿著幾方私章
說起石頭的故事
我也借出印泥
搬弄自己的石頭
最深喜愛王府井大街刻的
一枚雞血紅
你的一枚紋色字款一樣
雕上隸書文字
你輕嗔道夫妻姓氏相同
今生今世再不有夫姓
勻稱方正的私章靠肩
都漬紅了多少扉頁
都冰清地藏起來
人不聚在一起
石頭也冷了
當被巧手將胚石分割
許情份就盡了
再黏在一起，也緣天之幸
那還有甚麼可以怨懟呢

和佩兒共事數年
都沒有提起你
那日我說正在想著妳
佩兒才透露美美剛巧碰著你
從倫敦回來了

我說幾年了都沒遇上妳
只聽說過你的婚紗照
一大群朋友
原來就只有美美和佩兒參加婚禮
有你的婚紗照
佩兒好忍心
幾年來都不讓我知道
其實，我又怎會太黯然呢
那日佩兒在路上遇到你
大家站著說話
你穿著泥黃直身裙
短髮，不再咬指甲了
大抵也沒穿高跟鞋子
面龐稍稍胖了，眼睛更圓
你把新地址、電話都給了佩兒
下班後步行回家，就像從前練舞後一樣

佩兒問妳是否快樂
你說很好，但沒有說快樂
那日約了佩兒在火車站
便絮絮的纏著她說故事
坐在超級市場的石階上
要她憶述了幾十分鐘
不知道那日再會遇上妳
不知道會不會駐足
不是怕哽咽
但還有甚麼想知道呢！
不怕流淚
可是我該用甚麼樣的眼神看妳！

記著妳乖乖依偎的柔軟
帶髮香的耳語
怕一沾碰就塌掉了
你是朵惺忪的白蓮
我還會記得讚美你
說你最愛聽的諛辭
但能夠怔怔地站著看看妳
微風擺動時
觸著妳的裙腳
我還要說些甚麼話呢！

乞靈

灣仔摘豆芽的老婦人

我守著我小小的街角
皇後大道東汽車川流不息
從早到晚
就像我黑白相間的頭髮
垂下頭勤快地截去頭尾
只留下玉臂一段的豆芽
一斤一塊工資
每日吃著清早剩下的便當

夕陽煦煦地移過來時
我招呼我的朋友吃卷煙
從前和將來都是街道外的事物
從我的手中摘掉
我守著我小小的街角
只有一段一段潔白的心事

Tracy Cheung

A Wayward Girl

Sometimes I catch her looking at me in her characteristically sharp but bemused way. I guess I didn't turn out the way she had expected, though what she'd imagined I doubt she herself could explain.

"You don't even look like a woman!" she'd exclaim loudly. "You are so untidy, what man is ever going to want you?" Then she'd click her tongue in exasperation and roll her eyes to the sky. If anybody could be described as a drama queen, I guess that would be her all over. She infuriated me constantly, her brashness and her refusal to even attempt to soften her words with the velvet glove of English politeness. "Chinese people don't talk like that," she snapped once, when I'd chided her on her tone of voice. "Anyway, I am your mother and I am just TELLING you."

I liked the way I dressed, anyhow. So I was laid back about my appearance and had worn my jeans till they had holes in them and preferred heavy-soled shoes to the neat pumps my oldest sister wore. I was into Alice Walker and feminism and militant studenthood. She just didn't understand me.

Her home was always so pristine and had the feel of shiny-newness I detested. My student digs had junk from secondhand shops, candles, ethnic rugs from Oxfam and clothes from various kitschy stalls and shops in Leicester.

"Why you want to wear dead people's clothes?" she demanded.

"Because I like them!" I retorted with impatience.

"Hnnnh!" she snorted emphatically. There was more emotion in one snort from her than in an entire episode of El Dorado. "Did I bring you up to buy old clothes? You are not poor! People will think you are a peasant! That I have taught you badly, that you have not learned how to dress yourself!"

I threw my hands into the air helplessly. "OK," I sighed. "I'm going out. I'll be back later."

She crossed her arms and gave me that sidelong glance that dripped with disapproval. "Dinner is at seven," she stated.

"Yeah, yeah," I muttered and closed the door behind me. As I walked down to the gate, I thought to myself, I bet none of my English friends go through this every time they come home for vacation. Perhaps with the exception of Juliet Maynard from Hall. Her mother always talked to her as if she had a red-hot poker stuffed in the proverbial. It made me giggle to think of the last time she had popped up to visit Juliet.

"Is that an earring you have in your nose!" she'd shrieked, aghast. Juliet had been mortified at the time but I'd thought grimly, I know someone who'd give your ma a good run for your money!

I strolled along the high street. It was a brisk winter day and I lit a cigarette and inhaled appreciatively. Oh, she wasn't a bad old stick, my mother - but sometimes! When we were younger, my sisters and I used to back-chat her and tell her that she was old-fashioned, that our friends' mothers were more fashionable than her and that she told old wives' tales. That used to drive her mad and we had got a couple of good hidings out of that one. "No respect!" she'd scold us. Which wasn't true of us, in fact.

I caught myself in the window at Top Shop and watched for the few seconds it took to pass it. My hair needed cutting, I decided; I was sick of my centre parting and the grungy look. Perhaps I should just cut it very short. Now that would really get my old lady's goat.

I suppose I must be a million miles from the people she'd left in Hong

Kong. She went back last year and brought my cousin back with her for a few weeks. Her name was Gee-Ying, she was eighteen and impossibly prissy and my mother, of course, loved her. She spoke Cantonese in a way that my mother admired. I couldn't hear it myself, but apparently she was very well educated and her use of language was terribly effective. I spoke Cantonese mingled with English, with a South London accent, and struggled over finding the right words. My cousin found it quaint. I most certainly did not.

It served me right, I guessed. I never went to Chinese school, which was always on a Saturday. When I was younger I never had the inclination and my mother since gave up trying to persuade us to go. My oldest sister spoke Cantonese pretty well and she married a Hong Kong-born Chinese about a year ago. At university, I never joined the Chinese society as it seemed to be mostly aimed at overseas students and I didn't want to get pigeon-holed. It was a little strange whenever I came home though, and found that my grasp of Cantonese was slipping each time. It kind of embarrassed me, to be quite honest. But it was a little late to have regrets about not speaking it more when I was younger.

My language, as soon as I went to school, became English. I was surrounded by English voices, books, television programmes - how could I have ignored it? The Chinese newspapers that lay under the coffee table were indecipherable to me, bar a few characters. I even ended up studying English at university!

I went into Debenhams, bought a cappuccino and an eclair and sat down in the cafe. I'd finished my cigarettes so I would just have to console myself with a fat chocolate cake and get warm at the same time. As I sat there, munching my way into chocolate heaven, a little Indian girl stopped at my table and stared at me. Her eyes were round as she watched me take a huge, greedy bite. She was dressed in a tiny, pink silk outfit and she had curly bunches on each side of her head.

"Smitta!" Her mother grabbed her hand and pulled the little girl to her. "What did I tell you about staring, huh?"

The small girl shrugged all wide-eyed and her mother gave a "hnnnh!" sound in the way my own mother did and said something very quickly in her own tongue. Her words flowed quickly, it was like listening to something quite musical. Then she turned to me, smiled briefly and said in a very English accent, "I am sorry. I tell her all the time, but you know how kids are."

I just smiled right back. She was definitely going to grow up to be some cheeky kid.

"Yeah," I said. "I know what you mean."

王家新

卡夫卡

我建築了一個城堡
從一個滾石的夢中；我經歷著審判
並被無端地判給了生活；
我的鄉村之業躑躅不前；我的布拉格
自一個死者的記憶開始。

而為什麼我的父親一咳嗽
天氣就變壞，我不能問
我一問在我的日記中就出現烏雲！
徒勞的反抗使我虛弱下來，
於是有時我就想到了中國的長城。

現在，饑餓仍是我的命運。
我能做的，只是荒誕到最後一刻。
因此世界本身並不荒誕
尤其當一位美麗的女性照耀著你時，
為什麼你我就不能達到讚美？

我將離去，僅僅由於我的呼吸
我的變黑的肺；我比醫生更知道於此；
這是我自己的祕密，但這是否
我一生的罪？———我已無力再問，
我已不能從我的失敗中再次開始。

我的寫作摧毀了我！

我知道它的用心,而生活正模仿它
更多的人在讀到它時會變成甲虫
在親人的注視下痛苦移動———
我寫出了流放地,有人就永無歸宿!

因此,最後的日子已經到來
朋友,請替我燒掉我的這些書———
看在「上帝」的份上!記住,這是我
一生中最不輕易喊出的一個詞
而這卻是一個最後的時刻!

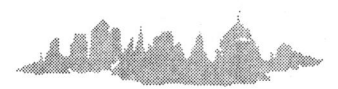

Wang Jiaxin

Kafka

I built a castle
within a dream of shifting stone. I am on trail.
I've been given life, and God knows why.
My nights in the countryside stumble, won't move on. Prague, for me,
begins with the memory of a corpse.

And why should the weather break whenever
my father coughs? I never could ask
because if I did, dark clouds would appear in my diaries.
The feeble resistance I put up just made me weaker.
And so there were times when I imagined the Great Wall of China.

These days, hunger is still my lot.
Down to my final hour, all I can accomplish is the absurd,
and for this reason the world itself is not absurd.
All the more so when the beauty of a woman shines upon you,
then why can't you and I learn to adore?

I must go, but only for the sake of my breathing,
my darkening lungs. I know better than my doctor.
It's my own special secret. Or is it rather my own
original sin? - I no longer have the strength to ask,
I am no longer able to set out again from the circle of failure.

My writing destroys me.
And I know what it wants from me. Now life imitates my art.
More and more of my readers metamorphosise -
dung beetles moving painfully under the eyes of their loved ones.
I have created alienation, people without homes to return to.

Because of this, the last days have come.
Burn my books for me, my friend -
for *God's* sake. Remember that is the word
that all my life, I have found most difficult to say,
but this is a final hour.

translated by John Cayley

王家新

日記

從一棵茂盛的橡樹開始
園丁推著他的鋤草機。從一個圓
到另一個更大的來回
整天我聽著這聲音,我嗅著
青草被割去時的新鮮氣味
我呼吸著它,我進入
另一個想像中的花園,那裡
青草正吞沒著白色的大理石臥雕
青草拂動;這死亡的愛撫
勝於人類的手指

醒來,鋤草機和花園一起荒廢
萬物服從於更冰冷的意志;
橡子炸裂之後
園丁得到了休息;接著是雪
從我的寫作中開始的雪
大雪永遠不能充滿一個花園
卻湧上了我的喉嚨
季節輪回到這白茫茫的死
我愛這雪,這茫然中的顫慄;我憶起
青草呼出的最後一縷氣息……

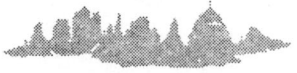

Wang Jiaxin

Diary Entry

Starting from the base of a luxuriant oak
the gardener pushes his mower out, from one circle
to another wider round-trip.
All day I hear this racket; I breathe in
the fresh smell of the new cut grass.
I breathe it. I enter
another garden in my mind - there
the new grass swallows up a reclining figure,
brushing the carved marble - deathly caresses,
more intimate than human fingers.

Waking, garden and mower are both laid waste,
all things submit to a colder will.
After the acorns crack
the gardener gets his rest, and the snows follow,
the snows that begin with my writing,
the heavy snows that will never cover a garden
but which well up in my throat
as the season turns back to the pale expanse of death.
I love this snow, a shiver in the void. I remember
the last breath of the new grass ...

translated by John Cayley

Paul Wong

Jerusalem

Here lies my grail, some tarnished cup of
Godly origin.

Here lies my pride, a vessel easily led.

Here dreams my whitened self, burning with
Stigmata.

Here holds my weakened heart, ill-supported upon a
Faithful crutch.

And in seeking this I have strength, dripping from my
Wounds, constantly self-replenishing,
I am reborn.

Paul Wong

Jugular

taking away the pain,
I took away my sanity, to leave behind
some enchanted evening in a bin
of broken parts.

there would be more than this if my heart were
true but
I've shown the lies the way in, so
drift away around me,
seek my tears in the dry wells of my eyes;
there is no one.

I juggled for your jugular
mounting
a lame horse just for effect.
I am full of you still but still
full of shit.

the world's a greyer place,
all too sane and full of pain.
the heart I own is as wooden
and glassy as
those I gave you.

all over, the clichés grow,
weeds on the landscape of our time together
and life goes on frighteningly
fulfilling every sad moment.

Paul Wong

Less Than Yellow

The bright lights of London's West End sparkle on the gilded surface of a hollow plastic gourd dangling from the rear-view mirror of a red BMW sports car. Madonna songs, reworked in Cantonese, boom forth from the in-car CD hifi and a small plastic bunny bobs up and down on a spring stuck to the dashboard. Power-steering the car into a multi-storey car-park, the driver finds a space, gets out, clicks the central locking and presses a button on a keyring. The car beeps its alarm and flashes its headlights and indicators like a reassuringly obedient pet.

Humming one of the Madonna tunes, the driver skips down the urine-drenched concrete staircase and heads out towards Chinatown. All along Wardour street, late-night revellers laugh at the window displays of roasted animals and stagger out of restaurants burping and belching, their bellies bloated with sweet-and-sour pork and egg-fried rice, all floating in oceans of lager and Coca-Cola.

It's St Valentine's Day and the driver passes through Chinatown and into Leicester Square, almost drowning in a sea of buskers, lovers and rugby-scrum groups of single men and women. Hordes of badly dressed flower-sellers pressure-sell cellophane-wrapped roses to drunkenly desperate men, who part, like fools, with exhorbitant sums of money for these puny, sickly blooms.

Stepping into the entrance of a nightclub, the driver joins a small line of people waiting to get past two huge tuxedoed bouncers. The mirrored foyer is festooned with hearts, cupids and lipstick kisses, and a glittering but amateurish sign declares tonight to be a "Rendezvous with Eros: A Lovebase Special Event". Paying the underdressed woman at the desk, the driver saunters along the red carpet and trots down the stairs, eyes adjusting to the ever-decreasing lighting.

Inside the club, music pummels the senses of the trendy clientèle and sends a shiver down the driver's spine. At the bar the driver orders a double vodka on the rocks and a "Golden Rain" cocktail (champagne, galliano liqueur and tequila). Musing on the next allowance from "mummy and daddy", the driver smiles at the thought of the extra "examination success" bonus already winging its way from the East.

Downing the vodka in one - the genital and breast-shaped icecubes clattering against expensive dental work - the driver banishes all thoughts of family, exams and the future, preferring instead to be absorbed by the evening's hedonistic atmosphere. A quick glimpse and preen in the mirror behind the bar, a gesture for another vodka and a sip of cocktail, prepares the driver to face the gauntlet of bodies leading to the dance-floor.

With the second vodka already sliding liver-wards, the driver slinks towards the core of the club: a body-heated, industrialised level of hell for hypersensitive sinners. The music leads the dancers from a psychotic-pacemaker frenzy to a groin-grinding bonk-tempo. Standing at the brink of the dance-floor the driver nods along to each rhythm, puffing stylishly on a cigarette and sucking-up the last dregs of the cocktail through a mini-calibred straw.

Behind the mass of writhing and flailing dancers, photographic slides flicker across white bedsheets on the walls: black and white images of romantic moments from classic films alternate with vivid close-up colour shots of hard-core pornography.

An appliquéd mass of sequins screams "Tyrannasvestite Rex" on a sash draped around someone dancing in a pair of size-11 stilettoes. This six-foot creature, with false eyelashes and a hirsute brick shithouse of a body squeezed into a purple lamé gown, inspires the giggling driver to slide onto the dance-floor as a picture of Cary Grant kissing Ingrid Bergman dissolves into an image of sweaty stretched flesh and glistening pubic hair.

Alcohol streams through the driver's soft dancing veins, and a trickle of melted gel runs into the driver's contact-lensed eyes, stinging them slightly. The driver blinks and loses focus for a few seconds. The lenses slide back into place, tears squeeze out to jettison the sweaty hair gel and still slightly misty Chinese eyes open to see a beautiful blue-eyed face, staring right into the driver's chestnut pupils.

Transfixed, the driver feels a blush wildfire its way from delicate cheeks to pedicured toe, causing a burst of goosepimpled cold sweat on the driver's buttocks. Helped along by the alcohol, the driver's inhibitions take flight and through body language and unsubtle glances he beckons the blue eyes ever closer.

Almost as if the DJ could mind-read the driver's intentions, the music suddenly slows to a classic jazzy smooch, all shuffling drum sweeps and deep black voices. Blue eyes sparkle within brown eyes as European hands meet and intertwine with refined Chinese fingers and the driver and new partner slide along each other's arms to fall into a gently rocking embrace. Their bodies hardly touch at first but then they move closer, edging beyond the limits of their clothes until their hips are swaying, melded together like Siamese twins.

The room twirls with erotic romance and the driver and partner smile at each other, lining up their lips which pucker, tease and finally kiss before any words are spoken. Firecracker bursts of romantic clichés explode in the driver's mind. Mouths yawn open and tongues unfurl to wrestle among the result of expensive orthodontics, tasting the thrill of untrammelled desire. Another smoochy ballad sends the driver spinning tighter into the blue-eyed body, and finely tailored fabrics, already weakened with sweat, become crushed, stretched and rubbed out of shape.

The music speeds up, dispersing the couples who either separate and continue dancing or slink off together to dark corners. The driver, giddy from continuous and breathless kissing, feels a body peel away and vaguely senses being led off the dance-floor and taken through a set of swing doors into a small room. Still dazed and staring at the mad mosaic of varnished seashells covering the walls, it takes a while for the driver and partner to realise they are standing in a "powder room". A few people stand over wash-basins, oblivious to the couple who are reflected in the mirrors an infinite number of times holding hands like two lost school children.

The blue-eyed blonde tugs at the driver's hand and they enter into a black toilet cubicle. A bare ultra-violet light bulb casts an eerie glow as the driver locks the door behind them. Facing one another in this ebony void, where only the white porcelain toilet and an aluminium tissue-dispenser break the visual vacuum, the two undress each other; pearl buttons, fastenings and zips melt and dissolve under caresses until two semi-circular piles of clothes lie crumpled on the floor. The blue eyes glow pupil-lessly in the ultra-violet, floating like UFOs in front of the driver's face.

Finally naked, flesh meets flesh. Fingers explore the moist places, seeking out those spots which trigger a groan or the arching of the spine. Tongues trace trails of curving brush strokes lapping up slightly perfumed droplets of sweat and leaving a sheen of saliva upon olive-yellow and white skin. Blonde furze brushes and drags against the black barcodes of the driver's downy flesh until the skin can no longer represent a barrier and the two bodies wrestle further into one another.

Dull thuds from the dance-floor counterpoint the rhythm of the couple, as brown nipples bang against pink nipples, feet trying to find platforms to push against, while hands alternately carress, grip and stabilise. The driver's eyelids are shut tight in fantasising euphoria as the thrusting rhythm and gropings become more insistent. Finally one orgasm triggers another and the feet lose grip and the bodies jerk and thrash like robots gone mad.

Their breathing returned to normal, the couple separate and using sheets of tissue paper from the shiny metal dispenser they wipe themselves dry. The driver smiles and receives a taut kiss from lips that suddenly seem over-familiar. Trampled clothes are sorted out and picked up from the black rubber floor. Quickly dressing, the couple hug and share another, more generous, kiss before leaving the cubicle.

The bubbly water with its slice of lemon refreshes the driver's parched mouth and the couple, facing each other, burst into nervous laughter. The blue-eyed blonde speaks with a voice that disappoints even before a single syllable is finished, "Hi...That was amazing...I just love your skin and...and those wonderful eyes of yours." The driver smiles to cover a wince. "Do you live here? I mean, are you staying in London? On holiday? Do you...do you speak any English??"

The driver feigns incomprehension, shrugs and looks around for help and an escape route.

"Where are you from? Can I see you again? Look ... tomorrow ... Understand? Ple ... eck ... sus, OK? Midnight??" The blue eyes squint in deep thought as their owner confusedly tries to work out some sign-language. Nodding and smiling, the driver blurts out a cod-accented "OK ... Bye ... Goodbye ... OK," and casually, but at a fair pace, leaves the club and the perplexed blonde lover.

Outside, the faint purple light of dawn breaks over the Swiss Centre and the driver meanders back towards the car-park, occasionally skidding on the grey-streaked, crumpled cellophaned roses that litter the ground. A rubbish van rumbles nearby and green-jacketed men clatter steel waste bins and yell at each other. At the car-park, the driver trudges up the concrete stairs, nostrils filled with the acrid stench of too many impatient bladders.

In the driver's shiny car, catching the artificial light from the overhead strip-lights, the golden gourd waits to trap evil spirits. The driver presses a button disengaging the car's alarm and the car bleeps and flashes in relief. The dangling gourd seems to sway a little and the driver, suddenly catching a reflection in the car's coachwork, stops to think of the future, bathed in sports-car red, and anxiously feeling less than yellow.

吳洪強

沒有那樣黃

倫敦 West End 的霓虹燈光落在一輛新的紅色寶馬車後窗懸著的一只金色葫蘆的塑膠面上,當葫蘆下的紅色絲穗蕩向右時,車子正好駛入 Leicester Square 後的一個多層停車場。車裡 CD 播出喧嘩的麥當娜最新廣東流行歌,儀表盤上的彈簧塑膠兔子就如駕駛人的腦袋一樣跟著節拍、一上一下的跳動著。泊了車,上了中央控制鎖,仍舊哼著麥當娜的一首歌,用他的鎖匙圈上的警鐘再次測驗一下,車頭燈和指揮燈立時反應地亮起來。

踏著名廠鞋,吹著無音譜的哨子,他沿著濕尿滿佈的樓梯搖擺地往唐人街的餐館行人道走去。在 Wardour Street 一帶,夜遊客打著嗝,抱著那塞滿了甜酸肉和蛋炒飯,加上如海洋多的啤酒和可樂的肚皮,取笑著吃館窗前懸著的紅燒的動物;最後的顧客走了。那駕車人輕鬆的走著,身上穿著價值500鎊的名貴外衣,頭髮光鮮,眼睛高傲地瞇起來,鼻子往上朝著。這才是夜的開始,一個在 West End 表演遊行的時間,這裡只有最美麗和最怪異的才會引起別人的注意。

這天是情人節,Leicester Square 四週是街頭奏樂家、情侶、併著頭的單身男士和女士們、賣花的執著膠紙包裝的瘦弱玫瑰以高價向一些半醉或願意付錢的傻子售賣。本來是好玩的卻演變為原始求愛的地方,好友們互相撕破對方最好的衣服,在行人路旁摟作一團,一些年輕女子們縮捲一起,又叫又哭,同時又吃吃的笑起來。

駕車人走過這些,也經過一所有的快餐店、意大利薄餅店、遊戲機樂場、熱狗攤檔和雪糕車和它忠心的顧客一最後踏進了一間夜總會的前門;那裡一列鏡,迎接一些等著被一班挺著禮服的保鏢視察入門的客人。門前的大廳掛著一幅畫滿了紅心,愛神和紅唇,色彩鮮艷但水準不高的海報,寫著今晚是「愛之聚會:愛情之地的特殊夜」。那車主拿出一束用銀色夾子挾著的紙幣,給檯後穿得不大合時的女人付了入場票,經過紅色的地壇,下了樓梯,瞇了瞇眼睛,應付著那突然暗淡的燈光,穿過一些活動扇門,走進了夜總會內。

數張臉孔轉過來迎著這新來賓,音樂在舞池和空中環繞著,在這些目光下,他感到有點怯意和畏縮。當他略為稍定時,也向那些熟悉的和漂亮的人點頭微笑,然後挺起胸膛一邊打嗝一邊輕笑地走到酒吧間去。他叫了一杯雙料伏特加酒,和一個「金色的雨」雞尾酒(香檳、Galliano酒和龍舌蘭酒);他想著媽咪和爹地將要寄來的生活費,也想到他最終通過了那煩悶的工程考試,可以得到額外的費用時不由得笑起來。

一口吞下一杯伏特加酒,杯裡的生殖器和乳房形狀的冰塊在他那花了不少錢的牙齒間打滾,他,這個晚上,要把所有的父母、金錢、考試或將來責任的問題全打消,只是要趁這時,在這裡去尋樂。他看一看酒巴後的鏡子,快快地整理一下自己,叫那酒巴待者多來一個伏特加酒,用一枝小飲管粗魯地吸吮那雞尾酒,點了一枝Sobranie香煙,準備好了,便轉身面向前往舞池的一群人。

在第二杯伏特加酒已滑落肝部時,車主,一手拿著雞尾酒,一手持著香煙,靜靜地走去舞池,那裡的體溫、燈色和音樂的組合給過敏的犯罪者創造了一個酷似工業化的地獄。以每分鐘一拍的音樂,由使你癲瘋和神經病的狂濤到兩體捲作一團的慢舞;他,現在站在舞池的邊沿,一面跟拍節點著頭,一面有形地噴出煙絲,和吸吮那最後一滴的雞尾酒。在那些扭動和抽動著的身體後──一刻是單色瘋人院病人的影像,一刻是「春節」狂歡的表演-牆上的白床單交替閃影著羅曼蒂克的古典黑白愛情片和彩色鮮艷的色情性交幻燈像。

「恐龍變性者」出現,只見釘滿炫耀珠片的衣裙披在一位穿11號高跟鞋的人體上。駕車的人,見到這六呎高毛茸茸的生物,臉孔化裝得很漂亮,粗大的身體竟可鑽進那苗條的紫色晚裝裡,不禁大笑起來,不期然的以他那滑溜的皮鞋向那「變性者」移動去,那時候加利格蘭和英格烈葆蔓接吻的照片轉為全畫面的肉體,女人的下體照。

他的學士學位是在夜總會裡渡過的，因此他很容易便能跟著音樂和其他的人在舞池上一起流著汗，進入了一種柔軟的和生理上性感官發洩的狀態。有如吸煙、購買用品、穿衣服和填鴨式的考試一樣，跳舞成為他在倫敦生活的重要部份。又如汽車是不可少的用具，去夜總會也成為生存的主要程序，一種新的第二個自我，全力意圖在短短的數年內遠離家庭的監視和壓力。當他在想延續這種生活而繼續他的碩士學位時，音樂的節奏加快起來，跳舞的群眾連結起成一旋轉的長龍，思想和行動都要棄置一旁。

酒精流到全身每一個動脈去，絲恤衫開始被汗黏貼在身上，一串溶了的濃汗流下了帶著穩形眼鏡的眼上，他閉一閉微痛的眼睛，一時眼前視線模糊起來。他整一整穩形眼鏡，淚水混和鹹味的汗水，當視線開始清楚時，見到眼前一張美麗的臉孔，藍色的美目正凝視著他自己杏形臉上的褐色眼珠。他震了一震，臉孔霎時紅起來，一直紅到腳趾跟去，屁股也頓時的冒出了點點的汗粒。舞池震盪的情懷，酒精的作怪，和大學的完竣，他忘記了那平日的拘謹，向那藍眼的美女投去一個挑逗的輕笑。雙方的默契，臀部的舞動和挑引的目光，他把藍眼睛環抱過來。

那裡，在一雙雙情侶和群眾快樂盡情的舞姿中，他，找到了一位舞伴；唱片騎師似乎知道他們之間的事，音樂慢了下來，放出爵士音樂的柔情，輕擦的鼓聲和黑人低沉的歌聲；藍眼睛和褐眼睛交投，西方和東方優雅的手指相握，車主和舞伴擁抱起來跟著音樂慢步地搖動，最初他們的身體是分開的，慢慢地軀體似乎衝出了衣服的隔膜，臀部相接有如連體人一樣的膠在一起。

舞廳裡浪盪著挑引的情調，無言，雙方捲入熱吻之中。他，有如愛情小說裡描述的，腦筋像爆炸一樣，煙花四起，舌尖在昂貴的牙齒中舞動，嚐著那性慾的新刺激。又一支柔和的歌調使他更緊緊地摟抱著藍眼睛柔軟的腰股，生理上的需求使汗水更一次的溶爛他那訂做的衣服，使它們變了形。

最後音樂的節奏加快，舞池上的人一些離開，一些仍舊跳著或走到黑暗的一角。那位駕車的人士，經過了那持續的和透不過氣的熱吻，一時頭昏和眼花瞭亂，只感到有人從他身邊移開，朦朧中似乎有人拖他走出舞池而穿過一度扇門。在熱浪、情慾和酒精下，他神智不清，當他定睛望著房間裡裝飾牆壁的古怪貝殼圖案和看到鏡中的反映，以及一些瓷洗臉盆時，才知道這房間實在是一個盥洗間。在臉盆前站了一些正在打扮的，或是在用刀分割毒粉的人，對後面站著的兩人全不理會，從鏡中的無數反映可看到他們有如學生般的拖著手，好像著了迷一樣，正在發出內心的微笑。

藍眼金髮的女子拉一拉他的手，兩人便鑽進了一個比一般廁所大些的小房，從地板到黑膠的隔牆和從天花板到隔牆的頂端只有一吋的空間，兩人反手鎖好了門，懸著的紫外線燈泡向他們籠罩一層陰沉的暗影。在這黑色的空間裡，他倆面對著，只有白色的廁所和一個鋁質的紙筒打破這視覺的真空，他們互相替對方解除衣物：珠的鈕子，扣子和拉鍊在對方的觸摸下溶解，直到地上出現兩堆半圓形的衣服，暴露出不耐煩的肉體。藍眼睛在紫光下變得沒有了瞳孔，在他的面前有如太空外來物一樣的浮動，現在快要沉溺在迫切的慾海裡。

帛肉相見，又迫切又憐惜的，火熱的手滑過痣、疤痕和洞穴，摸索那濕潤的地方，輕觸挑逗引起她呻吟的部份或是脊柱的彎處。舌頭在玲瓏的曲線上吮掃，舐乾帶有微香的汗珠，在褐色和白色的皮膚上留下一層閃耀的唾液。金黃色的花草在車主滑溜皮膚上的黑色標誌上又擦又拖的，直至皮膚不能再形成一種阻欄，他們互相擁抱對方，在延續的和搓掐的控制下，他們的身體再進一步的變而為一。

舞池沉重的響聲和這對男女的拍節正好配合，褐色和粉紅色的的乳頭相擦，他們的腳拼命在找一個地方來踏實，手卻在替換地撫摸、扭抓和平衡著。雙方閉著眼睛享受那絕妙的幻景，在那時候雙方的衝刺和摸擦的次數越來越劇烈，最後一次又一次的高潮相繼而來，腳失去了可以推動的地方，身體上下的抽動，撞向廁所內所有可以碰到的地方，有如一個發瘋了的機械人。呻吟，叫喊和喘息在這高潮中爆發，最後連續數次的深呼吸意味著這次淫亂的結束。

他們的呼吸平靜下來，兩人分開，從那金屬的紙筒處拉出長條的軟紙來抹去那汗珠和濕液；對方的唇在他唇邊輕輕抹過，他笑了笑，一煞那間她和他似乎變得過份熟悉起來。從黑色橡膠地板的衣堆裡拾起各自的衣服，快捷地穿著起來，他們再一次的擁抱，愛撫和親吻，才離開那小房間。

沒有人給這對從廁所出來衣衫不整的男女作任何的注意，車主快快的從鏡上望一下，便離開盥洗室。當他們踏進舞廳時立即被一陣汗味和音浪逼過來，兩人手挽著朝酒吧走去。駕車人希望他們之間的沉默最好能永遠地持續下去，因此當藍眼睛開口叫兩杯礦泉水時，他嘗試不去聽到那聲音。

水裡的氣泡和檸檬片使他那乾涸的嘴和喉頭頓時感到無比的清新，他倆手執著水，面對面的突然緊張地笑起來。藍眼睛打破了他們之間的沉默，她的聲音在第一個字還未說完時已經使他感到失望，「Hi…你說是不是奇妙…我就是喜歡你的皮膚和那對漂亮的眼睛。」車主只有以笑來遮掩他的不悅。「你住在這裡嗎？我意思是，你是否住在倫敦？…在渡假吧？你…你可以說英語嗎？」

車主，充作不明白的樣子，聳一聳肩膊，向四週視察有沒有可逃走的途徑。「你從哪裡來的？我可以再見你嗎？這樣吧…明天在…唔…柏拉加塞斯…OK…你知嗎，就在這裡轉彎的地方…明天，明白嗎？柏拉…加…塞斯，可以嗎？明晚半夜12時見？？」車主笑笑地點著頭，藍眼睛瞭瞭眼，在想辦法用手勢來使他明白。他笑著，更大力地點著頭，用滑稽的英文發音說：「OK，拜拜，拜拜，OK。」然後隨意的，漫步的，離開了夜總會和那位正在發窘的藍眼情人。

外面，淡淡的紫色晨曦籠罩著瑞士中心，車主漫步的走到泊車場去，一路上踐踏了的膠紙包的玫瑰花和夜間留下來的廢紙滿階都是，一輛垃圾車慢慢的駛過來，穿著綠外衣的人托起鋼鐵造的垃圾桶，高聲地互相呼喝著。他拖著滿身痛楚的身體和疲倦的頭腦，爬上樓梯，梯間一陣惡臭的尿味充塞每角落。找到了那光亮的汽車，它正在不耐煩地等著解除監視的責任。當車子的喇叭響過和閃燈後，駕駛人在紅色車身上的反影裡，用手梳一下現在蓬亂了的頭髮，他停下來想想自己的將來，急切地感到沒有那樣黃了。

Pui Fan Lee

From *Short, Fat, Ugly and Chinese*

Thing is, there was a time when I didn't think there was anything wrong. Anything different. Till this girl come up to me in the playground and asked me what I ate with.

Chopsticks and spoons. I said.
Should have seen her. Stupid!! Running off to her mates and laughing!
Tell 'em, tell 'em, she said. Tell 'em
Tell 'em what you eat with!!
Chopsticks and spoons! Chopsticks and spoons! Chopsticks and spoons!!!
Everybody eats with chopsticks and spoons, don't they!!?
Wanted a knife and fork after that, didn't I?

And then there was my knees.
Always thought people were laughing at my knees.
Always thought I had dirty knees. I fell over a lot, but I never had dirty knees, but they'd still sing about them.

Chinese! Japanese!
Dirty knees!
What are these!
Titties!
I didn't have any titties so they couldn't 've been laughing at them. Should've seen me in the morning scrubbing my knees with a nail brush. They were red raw. No wonder I wanted to be white.

I wanted to be ... VANESSA SAMANTHA HEELEY! She was fantastic! She had these cute, little blonde twin sisters, Stephanie and Sharon. She had a fantastic name too. Loads of syllables. White names always had loads of juicy syllables. I'd flick through the Kays catalogue to the children's clothes section, and pick a girl, a face, a white one, of course, and give her a name, a really long one. Like ELIZABETH ... or ...

ISABELLA ... and there she'd be, my secret ideal me.

My Mum and Dad didn't give us English names. All the other Chinese kids our family knew had them. They used them at school and put them away when they went home.
Some even picked their own names!
One of Lady Diana's bridesmaids was called CLEMENTINE. I was obsessed with that name. It was great.
But it was too late. I was used to my funny name and everyone mispronouncing it.
New teachers were the worst. I'd sit there counting the names down the register and they'd get to me. It was always a good laugh. Guaranteed a good laugh.
Mr Samuels the headmaster never did learn to say it properly over five years. Nor did Miss Thompson or Mr Pickering. Must have had a bad memory. Or deaf. Or just pig ignorant. It must be hard to remember one syllable.

I wouldn't go to the Chinese school. Wouldn't do that funny writing. Read that funny language. Read the funny books backwards. Speak the funny language. Drink the cartons of soya milk, eat the tofu, the seaweed. Now it's all the rage. All that funny food that wasn't on the adverts on the telly. That no one else's mum made.
I had Sunday lunch at Vanessa's once. It was brilliant. We had roast beef and gravy. I loved gravy. We used to have it in school. Gravy was dead special. Dead white is gravy. And cheese. Cheese is dead white too. Mum used to say it smelt because it was milk that had gone off and so was yoghurt. We had rows about cheese and milk and yoghurt and salad and anything that was raw. We had rows about lots of things. Especially about food.
Rice. Bowls of rice. Sacks of rice. The rice mountain. Rice with everything. Rice with fried egg. There was nothing more drab and boring and tasteless than rice with fried egg, except rice with boiled egg. Why do we always have to have it? Every day. My brother moaned too. But he was special because he was a boy and got everything that he wanted. I should've been a boy too. And didn't I know it. Got matching shoes one Christmas. Can you believe it. Big bufty tough tyre track

shoes. Trendy now but not then. Not when you're Vanessa's best friend. Then I became Fiona's best friend. Fiona was Irish. She had ten brothers and sisters. But she was white. I had tea at her house once. It was amazing. All fourteen of us with a choice of spaghetti hoops or beans on toast in front of the telly. I couldn't believe it. Looking around and seeing a sea of tomato sauce being slurped up around me and everyone concentrating on *Renta Ghost*. But I didn't have seconds. I couldn't. It might have been rude. The wrong thing to do. Just in case. Couldn't do anything...Just in case. I had the reputation of the whole Chinese population on my shoulders.

I went to work in a factory once. We made quiches for Marks and Spencers. Everything was clean and white. We all wore clean white overalls. Clean white aprons, white hats, white shoes, white minds. Dirty white minds. I didn't have a name to mispronounce anymore. I was the little Chinese girl in the big white factory. At least at school I was considered quite "brainy" so the thickos stopped calling you "Funny eyes". But here I was in the big factory, on the flan line with everyone else. On the slow flan line too. It was a summer job. First it was OK. I experienced "student prejudice", which was expected. You know, "They might have passed exams and go to universities and things, but they've got no common sense! Dead slow on cheese and tomato." That was all right. I was quite happy being slow on cheese and tomato and ham and broccoli and everything else that they shoved on top of the flans. But then there was the big question on the floor. I'd walk by the pork pie line and there they'd be. The Pork Pie Boys. I say boys, but some of them were old enough to be my grandad. Was she or wasn't she? I knew they were talking about me. Guaranteed a good laugh each time I went by. Is she or isn't she?
I was sitting in the canteen when one of them eventually came up to me. Young bloke. Wore his cap backwards and strutted around the place trying to look cool in that factory. Even "The Fonz" couldn't look cool in there.
"You're new here, aren't you?"
"Ish."
"Yeah, we seen you. We seen you come the other week."
"Oh, yeah."

"Thing is, we got a little disagreement to sort out, know what I mean, me and the lads on the pastry line, and you got to help us out, know what I mean?"
Honestly, I was pooing in my pants by this time. I could feel his mates on the table behind me holding their breath. A long line of them in their stained white uniforms with their knives and forks in their hands ready to attack. Listening and listening.
"Yeah ... um, what we want to know ... is ... are you ..."
Dear God in Heaven, help me!
"Um ... how shall I say this ... Is it true that you girls are cut crossways?"
I didn't understand. I felt so stupid. There was a big, enormous, gigantic, massive, MASSIVE roar of laughter behind me and I could just feel the cutlery come flying across the canteen into my back. Wish it had. I wanted to die that very second.
He didn't wait for an answer anyway. It was enough for him just to ask. Got a big laugh. Scored lots of points.
I went to the loo and sat there for ages and ages wondering what "crossways" meant ... and then I realised and at that moment I was so ashamed I pulled up my knickers and hid in the launderette. I wouldn't go to the toilet for the rest of the day. I was convinced there were spies in there watching. Placing bets. Did she or didn't she have a deformed vagina.

I left at the end of the week. You won't catch me eating pork pies any more. We even went off chicken for a while, me, my brother and sisters. There's this thing about fresh food. Nothing frozen or tinned. Fresh veg, fresh fish, fresh meat. You can't get fresher than live chicken, can you? It's all right if you live on a farm or in the country. But nobody had live chickens in Nottingham. There was this stupid custom where visitors bring food as gifts. They almost always brought a frigging live chicken. And it was always in a potato sack. Poor thing. Little did it know it was merely a status symbol, and its cries were to be drowned by Radio One in the kitchen so the neighbours couldn't hear what we were about to have for dinner. There we'd be around the table. Mum and Dad discussing the poor animal.
"How gnang a yuk ... gang hare how low... an sare jak ..."
Which roughly means the meat's a bit tough because the little thing was

getting on a bit. How could we eat the chicken after seeing it locked away in the outside toilet while the visitors were here, and then learning it was an old-age pensioner? In the end, we would just bung it in the boot and present it to the nearest Chinese family up the road. They were always impressed anyway. As long as we looked good. Looked wealthy. Looked rich. But we had an orange Morris Marina and that never looked good. Everyone else had big silver Volvos. You can see them all lined up outside the Wing Yip Supermarket, big shiny square cars with a little red Chinese lantern dangling from the windscreen.

We hired this big car for my sister's wedding.
Oh, yeah, it was still embarrassing because they stuck this doll in front of it, didn't they. OK, it was dressed as a bride and everything. But it was this big, fat, chubby doll that looked dead cheap and tacky. It was awful from then on. Dad hired this big restaurant in town. Everything was red. It was scandalous. Everybody wanted to know how much my sister was being sold for. How much my Dad was going to ask for. How much the groom was willing to pay. Or how little. How desperate we were to get rid of her!
And then there was this stupid Chinese wedding music that was driving me and my brother nuts.
"Chang, Chang, Chang, Chang, Chang!"
Oh, yeah, my sister was cheap. Dead cheap. "Bargain Bride", as she was known. It was awful, Mum and Dad were just dripping with paranoia.
What's everyone going to say?
What are the Chinese people going to say?
What's the "Jung Gok Yin" going to say?
And I swear there were a lot of Chinese people there. The place was just packed with all these people I'd never ever seen before. It was my sister's wedding and I didn't know any of them! Dad just about invited everyone to the wedding whether he knew them or not. So that no one would get offended.
To stop them talking. Anyone looking vaguely Asian in the Midlands was there.
There. Talking.
Talking about my sister in her red gown. Talking about her jewellery.

How much gold she was wearing. Talking about the food we were going to have. How many courses would arrive. We could afford. We had eleven! We passed the test! Just. What a traumatic experience! "Please, God, don't let me ever have to go through that in my whole life! Thank you, God. Amen."

So my sister escaped. So it left me to do her jobs. One of them was translator. I was bricking it because me Chinese was so crap. My Mum and Dad never quite got round to learning English. So there I would be. Talking to plumbers, electricians, doctors, RAC, opticians. I could just cope with doing it for my parents but I hated having to do it for other people. We've got this aunt. Not a real aunt. Never took to her. We thought she was out of order because she used to go on and on about us being short and she always fell asleep at our house. We called her "Sleepy". She was married to "Uncle Blackie". "Blackie" becuse he was always taking his kids to Hong Kong and so he had this amazing tan. Well, I was summoned to them one day. They had loads of kids. But they were all daughters so they kept sending them back to Hong Kong for the granny to bring up, which is quite normal but it meant old muggins here had to take old Sleepy to hospital. She had angina I think. It was awful. I didn't know what it was in English never mind anything else. I remember her lying there on the stretcher all crumpled up. She was normally such a dragon and here she was all bedraggled and out of control. Then she was wheeled into the ward and all these different people kept coming up to me and asking questions about "your mum". "My mum!?" I'm telling you now, I know she was probably dying at the time, but I wasn't having anyone calling her my mum! The nurses must have thought I was really callous. I resented having to stay there. She had a great big Volvo and the rest. Anyway, I had to be present when they examined her. That's right, I watched as they undresssed her and I felt sick. This isn't fair. This just isn't fair I kept thinking. And again I wanted to be white. Sleepy kept whimpering and I couldn't understand her. Then the doctor would ramble on and I couldn't understand her either. I wanted to be as white as a sheet. So white I was invisible. Daz-white.

She's got a son now. "Thank God," I thought, then they'd keep him in

England and he can do the dirty work for them. Their precious son. People felt sorry for those who didn't have sons. Sleepy was almost fifty but she wouldn't give up would she. My dad did have one English phrase he used quite often when I was much younger. "Good boy," he'd say. "Good boy." Me and my brother were a great pair of cowboys. My dad managed to fool me for a quite a while. Thought I was a good boy. Then I realised my brother got all the toys. And he realised he could sulk and get anything he wanted and I tried but it never worked. But it was dead confusing because I was the youngest and I was the cute one and I was the noisy one and I was the best. The Bestest!

But I wasn't a son. Mum's son. Dad's son. Anyone's son. Oh, to be a son! Or to have a son! Or two or three or four! How my parents gauped admiringly at the troops of sons as they paraded outside the Cantonese Restaurant on a Sunday lunch time. Splendid sons. Super sons. Stepsons. Grandsons. Great every son. Even greater still sons but always without exception sons with suns shining out of their backside sons.

We only had one in our family but he didn't love to parade. We just sat together in the back of the car, hiding. Just in case any of our mates came by. Shame. Sunday lunch time at the Cantonese restaurant was the dreaded non event of the week. We never wanted to go!

All our mates looked forward to their Yorkshire pudding as me and my brother sat there killing time, counting toothpicks. Or spinning the food around the table without anyone noticing. They hardly ever ate. My mum and dad. The purpose was to be seen there and small talk. This would get smaller and smaller. And we just squirmed with embarrassment as Mum and Dad shouted across to the other tables. They were always shouting. Didn't matter what they were about. The Chinese were always shouting! Used to scare the life out of my mates when they came to call for me. Used to think there was some domestic crisis going on. Or I was in big trouble or something. Probably right. Made them shout quite a lot. Hated home. Hated everything. But most of all. I hated the Shop. The Takeaway. Or, as the locals called it, "The Chinky".

Sitting behind the counter with the sizzly TV in the corner and the *Daily Mirror* on my lap. I wanted to be one of the girls who sat outside all night. Not inside. Sat outside with their bags of chips. Not doing anything in particular. Just hanging around outside the shops. But sometimes, they'd push the front doors open and shout "Chips with fried cats, please" and scarper. No, I didn't want to be one of them. I just didn't want to be one of us. In the shop.

Then it would get a bit later, and their big brothers and mums and dads would roll in, still clutching the same glass they were given for last orders with two gobfuls of murky cat's piss in it.

What do I want!
Hey! What you looking so miserable for?
Cheer up!
Let me see ...
I know what I want.
I want what I had last time.
I want.
Lads, listen to this.
I want some flied lice!!
Hey, you speak English good!
You from China?
You a boat person?
You do Kung Fu! Hi-yah?
You know Bruce Lee?
How old are you?
Time you were in bed!
Say my name in Chinese.
Go on! Go on! Go on!

Then there was the trouble, the fights, the broken windows, the police. The police telling me to calm down on the phone. Telling me to calm down when there's chairs flying over the counter. Telling me to calm down when there's a bloke being thrown through the window.

Once Mandy in my class came in. She had all these white carnations. So did her mum. And nana. The whole family. Her birthday. Then Kevin came in. With his mates and it all started.
Kevin and Mandy.
Then Kevin and Mandy's dad.

Then Kevin's mates versus Mandy's family.
In the shop.
My mum and dad back in the kitchen.
Only the sound of the woks clanging to be heard. The TV blaring and Mandy's granny screaming.
The boys playing hard.
Being big boys.
Mandy's dad holding out.
Me behind the counter.
Too scared to fetch Dad.
Too scared to pick up the phone.
The boys calling Mandy a slag.
Kevin, Fucking this, Fucking that, Fucking every word.
Mandy's mum holding down her dad.
Mandy holding her gran.
I watched as her dad's head was smashed against the radiator.
As her granny collapsed.
As the radiator shuddered behind me.
As all the radiators echoed in the house.
And I watched as Kevin booted her dad's head in as he fell.
And I watched as they tore out the door and ripped down the menus on the way out.
And they watched me as I pathetically dialled 999.
All the women were crying and Mandy's dad lay there. His head split open. Mandy was in my class. We didn't learn things like this at school. Twenty minutes later, they arrived in their special patrol fluorescent green tunics. Too late. Always too late. But the worst thing was, I couldn't tell them I knew who did it. That I went to junior school with them all. Didn't know their names any more. No names. They could smash up the shop. Smash everything up. But most of all. Smash me up. I wanted to run away but the shop didn't close for another long half-hour.
Oh, no. Couldn't close. Business comes first. No time for emotions. So I washed up the carpet with a bucket of water. Collected up the flowers. And pretended to watch the snowy telly.
All night I couldn't sleep. Kept seeing the bloody radiator.
Hearing myself tell the officer, "I didn't know who did it."

Mandy's face haunting me. Mandy was in my class. We never talked about it at school. We never talked to each other ever again.
Kept thinking how many other kids didn't have to go through this. English kids didn't have to watch behind the counters. English kids didn't have to mop up the blood. White English kids. What did I do to deserve this?
Why did God choose to make me different in this country?
And did everyone have to keep reminding me that I was different?

People always watched me in the shop. I knew they felt sorry for me. They used to ask me if I ever went out. If I had any friends. Didn't like it when they asked me that. "Course I had bloody friends." Made me feel like some kind of freak.
Must have probably looked like one. Sitting there day dreaming. Or with my head buried in a Jackie Collins novel. Or revising. O-levels. A-levels. My files were always scattered all over the place with food stains dotted around my notes.
It's funny, because when I was choosing which polys or universities to apply for, I didn't really sus out the courses, I just got out the Collins map of Great Britain, and if it was pretty far from the Midlands, I thought, "Yeah! Then I didn't have to come home at weekends to work in the shop!" I worked pretty hard for my exams. Didn't particularly know what I was going to do. What I was going to be. Just not where I was.

The afternoon of our last exam was really hot. A load of us sat out on the playing fields. All the white people turning pink. We had a whip round and the lads went out and bought all this drink. Well, some beer and a bottle of tequila. It was weird because I wasn't really excited about leaving sixth form. I still had visions of me stuck in the shop. Still angry. Angry at being me.
Anyway, there we were, in the sun. The alcohol making us even more hot.
Dizzy and hot and red and delirious.
Dizzy and hot and red and delirious.
Dizzy and hot and red and delirious.
Dezzy and red and rederilus and dizzy and hot.

And we're on the beach. Loads of us and I don't know what time it is and I don't care. You can tell the time with the sun or the moon. Or the stars or whatever you like, you can do whatever you like. Be whatever you like. Swim! Swim everywhere! Loads of us swimming! It is so hot!! And I love it! And it's hotter and hotter and we eat mangoes and big juicy melon and I love it! And we dance to everything and do anything. Somersault into the sea! Skinny-dip! Skinny-dipping! And we kiss! Lips kissing and skinny dipping! And frisbees spinning! And kissing! I should have gone home to open the shop ages ago. Mum was going to tell me how irresponsible and unreliable I was. How selfish I was. How incompetent I was. How old I was.
How short, fat, ugly and Chinese I was!
And if I carried on like that the worst thing in the world would happen, nobody would want to marry me.
Got a slap across the face, didn't I! Never been hit before. Ever. "That's it!" I thought. That's it! I'm just going to go away and leave them in the shit! That'll show them. I'm going to pack my bags and announce that I'm going!
No one tells me what to do! No one hits me!

Ha! So I'm on this train. It's going to London. I'm going to London. Can you believe it! I couldn't. Couldn't bloody believe it! Could I! I was going, just like I said I would! I packed my bags and off I went! Well, I didn't actually tell my mum and dad the way I said I would. I mean, that would have been stupid! Would have got another slap around the face, wouldn't I. But I did tell them I was going to the best college in London. (It wasn't really, but I thought I'd tell them that, anyway.) Didn't matter. They didn't believe me. Wouldn't have mattered if it was the best college in the world! The universe! They wouldn't have believed me!
I was going to sub-let this student's flat. Sub-let. In Tooting. Tooting. That sounds good, I thought. Tooting. He said it was south of the river. What river? Oh, the River Thames! You know the blue bit in the beginning of East Enders. Sounded cute. Quaint. Tooting. Tooting Bec. What's Bec? I wanted someone to come up to me and say, "Do you live in London?" "Yeah, I've got a flat in Tooting!"
And just as I was fantasising away, it happened! There's me listening

to my Walkman, and this man opposite, grins and says just that! I tried to pull out my headphones, but the wire got caught and then the whole thing fell under the table and smashed on the floor and I knew I was dead red and I was trying to tell him that I lived in Tooting and I know it sounded so completely stupid: "I ... live in ... Tooting ... South ... of ... the ... River ... Thames." I was shaking like mad! He had blonde hair. Blonde curly hair! Real curls. Not permed or anything. It was dark blonde. No, dirty blonde. Yeah. And we started chatting. Just like that. He rescued my Walkman for me. He was dead nice. I bet everyone was looking at us. Listening. Chit chatting. Like I always did that kind of thing! Talking to strangers! Like I was crazy or something! I suppose I was being chatted up! I bought him a coffee from the buffet car. I had one too. Never did drink coffee. We never drank it at home. We used to have this jar of Nescafé in the back of the cupboard for the English people, but hardly any ever came round so it had gone all hard and nasty. Probably still there. Oh, yeah, his name's Jan. I know, I thought it was a girl's name too. And he's telling me about his band, he's in a band. And how he's been to India, and plans to go to Thailand. And as we were pulling out of Kettering, he said he was going out to have a cigarette. But then, he signalled over to the automatic doors. It was dead funny, standing between the noisy carriages. Shaking.
Then guess what.
I got snogged.
Right there. On the train. Next to the toilet.
Never been snogged before. Chinese girls never got snogged. Yasmin Green and Jackie Belshaw got snogged. Not me.
Chinese girls don't get snogged. But I DID!
NOW THAT WAS FANTASTIC!
This was it. This was what all the fuss was about! I didn't really know what to do next, so I stood there, watching him. Smoking. It was great. And then he took one more drag from his fag and threw it out of the window. He's such a nice guy.

I was so nervous when I got to St. Pancras, I didn't know what to say. Do I give him my phone number? Oh my God, I didn't know if I had a phone number. Do I ask him round for a cup a tea, or coffee? It was awful, my eczema started to itch. And then he said: "What you doing

tonight?"
Tonight? Never even crossed my mind what I was doing tonight, I mean, watching telly would've made a change, you know, on a settee, in a lounge, instead of cricking my neck sitting on a stool in the shop. I never thought I might be asked to go out! So, I floated to Tooting. It wasn't what I'd expected. Tooting.
I found the flat. John, the ex-student, showed me round. Everything was brown. Or maybe it just looked brown. Perhaps it was the brown lightbulb. I followed him into the kitchen. It looked a bit more of a yellowy brown. The lino on the floor was sticking to the soles of my trainers. Then John showed me his bedroom which I was going to have. That was browner. That was chocolate brown. He jumped up and down on his brown double bed and said, "The springs are in good nick, if you fancy bringing any men home!"
I nearly choked. Me! ... Then I thought about Jan. He's not like John. John's nothing compared to Jan. I was going to meet him later, Jan, my...friend. So that made me feel better. John Brown left me his keys and said he'd be back at the weekend. Here's me, in the living-room. I didn't know what to do so I switched on the TV. It was this black and white portable. I couldn't get used to it so I switched it off. I felt all itchy again but I don't think it was my eczema this time.
I decided to go out. I'd be meeting Jan soon anyway. Well, in about four hours. What shall I wear? Didn't really bring that much stuff up here, I mean down here. So I put on my black leggings and a favourite top from Next and went to the West End!

No one looks at you in London. No one cares in London. I could've been wearing a big banana on me head and I don't think anyone would have noticed.
I went to Harrods.
Harrods is London, isn't it?
London is Harrods.
Now everything was green! Green and gold!
There were so many rich people there!
I went upstairs where all the top fashions were. I read it in a magazine. I felt dead good. Looking at all the clothes. Pretending I shopped here all the time. Trying not to look flabbergasted at some of the price tags.

I could have been anybody and no one would know. No one looks at you in London. No one cares.

It's great.

胡冬

圖書館外的面具

在一部題爲《琅嬛記》的著作裡,記載著這樣一個故事-

> 謝霜回有七寶靈檀之几,几上有文字,隨意所及,文字輒形隸篆眞草,亦如人意。譬如一人欲修道,則使其人自覩,几上便自有文字,因其緣分性資而曲誘之。又如心欲得某物,則几上便有文字曰:「某處可得」。又如欲醫一病人,或欲作一戲法,則文字便曰服何藥癒,念何咒,書何符即得也。甚至讀書偶忘一句一字,無不現出。霜回寶之。

順便應當提到,這部堪稱荒誕猥瑣的書,是我通過圖書館的電腦索引查找到的。書中的這一段,被我仔細地摘錄下來,和搜集到的其它故事一起,儲存在一個我自備的電腦軟盤裡,以俟逸興萌發時拿出來展玩,誦讀一番;在無窮的拼貼變化中,我不斷把許多故事合爲一個故事,然後再把它們隨意拆散,使每個故事都可以既是開頭,又是結尾。我以這樣的顚覆來從枯燥的學院生涯裡搾取著刺激,不必否認,我正是迷上此道才眞正染上了讀書的惡習的。我在一塊軟盤大的方寸之地上嬉遊,逐日累月,樂此不疲。這遊戲雖然是單調的,但它卻是單調的萬花筒。

我仍然在大學敎書。我之所以還在那種場合逗留下去,如同幾個偏激的學生對我叫嚷的那樣-賴著不走,完全是因爲大學擁有一座像樣的圖書館的緣故。最近,它又遷入了現代化的新址、成千上萬曾經亂堆亂放的書籍正在被重新發現。隨著無數的孤本、珍本、善本由百事可圖的電腦重新編目,圖書館龐大的古籍部將全部開放。對於敎師,在閱覽規定上還特別予以優待。夜裡,我在單人床上輾轉反側,圖書館陡然倍增的魅力使我思量著得再增添個軟盤才行。

上面分配給我講授的是「社會主義經濟」,學生們,則把這門令人厭煩的必修課程扼要地稱之爲「社經課」，用不著多想就知道，淫穢的影射輕而易舉就把我變成了課堂內外的笑料。對此我泰然處之－事實上，除了忍受，我們還能有什麼選擇呢？我只得向面朝我的二年級學生們這樣說，結果卻在階梯教室裡招來一片噓聲。從一張張由吃驚而變得憤怒的臉上，我明白他們把我當成了自我暴露的萎靡不舉者，是種族悲劇的恥辱根源。亂成一團的學生們不停地爭論和哭泣，一向聽話的班幹部居然在鼓動罷課，以後便是悲痛的集體歌聲。我拒絕了他們要我加入的肉麻邀請，獨自鎮定地返回到單身宿舍。我還能說什麼呢？我對鏡自語。教室裡已經沒有我的位置，矯揉造作的學潮轉眼就把我拋開了。到了期末，當我和一個被推舉來套問試題的女學生上床時，我不禁念起前嫌－早晚，我得把你那些一上課就咯咯發笑的同伴一個個弄到床上來補課，好叫她們後悔不早點堵上自己的嘴。我一邊抽送，一邊任她按捺不住地呻吟。

但我可不是一個混進教師隊伍的惡魔，我甚至連色情狂都不是。我對那手腳酥軟的姑娘的譫言，幾聲恫嚇，不過是想要控制住她罷了。旁人都清楚，我雖然一貫稱讚癮君子，卻在私下裡認爲酒色無度並不可取，要想易受指使的心靈不離正軌，就得承認不可傷身的限度。就算我早就厭倦了教師的職業，卻還沒有失去志向。我夢寐以求的是能夠走進圖書館，改行從事古籍的整理與研究，因而我實際的學術興趣與我的專業相去萬里。我花費時間披閱一部《琅嬛記》那樣的奇書，其實也並非只顧從中東挑西揀，我的純正動機，是要考証出它的眞實作者，從而確定成書的具體年代。

《琅嬛記》題爲元代伊士珍所撰，但也有人疑係明人桑悅所僞托。不同朝代的兩個人，被同一本猥褻的，荒誕不經的書拉扯到一起，這便是引人入勝之處。我對課程多少敷衍塞責，卻頻頻出沒於線裝書庫；幾乎達到了廢寢忘食的境界。然而一個學期過去了，我發現的材料卻不僅不能使我在兩個朝代中確立一個朝代，在兩個人中挑選出一個人，反而錯綜複雜地顯示出這部書可能擁有另外的，甚至更多的作者。它成書的年代也可能還要晚得多，要麼，上溯得更早。我飽嚐無從下手之苦，揣度著史學之乖戾豈是我這個門外漢能夠望其項背的。但我並不死心，從圖書館鋥亮的玻璃門瞥見自己憔悴不堪的模樣，我拿定主意不到自封爲乾嘉學派的歷史系去討教，免得白受那些迂夫子們的嘲笑。

趁著放假，那女生也回了家，我把更多空閑投注到越來越無望澄清的叢叢疑竇上。我自忖治學欠於慎嚴，因此把所得線索反覆梳理，查証，卻仍然不見答案。我懷疑自己在收藏了焚書坑儒以來全部古籍的各類書架間瀏覽時，可能偏偏放過了我應當挑選的，至爲關鍵的一本；要麼某位粗心的圖書管理員在編排電腦目錄的過程中單獨把它給漏掉了；或者，這本書仍舊沉睡在舊圖書館的陰暗地窟，跟那些準備大量燒毀的霉爛書籍混在一了一起；最後一程可能，也是我最不願接受的，就是一本我朝思暮想的書中之書，其實並不存在。

就在我進退維谷之中，要命的謎底反倒把我纏得更緊。謎語的虛幻磋砣，一點點侵蝕了我的起居，替代著我懷抱的，不可告人的內心生活，使的變得日益陰沉起來。假期很快又要過去，我憂心忡忡，不願再拖延下去了。於是，我憑著積聚的一點勇氣，在一個風和日麗的午後，拜訪了元瑞－一個僅與我有過一面之交，蟄居於博物館的雕樑畫棟下的考古學家。我從認識的人當中篩選出他，自然是因爲他惹人垂涎的工作雖然與史籍研究有著異曲同工之妙，卻在方法上與歷史系那班沾沾自喜的考據學者們相悖逆，具有令人望而生畏的深度和準確性。還有一個原因，很久以前，在一個我們共同識認的朋友家中的偶遇，這個人給我留下的印象是難忘的。他不僅有著放縱的，如同一匹古代種馬的相貌，當他說起話來，他奇特的聲音也像是一頭無人乘馭的麒麟，從重霄之外探出頭來咬嚙著懊惱的雲團，使人不得不傾聽他。

不出所料，他對我冒昧的造訪並不驚訝。他依然記得我，但也未故意特別寒暄。這正好讓我安心，他倒了一杯水，示意我請便，接下來我們的談話就進入了正題。

近年來的考古發現，主要都是一些未來作品。元瑞以一種引誘的口吻說，我馬上表示不解地等他繼續說下去，但他卻頓住了，用倨傲的下巴稍微暗示了室內的某個方向，我看到一些完**整的畫像磚，一些獸首人形，不大不小的石灰岩雕像，一大塊**

粘結著的銅鏽和硬土，乖張地露出某種器物的一角。然後是一堆可疑的木片，謹慎地攤放在辦公室正中。在牆上，還掛著一幅巨大的、鑲在鏡框中的金屬齒輪照片，制工精密的組合齒輪熠熠生輝，看上去像是一家大公司的傑作。

這些文物，元瑞又開始說，它們所展示的並不是古代生活，而是今天的成就，是向後推的，某個尚未到來的時代。他見我正詫異地注視著牆壁，於是毫不離奇地告訴我，異國的同行們從地中海深處撈出了這副齒輪，它仍然可以用於現代航運，但同位素鑒定卻証明它在幾千年就已經存在了。

對純粹的考古學而言，這本來不是一記耳光，元瑞撇開我拐彎抹角提出的疑問，彷彿他早就預謀了這場談話－但是考古界，已經完全被那些竊據了研究員頭銜的老傢伙們控制了。他們對我的工作進惱羞成怒，對我準時交出發掘報告的事實假裝糊塗；並且，世故得以借口維護學報的純粹來掩飾他們害怕動蕩的眞相，哪怕僅僅是一場考古學的革命。元瑞的眼睛散發出釉彩，不知是惱怒還是興奮，他凸鏡般的瞳孔對準我，嵌入了整座辦公室。

一個主人翁，一個滔滔不絕的人，一張嘴就使我陷入了應接不暇的窘態。實際上，元瑞那天的談吐正好對準了我的來意，把它轟得七零八落。即便是在向他辭別後，我也再也未能從忐忑不安的激動中平靜下來。失眠的焦灼，更是無端地賦予我元瑞式的靈感。

究竟是什麼進入了我的頭腦，彷彿永久性的，築起了堡壘？我心如亂箭，竭力想弄懂元瑞再也明白不過的話－矛盾的歷史不只是像徵著過去，也包含了在過去就已預先存在的未來。換句話說，未來已經發生了。我們與前人、今朝與往夕，並不是一種遞嬗的關係；而是－和後人一道，活在同一個瞬間。照元瑞看來，無論是今天還是未來，都強烈地左右著古代生活，程度上與古代對我們的影響是相等的。他反覆解釋，歷史並不應當因此被曲解為是在倒退著發生，而是相反，正如古人們惴惴不安是由於我們已經預先存在的緣故。今天，我們的憂患也是後人造成的。我請他舉例說明，他立即就引出了經脈學說，並說針灸師和按摩醫生已經熟練地在病人身上搗騰了好幾千年了，但他們卻至今還不理解自己爲何醫術附身。更有意思的是，一張遠比集成線路更複雜的穴位圖竟一直被相信是由公元前的人們一點點揣摩出來的。我提醒他，穴位，最早都記載在一部叫《黃帝內經》的書上。是的，元瑞反問我，哪麼《黃帝內經》又從何而來？元瑞吸了口氣，語調充滿難以抑制的感情－望洋興嘆的古老啞謎，遙遠地，矗立於未來的某一定點上，本來就是我們的後裔對於偉大先祖的饋贈，卻一直被無所察覺地歸咎爲奇跡，在一個自以爲了不起的時代則被危險地劃入了傳統。多麼漫長的煎熬！我們代代相傳，期望把它歸還給它本來屬於的時代，但那樣的時代卻遲遲不來。

那麼，一個你所消受的女人，一口啜飲的茶水，甚至，一幅卷軸上趺坐於刺柏下的古僧呢？它們卻不是後人設下的苦計。元瑞回答說，由於它們是及時的，享樂的，賞心悅目的，從而它們是無害的。你不會爲它們真的付出代價，因此它們也是無意義的。因此蕩婦與貞女，文物與古董，之間並沒有真的差別。僅有的，值得一試的事情，是像後人那樣，把非凡的作品埋葬在今天或者更早的時代，但是我們已經完成了，並且還是在我們未及生下，未及開口之前－事實，都記載在出於那些落舉文人和貶謫者手筆的書籍當中，還有－元瑞揚起他的右手，一枚碩大、發黃的戒指，套在他中間的手指上，正在得意地炫耀著，正如你已經看見的，元瑞坦然相告，這枚純金戒指，是我在一個原始墓葬中發現的－細石器時代晚期，階級分化才剛剛出現，財富的佔有就多麼驚人！但是，我要告訴你的是更有價值的事實，雖然冶煉在那個時代尙未出現，但戒指的工藝卻達到了今天的水平，以至於誰也不會相信它有如此老耄的壽命。看到我驚異的神色，元瑞再次滿足地笑了－的確，我佔有了它，由於它和一枚金店售出的普通戒指沒有什麼不同，在一個我們不得不苟活下去的世界，入不敷出才是最大的罪過，而按月領工資，簡直不過是貧窮和另一個代稱而已。因此，爲了多少改變一下困境，我不僅同老傢伙們周旋，我也同討厭的古董販子打交道。

他所透露的一切都令我無話可講，但無庸諱言，鐫刻在畫像磚上的並不是細腰溜肩的東漢人在煮鹽行獵，而是未來人類的起居圖景;一堆朽黑的木片,也不是什麼劈開的柴禾,而是魯班、墨翟曾經駕馭過的「木鳶」,一種更輕便的,大有發展的未來飛機的殘骸;那塊黏接在一起的銅鏽和硬土,也不是什麼已經糜爛的陰毒刑具,更非眾人猜測的那樣,是綠林好漢埋沒在路當中的害人機關,而是隱藏著一部十五世紀的微型收音機。這些無人留意的藏品,被元瑞仔細的從庫房中挑選出來,為他縱橫馳騁的思路擔當先鋒。至於那些闊嘴大牙,頭部呈三角形的遠古石雕,它們也不是什麼圖騰,而是未來世界中人類自身的形象。最後,元瑞順手合上了攤在桌上的,一本薄薄的書籍――一部《易經》,你瞧,他說,我也像每個人一樣,正在研究這部書,不過對於我來說,它卻是一部後人的著作。

新學期到來,我就開始在一種可以稱作昏厥的清醒中飛渡。我不修邊幅,無視課程安排和校歷的頒佈。臨睡之前,我也不再強迫自己洗腳,並自認為那和起床後戴表一樣,是一種從前我未能克服的惡癖。我把黎明和日暮混為一談。中午時分,當我仰面躺在荷花池畔的草坪上,元瑞的讖語,就在我的耳廓內轟鳴著,蓋過了樹幹上聒躁的高音喇叭,也蓋過了午眠時間結束的鐘聲,然而我依舊不曾醒來-時間,圍困和消熔了千秋萬代,消熔著成排的校舍,操場,新修的圖書館…消熔著小伙子的牛角刀和姑娘的連衣裙,但時間的烈焰卻無法消熔我。我無往無來,無生無死,卻嘀答、嘀答,在它的每一刻度上秒針般出現。在我的夢魘中,我不斷引用元瑞的銘言,以反擊那些慣於哀嘆的,循規蹈矩的學院人物。那銘言是:僅僅因為錯誤的一套把本來接近我們的事物估計得太遠,才使我們肉眼看見的星星無法到達。

女學生成了我夜以繼日的情人,我們如狼似虎,欲壑難填。這在校園裡已經不是什麼秘密。從人們交頭接耳的表情來看,我們的行為純屬是在制造沸騰人心的醜聞。一個神經衰弱的「社經課」教師和一個有粉刺的女學生交媾會是什麼樣子呢?每個人都在這麼想-而且,有時就發生在稀疏的綠化帶和擁擠的課桌上。換了從前,我恐怕會無地自容,但現在,管它呢!比這駭異得多的發現令我根本無心顧及他人;還有,我又怎會猜得出那些慣說空話的傢伙到底是什麼動機呢?

學生們似乎在策劃又一次行動,到課堂上來的人寥寥無幾。這正合我意。不僅如此,我還經常假裝不適,以換取更多的自由時間呆在圖書館的角落裡看書。我已經變成了一頭古籍的饕餮,率領著千萬只飢腸轆轆的書蠹,輕車熟路地穿行在線裝書庫的迷陣裡(自從我拜訪過元瑞後,它們對於我就不再是迷陣了)。我的快樂,上升到想要吟哦的程度－琅嬛呀!機密的高樓,雲蒸霞蔚的,神聖的藏書處,正是天帝本人消暇渡日的地方。如今我可以闔上眼,隨便抽出一本來就可以証明古人曾經何其率真地感受到了我們的體溫,我們的呼吸,咳嗽和鼾息。而今天,左右了我們的種種奇技淫巧,無不曾越阡渡陌,浸濡過古人的衣裾。這又有什麼奇怪呢?我模仿元瑞的口氣,對想像中的大庭廣眾說－一部電腦,一個貨真價實的微機系統,對於今天的小學生也不過是常識,但對於十三世紀收藏它的謝霜回來說,它卻是稀罕的寶物,是神秘的靈檀。

但我畢竟沒有像元瑞那樣,狼心狗肺地去頂撞巴結在一起的權威們。謹小慎微的品性在我的早年便已培養起來,現在只是在元瑞的點撥下,在故紙堆中找到了它的一席之地。多虧了他,我的嗜好已不再是追隨那些陰陽怪氣的考據癖,而是從古人的一笑一顰中捕捉未來的訊息。我發現,生活在一個後人設置的時代裡,是多麼容易把他們的獻禮當成是今人的杜撰,誇大其詞,或是故作熱情的欺騙。只有我們才活著－這堅貞的信念把人人都螫成了瞎子。時間的機器彷彿停止了,我們懸浮當中,在雞毛鴨血的世界上互相糾纏,既無以往也無將來－這才是難堪的!我開始,毫無顧忌地,放任自己這樣自言自語下去。一天,在雷雨前昏暗的圖書館裡,當我噙滿淚水愧對祖先,卻在一副慈眉下看見我自己的末代玄孫轉動著骰子似的眼珠,撒手無援地站在一場白色的大火中。

人要搶在大火之前找到他要的那本書,為此不得不先釋破萬卷。元瑞的話可能是對的。但那場大火卻沒有到來,圖書館反倒因為有人提醒而遷移到了一個安全的地點。可見多少我們還是能夠做點什麼。正如活下去的趣味,恐怕也不只是放縱後代,而且也是利用時機替古人反撲,同時攫取現存的享樂。我想,元瑞就是深明此道才荷上了他迷人的幻想之戟的。而且我,也是因此才甘願陷身在圖書館裡,好比藏身於木馬進入特洛伊的勇士，為了攻陷這座神話之城才忍受著長久的緘默，恐懼和焦灼的黑暗。

我的戰績不斷擴大。我搜集到許多令人扼腕的故事。譬如，唐人李濬所著的《摭異記》中寫到，漁人在秦淮河中網得一鏡，十分驚訝，拿來一照，「歷歷盡見五臟六腑，血縈脈動」，因而嚇得魂飛魄散，手一鬆，鏡又墜入了河中，此後便再也打撈不到。既然這則史料並未說它「照之則左、右、前三方事皆見…兵甲如在目前」，那麼它跟我在另一部唐人著作中讀到的關於望遠鏡的記載是不同的。這一次，它是一台具有透視功能的X光機。此外，許多珍貴的材料，竟然早就不知不覺地被我輯錄在自己的軟盤裡，令我不禁自得，打算寫一本書來總結一下我的發現。這個計劃使我的情人大為感動，很快，她為我打字的次數就變得和我們做愛一樣頻繁。每當我停下手中的工作，注視著她在電腦前專心致志的神態，以及她可愛的膝蓋下露出的腿部，我就得抑制住想要吟哦的毛病－神啊！把她和我永遠關在這座圖書館裡吧！此外，我什麼都不需要了。我，區區書生，有幸能營巢在書堆裡，和自己心愛的人甚至不存在咫尺之遙。尤其是，她美不勝收的軀體就像炎帝本人制造的試管女嬰一樣結實可靠，性能無可挑剔。在我的懷抱裡，她慨然領受雨露的模樣真是既像擄掠來的嫦娥，又是未來的飛天。

隔了半年，我再次萌生了拜訪元瑞的願望。臨行前，我為一次旗鼓相當的傾談作好了準備。不必說，又是一個好天，我心情愈佳，輕輕叩開了虛掩著的，同一間辦公室的房門。

一位老者，藹然可親地接待了我。他吐出的每一個字，對於我，都如見鎖鑰－元瑞，由於利用工作之便，直接盜賣國家文物，已經被有關方面逮捕了。接著，他評價了這個他曾經著力栽培過的下屬－－個後生，本來是佼佼者，卻不幸迷上了偽科學，挾持著種種臆造的發現，沉浸在褻瀆的狂喜中，其實是奇門遁甲。他所褻瀆的，不僅是考古界的榮譽，而且也是他自己崇拜的人類的偉大神話，到後來，他竟然固執地相信自己是早已消失的賓人的後裔。

老者繼續說著，口氣是繼父般的。我恍恍惚惚，以為自己走錯了房間，因為牆上，分明貼著一張白底紅字的《文物管理保護法例》，地上，也不再有古代收音機之類的東西。只有一件剛剛出土，轟動於世的，巨大的青銅面具，穩當地擱置在元瑞過去堆放木片的位置。而具以不變的姿態微笑著，似乎在嘲弄著這間辦公室。

此後，我再也沒有去參觀過它。對於我來說，一次就已經足夠了。而具不斷以它的本來面目出現在我的幻覺中，並發出昏昏沉沉的笑聲。它那雙獸耳，特別是一對向外聳出的，柱狀的眼球，常常把我從爛醉和狂睡中逼醒，回到心驚膽戰的，畫外音般的現實中。從報紙、電台，甚至路人的閑談也常常傳來它在各地流動展出的消息。但在我周而復始的白日夢裡，那些變幻的地名和元瑞的辦公室始終是同一地點。這沉睡千載，仍然來歷不明的面具，凸出它傲岸的，巨喙般的鼻子，和元瑞現世的貪財面目重疊在一起，構成了一個完美古趣的畫謎；謎面上瀰漫的氣氛正是觸痛的老者所說的－「褻瀆的狂喜」。

幻想的洪水（更為專制的），曾經褻瀆了圖書館和野外的發掘工地。水勢正在褪去，水面上飄浮著的不只是虛妄的書籍和陶罐，而且也是現實的，肉身的肥豚駑馬，在赤日炎炎的季節散發出令人掩鼻的氣味。一天，當我無所事事地空著肚子在街上蹓躂，忽然被一個舊日相識大呼小叫地認了出來，寒喧了一陣之後，他便問我知不知道元瑞已經自殺了。

事後我也沒有去印証他顯然添油加醋的消息是否屬實。我獨來獨往，遠離書海和同樣浩翰駁雜的街談巷議。我私下認為，一個為犯人們所瞧不起的犯人，也就是犯人中的犯人。面對高傲的元瑞，我們全都是愛國者。在對一個把國寶輾轉盜賣給洋人的敗家子進行正當的侮辱時，犯人們並不在乎他曾把一枚無價的戒指順手摘下來送給一個後來出事的妓女，更不因為他是一個持有異端邪說的狂徒。

在這之前，我曾經去勞改農場看過他一次。他光著頭，但還是容易認出來。當時我想，時間，哪怕是監獄裡的鐘點，對於一個雖敗猶榮的人也是奈何不了的。元瑞看上去比過去還要灑脫。他一反從前的矜持，熱切地翹起中指，做了一個考究的、褻瀆的動作,既用來跟我打招呼,也表示他正在毫無悔意地褻瀆此地。在被看守帶走之前,他像才想起來似的,問我看過一部叫《琅嬛記》的書沒有,沒等我回答,他又告訴我那部書就存放在大學圖書館的線裝書庫,緊挨著一部私版的官修《元史》－元瑞說出了《琅嬛記》的準確位置,不過他怎麼也想不起它的版本和作者了。他還是那麼能說會道－即使是私版的正史也是垃圾,而《琅嬛記》卻不是,其它千千萬萬跟它一樣煙沒無聞的書也不是,只有這樣的書－元瑞說,才會使人思念女色,揮霍財寶,縱飲美酒;只有它們才敢把你掏出去,賒押給紙醉金迷的過去和將來;也只有它們,才會把你引誘到勞改農場來,享受到城市裡沒有的新鮮空氣;只有…瞧,你笑了。我們都知道那是怎麼回事,因為我們都是賓人。多麼奇怪的蠻族!瞧在它的份上,讀讀那部書吧!…

我最終沒有告訴他,隨著那女生的肚子一天天大了起來,等待她的是遣返原籍的嚴厲處罰;而我,隨之也被開除了公職。除了有時在大街上,我已很少見到成群結隊的大學生隊伍。永駐圖書館的美夢已經破滅。軟盤上辛苦積攢起來的故事,也被我在一怒之下頓時勾銷了。為史詩所篡改的歷史還原為真相:木馬計被識破,特洛伊依然高聳,蠹蟲的大軍徹底潰敗。我僥倖逃生,徘徊在大學森嚴的高牆外,沿著乾涸的護城河遊蕩,思念著放蕩的海倫,也思念著元瑞。晝夜變遷,那部束之高閣的《琅嬛記》,我恐怕是再也難以讀到它了。

注:本文多處材料直接引自一部飛碟學著作《有客太空來》。王江樹,可曉敏著。

Hu Dong

From *The Mask Outside the Library*

The following extract appears in a book entitled *Lang Huan Ji (Notes from the Imperial Library)*:

> Xie Xianghui had a magic table. The top was inscribed with original freehand notes and jottings in the Li and Zhuan calligraphic styles. There was something to interest every reader. For the person contemplating taking orders, there were words to guide along the winding way of self-reflection. For those searching for something, there were comforting phrases such as "You will find it somewhere". And for the person seeking a cure for a particular ailment, or for the person looking for magic formulae, there were references to medicines and magic charms. And there were even notes in full to remind the student of forgotten lines and words. Xianghui treasured his table.

At this point I should mention that I found this extraordinary book on the computer database in the library. I painstakingly copied down this excerpt and saved it on a floppy disk along with the rest of my stories, so that I could read through it again in idle moments. I used to amuse myself by joining a number of stories together in one long tale, then breaking it down again into individual pieces, arranging it so that each story could serve both as the beginning and the end. The permutations were endless. Through these subversive acts, I managed to squeeze a little stimulation from my dried-up academic life. I tell no lies when I say that my infatuation with studying grew out of this obsessive pursuit. I roamed enchanted around this square inch of floppy disk for days and months on end, never tiring of it. Although the game was monotonous, it was a monotony of kaleidoscopic proportions.

I was still teaching at the University. The sole reason for my continued presence (my more outspoken students called me a hanger-on) was the excellent University library. Since moving recently to new, modern premises, its vast, previously chaotic collection had been rediscovered.

By means of its new, comprehensive database of good, rare and one-off editions, users could access its entire extensive holding of old books. All the special reader privileges for University staff were preserved. In the middle of the night, as I tossed and turned alone in my single bed, I was driven by the considerably enhanced attractions of the library to contemplating the necessity of filling yet another floppy disk.

I had been appointed by the powers that be to teach the "Socialist Economy". Punning on the sound of the Chinese characters, the students shortened the name of this hateful compulsory course to "Lessons on Ejaculation". In no time at all, of course, the place was buzzing with obscene innuendos: I was the laughing stock of the school. I stuck it out bravely - I didn't have much choice, did I? One day I confronted the assembled second year who responded with boos of derision. As their surprised expressions turned to anger, I realised that they regarded me as a self-centred impotent responsible for the humiliation of our race. The rabble continued to remonstrate and cry. Then, quite unexpectedly, the normally obedient class prefect called on the students to strike, which was followed by another round of anguished debate. I turned down their nauseating invitations to join them in their discussions and repaired calmly to my single room. What could I say? I talked it over with my reflection in the mirror. My position in the school was completely untenable. I had been written off by a bunch of hypocritical student activists. At the end of term, as I seduced the female student who had been dispatched to weedle information out of me about the exams, I couldn't help remembering this incident and regretting that I hadn't put the gag on all of her giggling classmates by inviting them in for a bit of bedroom tuition. As I humped away on top of her, she couldn't resist letting out a few moans of pleasure.

But I was certainly no evil spirit that had invaded the pedagogical ranks nor even a sex maniac. True, I did threaten that nubile young girl a few times when she began to rant and rave, but really I just wanted to exert some control over her. It was clear to all that whilst I was forever commending other people's addictions, privately I was very much against drink and sex. Suggestible souls like myself struggling to stay on the straight and narrow had to be conscious of limits when it came to self-abuse. Although I was bored with teaching, I still had my ambitions. I dreamed of embarking on a new bibliographical career cataloguing and researching old books, an interest far removed from my professional life. I spent all my spare time immersed in strange books like the *Lang Huan Ji*. I wasn't only interested in dipping in to pick out the more stimulating passages: I was particularly keen to clarify the true identity of the author and to establish the exact date of the book's completion.

The *Lang Huan Ji* was attributed to Yi Shizhen of the Yuan dynasty, but some people suspected that this was a forgery and that it was actually the work of Sang Yi of the Ming Dynasty. It was an intriguing situation: two persons from different dynasties thrown together by a bizarre, salacious book. I would dash off my teaching duties in a perfunctory manner, then bury myself in amongst the stacks of threadbound books, losing all track of time, often going without regular meals and sleep. But after a term's work, the material I had collected was still insufficient to enable me to verify which of the two dynasties or which of the two authors was correct. Rather the textual complexities threw up hosts of other possible authors and dates either considerably later or earlier than suggested. I was completely flummoxed. I began to question whether a non-expert like myself was up to the rigours of historical study. But I refused to be beaten. Contemplating my painfully wan and sallow reflection in the gleaming library windows, I decided against soliciting the assistance of the self-confessed conservatives in the history faculty in order to avoid exposing myself unnecessarily to their derision.

The female student went home during the vacation, so I devoted even more spare time to the increasingly hopeless task of deciphering endless volumes of impenetrable texts. I collected and went through them all with a fine toothcomb, but nothing conclusive emerged. I began to suspect that I had overlooked a key volume as I was browsing through the library's extensive collections of everything published since the Qin Shi Emperor burned all the books in the third century BC; or that one of the library assistants had omitted to include the reference when editing the catalogue; or that this key volume was languishing in some dark recess of the old library building among the moth-eaten, moldering tomes awaiting incineration. And there was another possibility, one I was reluctant to contemplate: that the book of all books that I yearned for day and night did not in actual fact exist.

These terrible riddles wound themselves around me more and more tightly, compounding my dilemma. Baffling hallucinations seeped gradually into every pore of my daily life, dominating the inner life that I kept concealed within me, making me appear gloomier than ever. With the vacation almost over, I became even more dispirited. Not wishing to prolong my agony, I summoned my courage and set off one sunny afternoon to call on someone I had met only once before - Yuan Rui, an archaeologist who worked amidst the architectural splendour of the museum. I picked him out from my circle of acquaintance because as far as I could see, for all the methodological differences between archaeological and historical research, Yuan Rui's outstanding work was totally devoid of the smugness that attended the scholars in the history faculty. It was formidably incisive and exacting. And I had another reason for wanting to see him: the impression he had made on me at our first chance meeting at the house of a mutual friend many years earlier. Not only had he seemed completely unconstrained by convention, reminding one of a stud horse, when he spoke, his voice was reminiscent of an exotic, untamed kylin, stretching out its neck from beyond the skies, snapping away at the bad-tempered clouds. People could not but prick up their ears to listen.

As expected, Yuan Rui was not at all taken aback by my presumptuous visit. Whilst he remembered me, there was nothing special in his greeting. This helped me to relax. He poured a glass of water, told me to make myself at home, then moved straight onto discuss the matter in hand.

"The most important archaeological discoveries in recent years belong to the future," he declared seductively. Showing my puzzlement immediately, I waited for him to continue, but instead he lapsed into silence. He gestured with his chin towards another part of the room. I saw that in addition to some fully intact portraits painted on bricks, there were some human figures bearing animal heads and some limestone sculptures, neither small nor large. Then there was a huge lump of rusting copper and hardened earth revealing the corner of an ancient implement. Finally, there was a heap of suspicious-looking pieces of wood, displayed carefully in the centre of the office. On the wall hung a large set of framed photographs of assorted gear wheels. The exquisite metal work on the gears gleamed, like the prize product of a large company.

These cultural relics, Yuan Rui began to explain, were emblematic not of an ancient way of life, but rather of the achievements of the present day. They represented forays into the future, into a period yet to arrive. Seeing me fix my gaze in astonishment on the wall, he told me quite nonchalantly that the gears had been dug out of the Mediterranean bed by a fellow archaeologist from overseas and that they were usable in today's ships, although carbon dating had proved that they went back several thousands of years.

"It's a slap in the face for the archaeological purists." Yuan Rui dismissed my misgivings which I voiced in an indirect manner, as if he had prepared his spiel in advance. "But the field of archaeology is dominated by the old school. They disregard all developments from overseas and are most put out by my new way of thinking. They feign bewilderment when, as scheduled, I submit my reports with the evidence there for them to see. And then on the pretext of safeguarding the academic reputation of their journals, these wise old men of the archaeological establishment refuse to publish my findings fearful lest they bring new ideas into the field." Yuan Rui's eyes flashed, whether with anger or excitement, I couldn't tell. He fixed his bulbous gaze on me and surveyed the entire office.

Yuan Rui's authoritative and loquacious manner stunned me into an embarrassed, baffled silence. I had no choice but to abandon my original plans completely. In actual fact, however, Yuan Rui's verbal outpourings did address the points I had wanted to make. He pulled them apart mercilessly. Indeed, after I said goodbye to him that day, I was so agitated and preoccupied I couldn't settle or sleep. It was as if

Yuan Rui's spirit had taken hold of me.

What was this invading force that seemed to have garrisoned itself permanently in a pillbox in my head? I set about trying to clarify what Yuan Rui had said.

"Historical contradictions are not only symbolic of the past, they embrace the future embodied in the past. Or, to put it another way, the future has already happened in the past. As far as ourselves and our forbears or the present and the past are concerned, it is not that the former succeeds the latter, but that they coexist at the same point in time." According to Yuan Rui, both the present and the future exert powerful influences on past lives, just as the past affects the here and now. He explained repeatedly why, in view of this, it was inappropriate to regard history as a retrospective phenomenon. On the contrary, just as the fears of people in the past were the product of premonitions of our existence, so our present day troubles and disasters are the legacy of our descendants. I asked him to give an example to illustrate. He honed in immediately on the subject of the circulatory system, asserting that whilst acupuncturists and masseurs had been practising their healing arts for thousands of years, they were still unable to offer medical explanations for their procedures. But what fascinated Yuan Rui in particular was the fact that the system of acupuncture points, more complex than an integrated circuit, was discovered in the pre-Christian era. I reminded Yuan Rui that the earliest references to acupuncture appear in *Huang Di Nei Jing (The Classic of Emperors)*. "True," Yuan Rui acknowledged, "By the way, who wrote that book?" He took a deep breath and in an emotional tone went on: "Those awesome riddles from the past, long ago, belong to some point in the future and were originally bestowed on our ancient ancestors by our descendants. But all along, out of sheer ignorance, they have been interpreted as miracles and tidied away quite dangerously in the cupboard of tradition by eras too proud of their own achievements. It's insufferable! As we pass from one generation to another, all we can hope to do is return those baffling phenomena we are unable to fathom to their original time. But those times have yet to arrive."

"So what about things like women one has enjoyed, refreshing mouthfuls of tea, or even a set of scrolls depicting a Buddhist monk sitting cross-legged under a pine tree?"

"These are not the work of trouble-making future generations," Yuan Rui replied. "They are timely, enjoyable and aesthetically pleasing. They are completely harmless. And because one cannot attach a price to them, they are meaningless. It follows, therefore, that there is no real difference between loose women and chaste virgins and cultural relics and antiquities. The only worthwhile thing to do is copy our descendants by burying our outstanding achievements for the benefit of times past. But in fact we have already done that, many years ago, before we even came into being or were able to open our mouths. The facts are there for all to see in the writings of disaffected scholars and exiled officials. And..." Yuan Rui lifted his right hand triumphantly to show a large, yellowed ring, gleaming shamelessly on his prominent middle finger. Smiling openly, he went on, "This solid gold ring was discovered in a grave. It probably dates from the late microlithic period. At that time, class divisions were just beginning to appear, and yet the ring testifies to the existence of a surprisingly comprehensive and stringent taxation system. But what I want to tell you is more important. Although smelting processes had not been discovered then, the standard of workmanship on the ring is as high as we see today. Indeed, no one will believe that the ring is as old as it is." My surprised expression evidently pleased him. "In truth, I've stolen it. Well, you can't tell the difference between this ring and the common or garden rings you find in the jewellers. Trying to make ends meet on an inadequate income is the most depressing thing known to humankind. Here we are, stuck in a dreadful city, living on what can only be described as poverty wages. So to pull myself out of this ignominious existence, not only have I got myself involved in antiques, I also do some business with those despicable antique dealers."

Yuan Rui's candour left me speechless. It was obvious. The pictures engraved on the bricks were not depicting fine-waisted, slim-shouldered salt-makers and hunters from the Eastern Han at all, but rather the lifestyles of future generations. The pile of rotting wood was not kindling, but the "wooden bird" that Lu Ban, the sage of carpenters, and Mo Zi, the philosopher and carpenter, once rode - the remains of a future light aircraft. Neither was that lump of hardened earth and rusted metal the decayed remnant of a poisoned torture instrument, nor was it as some people would have it, a weapon concealed in roadside undergrowth by some "Robin Hood" character. It was a poorly disguised miniature radio from the fifteenth century. Yuan Rui had picked these things out of the museum stacks to substantiate his wild, arrogant hypotheses. No one had ever bothered with them before that. And of course those wide-smiling, triangular-headed figures from the distant past were not totems, but self-portraits of people from a future age. Finally, Yuan Rui closed the slim volume that had been lying open on the desk - a volume of the *I Ching (The Book of Changes)*. "You see, I'm researching this too, just like everyone else. But, as far as I'm concerned, it was written in the future."

translated by Jenny Putin

胡冬

我想乘上一艘慢船到巴黎去

（節選）

我想乘上一艘慢船到巴黎去
去看看梵高看看波特萊爾看看畢加索
進一步查清楚他們隱瞞的家庭成份
然後把這些混蛋統統槍斃
把他們搞過計劃要搞來不及搞的女人
均勻地分配給你分配給我
分配給孔夫子及其徒子徒孫

我想乘上一艘船到巴黎去
去看看盧浮宮凡爾賽宮其他雞巴宮
是否去要回唐爺爺的茶壺宋奶奶的擀面棒
不，我不，法國人也有恥辱
我要走進蓬皮杜總統的大肚子
把那裡的收藏搶劫一空
然後用下流手段送到故宮
送到市一級博物館送到每個中國人家裡

我想乘上一艘慢船到巴黎去
去凱旋門去巴黎聖母院去埃菲爾鐵塔
去星形廣場偷一輛真正的雪鐵龍
然後直奔滑鐵盧大橋
活動安排在一天內完成

我要在巴黎的各處名勝
刻上方塊字刻上某君到此一遊
……
我想乘上一艘慢船到巴黎去
我算過這大約需要十萬分鐘
沿途將經過七大洲五大洋
經過我知道的全部外國
沿途我將認識印度人、阿拉伯人
美國人加拿大人以及其他甚麼有趣的蠻夷
我們將討論共同關心的公家問題私人問題
我會同每個國家的領導發生爭吵
會違反任何地方的交通規則
印度公安局埃及公安局包括美國公安局
都會派出成打成打密探跟蹤我

我想乘上一艘慢船到巴黎去
沿途我將同每個國家的少女相愛
不管是哪國少女都必須美麗
她們將為我生下品種多樣的兒子
這些小混蛋長大後也會到處流竄
成為好人壞人成為傑出的人類
無論走到哪裡人們都會注意他們
他們的眼睛會是黑漆漆的顏色
從滾滾的人流從任何場合
我也會加倍提防這些雜種他們是誰
他們是我的兒子我的好兒子

Hu Dong

From *I Want to Take a Slow Boat to Paris*

I want to take a slow boat to Paris
To see Van Gogh, see Baudelaire, see Picasso
To investigate further their hidden family backgrounds
Then I'll shoot all these bastards dead
And share the women they'd planned to screw but never got round to screwing
Equally between you, me
Confucius, his followers and their followers

I want to take a slow boat to Paris
To see the Louvre, Versailles and other fucking palaces
To get back Grandpa Tang's teapot or Grandma Song's rolling pin
No, not me. The French too can have their shame
I want to get into President Pompidou's big belly
And plunder it bare of all its collections
Then use underhand means to send them to the Imperial Palace
To the top municipal museums and every Chinese home

I want to take a slow boat to Paris
To go to the Arc de Triomphe, Notre Dame and Eiffel Tower
To the Place d'Etoile where I can steal a genuine Citroen
Then head straight for Waterloo Bridge
Operation scheduled for completion in a day
And in every scenic spot throughout Paris
I want to carve Chinese words saying so and so's been here

I want to take a slow boat to Paris
On the way I'll make love to the young girls of each country
No matter where they're from, they must all be pretty
They'll bear me a motley variety of sons

When these small bastards grow up, they'll also roam far and wide
And become good types, bad types, become outstanding species
Wherever they go, people will notice them
The colour of their eyes will be pitch black
Among teeming crowds in any place
I too will be specially wary of who these mongrels are
They are my sons, my fine sons

translated by Peng Wenlan

作者簡介

小芸： 香港新界客家人，1955年出生，71年隨家移居英國，從事飲食業十多年。93年畢業於倫敦東非研究學院歷史系；對文學、藝術、戲劇等甚有興趣。現在華人社區中心工作。

乞靈： 原名吳呂南。1952年生。香港大學中文系畢業，英國城市大學藝術評論碩士，現於倫敦大學亞非學院攻讀博士學位。

王玲： 利物浦華人。利物浦大學經濟歷史系畢業，曾出版《利物浦華人》一書，有關當地華人的歷史。有兩位年青兒子；和她的朋友蘇和貓露絲住在一起。她現在努力找時間寫作。

王家新： 1957年生於湖北，1982年畢業於武漢大學，1985-1990年任北京《詩刊》編輯；1992年來英後先後應邀在英、荷、比、德等國朗誦，出版有多種詩集及詩論集，並被譯成多種文字。

文坤李： 1965年生於香港，母親為法國人，父親為華人。她在倫敦長大，取得現代語文（中文和意大利文）學位，現在任職林拔芙華越青年的社工。

曲磊磊： 1951年生於中國東北，長在北京，祖藉山東。自幼博學多覽。文化革命輟學，以後下鄉、當兵、回城。當過知青、赤腳醫生、戰士、工人，美術設計師等。79年投身現代美術運動，組織並參加「星星美展」。1985年後旅居英國，為職業畫家，業餘寫作。

巫立基： 現時在林拔芙享受那定期的入息補助金，其中大部份花在唐人街的旺記飯店，那裡他時常和那七位人士一起進餐。

李佩芬：　　生於伯明翰，在諾定咸長大。1987-90期間在倫敦的音樂和戲劇藝術學院受演員的訓練，她的獨角戲《又矮、又肥、又醜怪，又是中國人》在第五電台播出後，獲得種族平等委會的媒介獎。李佩芬曾在電台、舞台及電視上演出。

吳洪強：　　格拉斯哥華人。做了七年的職業舞蹈家，後在倫敦印務學院學習新聞媒介。他曾為城市範圍、絲語時報、倫敦週末電視和BBC工作。

柳揚：　　1961年出生於浙江省蘭溪市。1988年獲西南師範大學文學碩士學位。曾任北京第二外國語學院講師。現在倫敦大學亞非學院攻讀藝術史博士學位。

虹影：　　1962年生於四川省。最初由寫詩始，後於1988年轉寫小說。她的中文作品包括詩集《天堂鳥》、《魔菌》、《倫敦，危險的幽會》；短篇小說《一直對溫柔妥協》和小說《裸舞代》。她的詩曾獲英國和台灣的獎項。

胡冬：　　1963年10月生。四川成都人。為中國「第三代人」及「莽漢主義」。現代詩歌運動的發起人及主要參與者之一。1990年移居倫敦。

浴缸：　　1962-2063，原名陳文瑞，來自馬來西亞，在英從事電影欣賞、繪畫及首飾設計。

細胞：　　1991年從香港來英，曾在英國不同地方居住，現職父母親的外賣店。

張翠詩：　　生於倫敦東部，在倫敦東南部長大，父母做飲食業生意。現住北倫敦，任職房屋部門。在Loughborough大學讀英文和戲劇時，因同學的挑戰而引起她對華人身份的探討。

陳雲西：　　生於倫敦的東部，在六十年代的搖擺樂的影子下長大。她的父親是華人，母親英國人。十六歲離校後，當過歌星／作曲，最後受訓成為劇作者。她講授電影和戲劇，亦為媒介寫作。她的新作品《蘇茜黃－人類炮彈》，將由木蘭劇團上演。

黃慧文： 她的父母都是中國來的移民，她於1965年出生於倫敦市。在King's College讀法國語文。做了三年的公共關係工作，現在於亞非學院唸社會人類學碩士。

喬林： 台灣旅英女詩人，南京市人，現於倫敦大學亞非學院攻讀博士。散文、小說及新詩，散見於港台、中國大陸、星馬及歐美各地。文筆老辣，幽默，富理趣。

游鴻潤： 1954年生於紐西蘭，移居馬來西亞。1969年來英唸，在倫敦住了17年。

劉洪彬： 一九六二年生，有詩集《東方的鴿子》、《鐵環》。另有小說、文學評論和媒介的西方現代詩等作品發表。其詩作八九「六・四」前張貼在天安門廣場。被詩人史苪芬・司班德爵士譽為「天賦的、嚴肅的詩人」。

劉索拉： 1955年生於北京，畢業於北京中央音樂學院。第一篇出版的短篇小說《你別無選擇》，是當時八十年代新小說浪潮的代表作。她於1988年來倫敦，她是聲樂家，作曲家，演員亦是作家。

顏展民： 廣東省普寧縣人，香港出生，一直在香港長大。一九八五、六年擔任香港青年作者協會主席。歷任青年文學獎、理工文學獎和職青文藝獎小說組評判。著作《天地與我何相幹》和《捲進迷濛的漩渦》散文小說集。一九九二年夏旅居英國。

蘇慧君： 在英國郭羅西斯達郡的朝頓咸出生，在利物浦大學得到英國語文、歷史和媒介榮譽學士位。曾任職於劇院、印刷和電影業。

About the authors

Bathtub (1962-2063) is the pen name of Tan Boon Swee who is from Malaysia. Since coming to England, he has been actively pursuing filmgoing, painting and jewellery design.

Anna Chen was born to a Chinese father and an English mother in London's East End where she grew up in the shadow of the Swinging Sixties. She left school at sixteen to be a singer/songwriter and eventually trained as a screenwriter. She has lectured on film and theatre and written for the media. She is looking forward to performing her own work, *Suzy Wrong - Human Cannon*, with the Mulan Theatre Company.

Tracy Cheung was born in London's East End and grew up in the suburbs of southeast London, where her parents owned and ran a takeaway. She now lives in north London and works in housing. While studying English and Drama at University of Loughborough, she met people who challenged her and made her think more clearly about her Chinese identity.

Chiao Ling, a woman poet from Taiwan, is working for a PhD in Chinese Literature at the School of Oriental and African Studies, University of London. Her essays, short stories and poems enjoy a wide readership in China, Hong Kong, Taiwan, Singapore and Europe.

Beverly Yew Guild was born in New Zealand in 1954 and grew up in Malaysia. She came to school in England in 1969 and has lived in London for 17 years.

Hong Ying was born in 1962 in Sichuan Province in southwest China. She started writing as a poet and turned to fiction writing in 1988. her Chinese publications include the poetry collections *The Paradise Bird*, *The Magic Mushrooms*, *Meet Me in Danger*; a collection of novellas and short stories *You Always Yield to Gentleness* and the novel *The Summer of Betrayal*. Her poems have won prizes in England and Taiwan.

Hu Dong was born in 1963 in Sichuan Province. He was one of the proponents of the radical *Manghan* poetry movement in China in the 1980s. They advocated a realistic, down-to-earth treatment of poetry, primarily through the shedding of refined language and content. He came to London in 1990.

Vivienne Tamar Huang's parents are both from China. They met in London and Vivienne was born to the sound of Bow bells in 1965. She studied French Literature at King's College, London and after three years in public relations, Vivienne is now working for an MA in Social Anthropology at the School of Oriental and African Studies.

Pui Fan Lee was born in Birmingham and grew up in Nottingham. She trained as an actress at the London Academy of Music and Dramatic Arts during 1987-90. Her one-woman play, *Short, Fat Ugly and Chinese* won the Commission for Racial Equality's Race in the Media Award after a Radio 5 performance in 1992. Pui Fan Lee has performed on radio, stage and television.

Liu Hongbin was born in 1962 in Qingdao, China. Besides poetry, he also writes short stories, literary criticisms and translates western poetry. His publications include *The Dove of the East* and *An Iron Circle*. His poems were put up at Tian'anmen Square during the pro-democracy movement in 1989. He moved to London that year. He has been described by Sir Stephen Spender as "a gifted and serious poet."

Liu Sola, born in 1955 in Beijing, studied music at the Central Conservatory of Music in Beijing. She began writing in the early 1980s and her first publication, the short novel *You Got No Other Choice* (1985), is characteristic of the New Wave Fiction of that period. It was a bestseller in China. Liu Sola came to London in 1988. She is a singer, composer, actress as well as writer.

Liu Yang was born in Zhejiang Province in southeast China in 1961. He graduated with a degree in Chinese Literature from Southwest China Teachers' University and has taught at the Beijing Second Foreign Language Institute. He is now working for a PhD in Art and Archaeology at the School of Oriental and African Studies, University of London.

Lili Kwanli Man was born in Hong Kong in 1965. Her mother is French and her father Chinese. She grew up in London, has a BA degree in Modern Languages (Chinese and Italian) and is working part-time as a youth worker with Chinese and Vietnamese youths in London.

Lab Ky Mo is currently enjoying income support from the Borough of Lambeth, a substantial proportion of which goes to subsidise Wong Kee Restaurant in Wardour Street, where he frequently dines alone with seven men.

Qi Ling (pen name of Wu Lunan) was born in 1952 in Hong Kong. he studied Chinese Literature at the University of Hong Kong before coming to London for a second degree in Art Criticism at the City University. He is now a PhD student at the School of Oriental and African Studies, University of London.

Qu Leilei born in northeast China in 1951, grew up in Beijing. His education was interrupted during the Cultural Revolution and he was sent to the countryside. He had worked as a soldier, barefoot doctor, worker and graphic designer. In 1979, he joined the contemporary art movement and was one of the renowned Star artists, whose cry was "in art we want freedom, in politics we want democracy." He came to London in 1985 and now works as a visual artist.

Helen Soo was born in Cheltenham, Gloucestershire. She graduated from Liverpool University with a BA Honours in English Literature, History and Media. She has since worked in theatre, publishing and film.

Wang Jiaxin was born in 1957 in Hubei Province, China. After graduating from Wuhan University he worked on the editorial team of *Shikan* (*The Poetry Journal*) in Beijing. He is currently studying and writing in London. His poetry publications include *Selected Poems* (in Dutch and Chinese) and *Stairway*.

Maria Lin Wong was born in Liverpool. She is the mother of two teenage sons and lives with her partner Sue and their cat Rosie. She has a degree in Economic History from the University of Liverpool and is the author of *Chinese Liverpudlians*, which traces the history of the Chinese community in Liverpool. She is working at creating more space for writing.

Paul Wong was born in Glasgow and danced professionally for seven years, before studying journalism at the London College of Printing. He has worked for *City Limits*, *SiYu Chinese Times*, London Weekend Television and the BBC.

Yen Chanmin was born and brought up in Hong Kong, although his family is originally from Po Ning county in Guangdong. In 1985 and 1986 he was chairman of the Hong Kong Young Writers Association. He has been on the fiction selection panels for the Youth Literature Award, the Polytechnic Literary Award and the Youth Arts Award. His works include two prose collections, *The World and Me* and *In the Whirlpool's Haze*. He went travelling in 1991 and is now living in England.

Xiao Yun, born in 1955, comes from the New Territories in Hong Kong. She moved with her family to Britain in 1971 and worked in the catering trade for over ten years. She graduated with a BA in History from the School of Oriental and African studies in 1993. She now works with the Chinese community in London.

Zibao came to Britain from Hong Kong in 1991 and has lived in various parts of Britain. At the moment, she works at her parents' take-away shop.